CN

CW01507410

West Sussex County Council Library

Please return/renew this item.
Books may also be renewed in person, by
phone and online.

www.westsussex.gov.uk

west
sussex
county
council

MOTHER KNOWS BEST

J. A. BAKER

First published in Great Britain in 2025 by Boldwood Books Ltd.

Cover Design by Head Design Ltd

Cover Images: iStock

A CIP catalogue record for this book is available from the British Library.

Paperback ISBN 978-1-83561-198-2

Large Print ISBN 978-1-83561-197-5

Hardback ISBN 978-1-83561-196-8

Ebook ISBN 978-1-83561-199-9

Kindle ISBN 978-1-83561-200-2

Audio CD ISBN 978-1-83561-192-0

MP3 CD ISBN 978-1-83561-191-3

Digital audio download ISBN 978-1-83561-193-7

This book is printed on certified sustainable paper. Boldwood Books is dedicated to putting sustainability at the heart of our business. For more information please visit https://www.boldwoodbooks.com/about-us/sustainability/

Boldwood Books Ltd, 23 Bowerdean Street, London, SW6 3TN

www.boldwoodbooks.com

Mother Knows Best is dedicated to my husband Richard who, after feeding me the initial idea for this book, has proven that he is clearly as dark and depraved as I am. Also to my good friend Dawn and her lovely hardworking daughter Emma, who is nothing like any of the characters in this book but whose gruelling work schedule provided the inspiration for this twisted little tale...

All suffering originates from craving, from attachment, from desire.

The scariest monsters are the ones that lurk within our souls.

— EDGAR ALLAN POE

PROLOGUE

It takes a few seconds to register, for the realisation to embed itself into my brain. Things like this only happen in movies. They don't happen here, so close to my workplace. They don't happen in this town. And they don't happen to me. Except it is happening. This is real.

I am lifted off the floor and hauled backwards, my feet scrambling for purchase, my fingers clawing at the large hand that is clasped over my mouth. Fireworks explode in my head, ice-cold terror claws at my gut. Fragments of thoughts, thousands and thousands of them shatter in my brain, the main one being – I am going to die. I am going to die.

I brace myself, ready for the pain, for the terror, and for the endless blackness to enfold itself around me.

The night had been warm, the roads silent before I was ripped from my safe, comfortable life. I was relaxed, trusting of my environment. Too trusting. And now here I am, waiting for the moment when this person will end me.

He peers in as I am bundled into the boot of a car, his eyes as black as coal, his gaze roving over me. A predator sizing up their prey before they strike. I swallow down bile, hot and sour. It scorches my gullet. Then the boot is slammed shut, the dull thud of its closure merging with my screams. I kick and shriek. I claw and push and twist and turn in the darkness, in the horribly confined space, hoping somebody will hear me.

Nobody comes.

I am alone and the only thing I can think of as the engine kicks in and we begin to move is this: when the moment comes, please make it painless and please make it quick.

1

HELENA

The room spins. A wave of dizziness forces her upright, the wooziness in her head a swirling kaleidoscope of muted colours. Helena shivers. The shrill caw of the phone has cut through the deepest of sleeps, the coarse interruption a bludgeon to her skull. She was dreaming about her mother. Her absent mother. Physically present but emotionally lacking. Absent in matters of the heart for as long as Helena can remember. She has always vowed to be a better mother to her own daughters. To be there, do what she can for them. Be a competent parent and give them some stability. Even through the most torrid of times. And they were torrid. Still are on occasion.

An ache spears the back of her head as she slides down beneath the sheets to stave off the chill of the unheated bedroom. Her fingers tremble when she reaches for the phone, her gaze drawn to the clock on the bedside cabinet. She tries to not look but the glare of the luminous digits pierces the room. Twelve thirty a.m. A callout from her daughter. Either that or somebody has died. Nails scratch at plastic as her fingers scramble to pick up the receiver. Her tone is husky when she presses the button and speaks.

'Hello. Vanessa?'

The sound of anybody else's voice would curdle her blood, send her into a tailspin. It's late, or early depending on how you view it, and calls at this hour are a precursor to bad news. Accidents. Deaths. All manner of life-changing, heart-stopping pieces of information.

'Sorry, Mum. Just got the call for work. They need me at the care home. I have to go.'

Her daughter sounds alert, as if she has been up for hours. Not groggy like Helena. Not tired and dizzy and longing to slide down under the duvet and go back to sleep. Vanessa is up and eager; prepared and ready to do what needs to be done. At any other time she would brim with pride at her daughter's professionalism and loyalty. But not at 12.30 a.m. Exhaustion has obliterated all positive thoughts, its sharp claws digging into her flesh and touching bone.

With cold, tight fists, Helena rubs at her eyes, trying to shake off the heavy mantle of sleep that has enveloped her for the past few hours. 'Give me ten minutes and I'll be on my way.'

Senses still dulled, vision blurry, she stumbles around the bedroom grabbing at clothes, throwing overnight items into a bag. A pounding sensation beats hard at her temples. She wouldn't have thought it possible to sink into such a deep slumber after only two hours in bed, but exhaustion swamped her after spending a day tidying the garden in readiness for winter. Who knew that cutting back shrubbery and dead-heading roses would leave her feeling so fatigued? Part of her hoped the call from Vanessa wouldn't come, but it has and as her mother, she has to do all she can to help. It's what parents do. Decent parents, that is. Not the shabby figure of a woman who was at the helm of her own upbringing. A woman who refused to reveal the name of Helena's father. The same woman who even now in her declining years lives in a tiny flat surrounded by mouldy pizza boxes and stray cats that she brings home after venturing out to the corner shop for cigarettes and cheap wine. The last time Helena visited, she had to clamber over piles of filthy clothing and plates of rotting food to get to the shrunken figure who was sitting in the corner of the room, glowering at her.

'Come to gloat, have you? Or is this one of your annual visits to the mad old harridan who happened to give birth to you, with you arriving all stony-faced wishing you were elsewhere?'

'Hi, Mum,' was all she could manage as she picked her way through the detritus, gagging at the stench whilst making sure not to show any emotion or rise to the sharpened jibes and caustic comments. The sound of her mother's voice still managed to jangle Helena's nerves. Even after all these decades, Sylvie still had the ability to sneak beneath her daughter's skin, stealthily pulling at raw emotions, her voice like the needle of a record player skidding across vinyl.

'Make it quick, whatever you're here for. I've got a visitor coming in ten minutes. One of those people from the community centre is paying a visit with a photographer from the local newspaper. They're coming to nominate me for an award for being the most caring neighbour and parent in town.' Her laugh was a hacking bark, her head shaking as she surveyed Helena with dark pebble-like eyes, watching for signs of a response. Anything she could grab onto and tear apart with her acerbic tongue. Spittle had formed at the corners of her mouth, small, white foamy mounds that gathered and then dissipated leaving a wet oily residue that ran down the sides of her lips and over her chin in silvery rivulets. Helena had wanted to gag, to turn and flee, but instead she did what she had always done: she stayed and made small talk with the woman who had given birth to her. The woman she barely knows or understands. They are oceans apart, their thinking and parenting methods on vastly different levels. And yet she still turned up to visit her ageing mother. A daughter doing her duty. Trying to care. Hoping to change a woman who is set in her ways and resistant to anything that would steer her off course.

The visit was brief. The rancid conditions and her mother's lack of compassion or anything remotely resembling love or kindness, starkly lacking. Keeping the visits to once a month is just enough to assuage Helena's guilt, to ensure her mother doesn't become a statistic, yet another frail undernourished pensioner left to rot after dying alone in her armchair, her shrunken body buried beneath mounds of debris.

A stab of anger pierces Helena at the thought of how much family life her mother misses out on. How it is all passing her by. And how much Gavin, her late husband and father of her two daughters, has missed out on too. It's something that continually irks her, the fact her mother has wasted her life, while Gavin would have given anything to prolong his. He would have adored their grandchildren while her own mother can barely remember their names. He would be proud of Vanessa and her work ethic. How she came through after those traumatic early years, their daughter regaining her footing and becoming a stable force in Helena's life, while forging ahead with her own existence as a single parent. Helena doesn't tell her often enough what a decent person she is, how she has overcome adversity and risen above it, shining brightly like a beacon of hope. Life gets in the way of truth and those much-needed emotive moments when people are able to vocalise their inner thoughts and reconnect with one another. The important times. The fragments of our existence that make us human. Vanessa isn't perfect, but then, who is? We are all flawed in countless ways.

Helena dresses and shrugs on her coat after taking the stairs in record time. At the foot of the staircase, she slides her feet into an old pair of gardening shoes and then leaves the house in a blur of exhaustion, locking up as quietly as she can for fear of waking any neighbours.

Frost glints on the windscreen of her car, near-translucent particles twinkling under the glow of the streetlight; the threat of an oncoming winter. She rubs at it with her sleeve and quickly inspects the roads for any signs of ice, before climbing in the driver's seat and reversing off the driveway.

The journey to Vanessa's house takes precisely four and a half minutes. When the sun is up and the streets are light and welcoming and she has enough time and energy, she walks it, but right now it is pitch black and time is of the essence, so she quietly navigates her way through the dark lanes to the main village, pulling up outside Vanessa's house, their changeover rapid and seamless.

'Thanks, Mum. I'll not be long. All depends what the night brings. You never can tell how things will pan out, unfortunately.'

Her daughter is standing at the gate, the front door behind her allowing a sliver of light to escape and pool on the path, its soft golden hue a patch of liquid gold amidst a pall of darkness. Like a soft breeze caressing Helena's skin, her daughter leans forward and touches her arm before disappearing into the night, the low rev of her car engine the only sign she was ever here.

Inside, Helena removes her coat, the chill of the house causing her to shiver. As expected, all is quiet, both children asleep in bed, their usual screams and chatter replaced by a heavy silence that settles around her like a shroud. They will be up and running about at 7 a.m. Even if Vanessa returns before then, Helena will stay over, get the children ready and take them to school. She will tidy the breakfast dishes and let her daughter get some sleep before her next shift at work. She and Vanessa have had their differences in the past, but as a single parent, Helena has enough empathy, understanding and compassion to know that when it comes to running a house and bringing up children either alone or even as a couple, people need as much help as they can get. Besides, Vanessa is her daughter and if her own mother won't support her when help is needed, then who will? There are families up and down the land, families the world over, who are riddled with strife, but if everyone pulls together then the tapestry of their existence becomes strengthened. As taut and as strong as cat gut.

Vanessa was only seven years old when Gavin died, Rachel, her sister, just four. They cried, they grieved. Helena sobbed into her pillow every evening when the children were both tucked up in bed, then arose for work the next morning feeling stricken and hollowed out. Every day brought a fresh wave of grief. And yet life went on. The earth continued to spin on its axis even though their own little world had been savagely torn apart. People mowed lawns and washed windows. They drank coffee in smart cafés, shopped and chatted and danced and laughed. It took Helena weeks and weeks, possibly even months, to realise that grief is invisible to others, that despite her weight loss and gaunt ghost-like appearance, people around her still had their own lives, their own routines and families and jobs to occupy their time. Her daily emotions ranged from bewilderment to utter rage born of the fact that they couldn't see how much she was hurting. But gradually, she began to understand that people cannot feel the pain of another. Nobody is able to comprehend what is going on inside the head of a person who has lost a loved one. Grief is both universal and unique. A complex sensation that covers a wide spectrum of emotions. Which is why Helena does what she can for Vanessa despite their differences. Despite all the arguments they have had. She suffered after losing her father. Rachel was younger, her emotions not fully developed, her awareness of events limited. But Vanessa was older, at an impressionable age, and to hear her eldest daughter's cries mingling with her own night after night was something Helena will never forget. Arriving in the early hours to babysit her grandchildren is small potatoes in the grand scheme of things. They have a bond, Vanessa and Helena. It has frayed over the years, sometimes coming close to splitting completely, but there is always a strand there, the smallest of fibres that keeps them connected. A fundamental umbilical attachment that will never break.

Both Noah and Mabel are fast asleep when she checks on them, their small faces buried into their pillows. She undresses and climbs into the single bed in the spare room, succumbing to a wave of exhaustion that drags her into a pit of darkness for the next few hours.

2

ALEX

Twenty Years Prior

'You need to put it down, Alex. It doesn't belong to you.' Saskia's voice, usually delicate and barely more than a whisper, vaulted around the classroom, bouncing off the high ceiling and reverberating against the expanse of plaster walls of the Victorian building.

Blonde curls bounced around her face when she spoke. She shifted in her seat, leaning forward to retrieve the silver pencil case that was clutched in Alex's hand. He grasped it even tighter, desperate to take ownership of the item. Desperate to have something he could call his own.

Eyes like slits, his gaze lowered, he could sense the teacher watching him from the other side of the room. His spine was rigid, every muscle in his body tense and unyielding. He was ready for it; braced for the fight that would break out in just a few seconds. He wouldn't give in, not unless he was forced into it. Didn't matter who it was – boy, girl, teacher or parent; Alex knew that he was a ticking timebomb, always ready to explode at the slightest provocation. He couldn't help it. It was just how it was. Sometimes he visualised his anger like a dragon or a prowling tiger, ready to strike. The teacher was too far away from him to intervene. She couldn't be everywhere. And she had had a busy day. He had watched her getting more and more exasperated. Exhaustion leaked out of her, like tiny invisible trails that left her feeling empty, and made her short-tempered and lacking in energy. Alex had once heard her talking to another teacher in the corridor after class, saying that trying to pre-empt a child's bad behaviour and stop it before it happened was like spinning plates or playing a game of whack-a-mole. No sooner had she sorted one issue than another arose. That had made him laugh. He had thought about it all the way home, imagining Miss Lathaway as a circus performer or Miss Lathaway at a funfair, getting angrier and angrier because she couldn't hit the mole properly with a toy hammer.

She wasn't soft though. He knew that. He had seen her in action. She often broke up playground fights. He had seen her pulling kids apart, threatening them with all sorts of sanctions. But incidents with Alex were always different. *He* was different. He didn't do it on purpose; it was just how it was.

Anything that involves that child is on another level. That was another thing that Miss Lathaway had shouted as Mrs Brown the headteacher came by last week, popping her head around the door to see what all the noise was about.

That was the time when Alex had torn up his work, refusing to complete it, shouting that it was 'all a complete waste of his fucking time.'

He shouldn't have done it, he knew that, but sometimes dark things happened in his brain. Bad things. And whether he liked it or not, he had to obey.

He watched her stand and slalom her way across the room,

her hips swaying from side to side to avoid the corners of desks, and now he could feel her presence without even looking up. He was able to smell her coffee breath, sharp and strong. There was another aroma too – perfume. He liked that about her, the way she always smelled nice, but today it was combined with something else. Something not so appealing. A dark wet patch appeared under her arm as she leaned over him and hissed in his ear, the new and unusual smell becoming stronger the closer she got to him.

'I'll take that, thank you. I'll return it to its rightful owner.' Her usually powerful voice suddenly wasn't so powerful. She was tired. He could see it in her eyes, the way she sighed, her chest going in and out, her voice squeaky and sounding more like an angry bird than an angry teacher.

Alex held fast to the pencil case. He wanted it so badly. He didn't even know why he wanted it, but he just knew that he couldn't let it go. His fingers were curled tightly around the silvery glitter-covered casing, his refusal to let go a growing force between them.

He glanced up at her, doing his best to give her one of his dark dead-eyed stares. The ones that made his mum so angry, causing her to shout at him that he was a fucking nasty little nuisance. A waste of space.

'Alex has very kindly found somebody's lovely pencil case and is looking after it for them.' Miss Lathaway's voice rang around the room, her pitch causing everyone to fall silent. A sea of wide-eyed pupils observed her, listening intently as they waited for what came next. 'Do we know who this belongs to?'

He felt his arm being hoisted up, catching him unawares, the case brandished in the air. She shook it as if to emphasise her point. Its contents shuffled and rattled, an abrasive noise that rang around the silence of the startled classroom.

Alex could hear his own breath rattling in his ears. He wasn't frightened. He wasn't anything. He simply sat and waited for what would come next, his fingers still curled around the case.

Then Oscar put up his hand. Oscar with his shiny new clothes and shoes, and the array of toys he regularly brought into school. Alex watched as the boy's eyes searched Miss Lathaway's for answers as to how his property had come to be in the hands of Alex Broadwood. That made Alex smile. Oscar might have had loads of new things but what he didn't have was any cleverness. Not like Alex. He had had to develop ways to make sure he got whatever he needed. Alex was clever in ways that others didn't even know existed.

'It's mine, Miss Lathaway. I lost it this morning. I put it in my bag and then couldn't find it after we came in from the playground.'

He couldn't find it because Alex had seen it and wanted it and taken it. Sometimes he took items he didn't even want, just because it felt good having things. But now he was going to have to make a choice: either hand it over or put up a fight. Sometimes Miss Lathaway would try to strike bargains to get pupils to do things they didn't want to do, but Alex was impervious to bribery and threats. He danced to his own tune, always had, and now he had to make a decision – keep hold of the case and risk being kept back after class for one of her teacher's 'talks', or hand it over and look like a weakling, the kind of kid who was frightened of being told off.

There was one positive, though – as he watched the young teacher, he could see panic hammering at her chest, how he, a young boy, still in primary school, had the power to reduce her to a frightened young woman. Her neck was thudding, as if a small creature was trapped inside her throat and was trying to claw its way out. Maybe handing over the pencil case wouldn't be such a bad idea after all. He was already winning, making his teacher worried and anxious to the point where she had palpitations in her neck. Now he understood the meaning of somebody's heart crawling up their throat. And he had done that. He wasn't a weakling after all; he was powerful and strong, and better than anybody else in the room. Especially his teacher. She was a scaredy cat. A grown-up who was worried about what he might do next. *That* was real power and strength. It was like standing at the top of a mountain with the wind rushing past him and the sun warming him through. He was clever and controlling and superior to everyone else in the class.

Alex waited, eager to see what she did next. How she was going to react and what she was going to say to make this whole thing better. He wasn't scared. If anything he was excited. Thirty sets of eyes were fixed on him as they waited, thirty half-open mouths eager to see what was about to unfold. Alex knew what they all thought of him. He was the boy who regularly stole from other pupils, salting away their small items in his pockets, ready to take other children's property home when the bell sounded at three o'clock. It was just something he did, something he neither understood nor was able to control. It just was.

The air in the room suddenly felt thick, the ticking of the wall clock the only sound to be heard. Apart from the clunk as Miss Lathaway swallowed. It was like she was trying to gulp down that small creature that was kicking at her neck with such ferocity she kept holding her fingers to it, pressing and manipulating the soft flesh there in the hope of squashing it and making it go away.

'Thank you for taking care of it, Alex.' He felt the tension of her grip as she tried to wrestle it out of his hands. It wasn't going to happen. He wouldn't let it. His grasp was firmer than hers, his hot little hands holding fast to the plastic, squashing it flat, doing what he could to keep control of the situation.

Then suddenly, as if he had been handed this golden moment, her fingers slackened. Whether it was intentional, he didn't know but slowly and quietly, Alex stood, the silence in the room as heavy as lead. He would give the pencil case back but only because he chose to, not because she had made him do it. Feet squeaking on the vinyl floor, Alex strode over to Oscar and laid the small sparkly item on the desk. It landed on the laminated surface with a slap, an array of small coloured pencils spilling out and rolling onto the floor. Alex watched as Oscar scrambled about beneath the desk, trying to retrieve his precious belongings. He was a stupid boy. They were just pens and pencils. Nothing to get excited about. Alex never really wanted them anyway. It was never about the *stuff* when he took things. It was about control. Besides, he knew that this wasn't the end. He had something else planned. Something gutsy and exciting. He would show Oscar that Alex Broadwood was somebody who always won. Alex always put up a good fight. Always.

* * *

The next hour passed without incident, the final bell of the day welcomed by a collective sigh from the other pupils. They all feared and disliked him. He supposed that was a good thing but at the same time, if he was being perfectly honest, it sometimes made him quite sad. Sad that other children melted away whenever he attempted to join in their games. Sad that they walked in the opposite direction when they saw him coming. He had watched how they all played together, linking arms and laughing. He wanted some of that; it was just that he didn't know how to get it, his anger and envy always making him do things that scared everyone off.

The ringing of the bell softened his teacher's stance. He had watched as she had sat for the remainder of the afternoon, her body rigid, eyes darting everywhere to try to avoid another incident. It was a Friday. Everyone was more upbeat on Fridays. Everyone except Alex. Fridays for Alex meant two whole days being cooped up at home with his mother. Two days of darkness and unpredictable behaviour. A little of the latent festering anger that sat in his abdomen, rose up his chest, thumping behind his breastbone. The other pupils bustled about, gathering up coats and bags, smiles a mile wide. He hated them all. He hated their neat manicured little lives. And he especially hated Oscar with his stupid shiny pencil case and the way he marched about like a robot, never doing anything wrong, smiling at Miss Lathaway as if they were best friends.

He would make his plan work as everyone bustled out of the door, eyes scanning the crowd of waiting parents while he would have to walk home alone, dread a clenched fist at the base of his stomach at the thought of what would be waiting for him when he walked through the front door. He didn't even try to make what happened next look like an accident or inadvertent clumsiness, tripping over his own feet in his excitement. He wanted it to look like a push. A hard one. Alex's hand, his shoulder and the top half of his body slammed into an unsuspecting Oscar, who collided with the concrete. A quick glance at the crumpled figure was enough to convince Alex that he had done a good job. Oscar's hands were scuffed and gritty, his knees grazed. He looked up at Alex, eyes glassy with tears and confusion. Smears of blood were visible through the torn fabric of his trousers. Alex smiled. A job well done.

Behind him a crowd gathered, murmuring words of comfort

to the injured boy followed by shouts for him to stop as Miss Lathaway opened the door and ran outside calling for him to come back.

Too late. He was already halfway through the gate, his body weaving through a throng of parents and merging with a crowd of people before disappearing out of view. Come Monday he would undoubtedly have to pay for his sins, but Monday was a long time off. He had more pressing problems waiting for him at home. A drunken mother. A filthy house. A lack of food in the cupboards. A small push and a crying kid paled into insignificance beside such issues. None of them knew him. And they didn't know his longings, the nasty vicious notions that bulged in his brain.

Alex smiled as he turned into a quiet cut-through between a snarl of bramble bushes and overgrown hedgerows. He had left them all behind. He was on his own now. It was just him and his thoughts pitted against the rest of the world. Relieved to have left it all behind, Alex emerged from the muddy track and turned into the back alley that led to his house before stopping outside, taking a long deep breath and turning the handle of the gate, ready to step from one set of problems into another.

3

HELENA

'You have to eat it. Grandma will be cross if you don't have at least some of it. Just take a bite, Noah. One little nibble won't hurt.' Mabel's stern school ma'am tone does nothing to alleviate the tension of the moment, her words of encouragement failing as Noah shakes his head and bangs his small fist on the table in retaliation.

Then, small thin fingers slide along the surface of the wood, and a piece of toast topples to the floor, landing butter-side down with a wet smack. A series of rattling breaths fill Helena's chest as she inhales. Her smile is a near grimace. It's only toast. The floor can be cleaned, butter wiped up. It's a minor incident, no need for anger or raised voices. He is a child, she is his grandma; she is allowed to let certain things go. Not like when her own children were young and she lacked experience and time, always in a rush. Always eager to do the right thing and make sure their stomachs were full before they set off for school resulting in her feeling permanently exasperated. A single mother teetering on the brink.

'Noah, your tummy will hurt and you'll be hungry at school

if you don't have something to eat.' She says the right words, doing what she can to encourage him, knowing that a member of staff will dole out cereal bars or a piece of fruit should he show signs of hunger at school. This is how their usual morning routine goes. Noah is bright enough to see through her pleas and cajoling, visions of his other breakfast looming large in his mind. Visions of special treatment an enticing thought in his tiny developing brain. He loves his grandma but these midnight callouts have an impact on him. On all of them. He misses his mummy, often becoming distressed when he wakes to find her not there.

'Right, come on then. Let's get your bags and coats and get into the car or we'll be late.'

'Is Mummy in bed?' Mabel's voice cuts through the noise and general hubbub.

'Yes, so we have to be quiet. She got called out to work very late last night and is really tired.' A finger raised to her lips is accompanied by a shushing sound, knowing it will make scant difference to their volume levels. They are children. Noise is what they do.

'She's always at work. And she's always tired.' Noah frowns, his bottom lip jutting out, eyelids lowered in protestation. Dark lashes flutter between tapered eyes as he turns away, giving Helena the slightest of side glances that she immediately recognises as frustration bordering on a slow but sure build-up of simmering rage.

'And she's always angry.' Mabel's sing-song voice contrasts against her brother's hissed declaration. A child-like tone that is light and airy, as if her words are no more than a statement of fact, their mother's fury something to which she has simply become inured.

A slight crinkling of Helena's scalp, a frisson of something she can't quite name. Vanessa has a temper, always has. Helena hoped it had diluted over the years, that motherhood would help soften her daughter's sharp edges, but Mabel's statement has ignited something hot and worrisome in Helena's soul. Memories from when Vanessa was younger. Arguments. Foul thoughts voiced out loud. Insults doled out to whoever got in her way when she was in one of her rages.

She winces at the recollection, her arms outstretched to give each of her grandchildren a quick hug, ignoring both state-ments, doing what she can to chivvy them along. 'Come on,' she says breezily, 'last one out of the house is a stinker.'

Shrieks of delight expand around her. Both children head for the door, a pattering of small feet on the wooden floor echoing around them as Mabel and Noah run onto the path where they wait in silence, their eyes raised to Vanessa's bedroom window. Helena doesn't glance up at the tightly drawn curtains. Only when they are strapped in the car and on the move, and over halfway to school, does she address their concerns.

'Your mummy works very hard, you know. She is the manager of a really busy nursing home where a lot of elderly and frail people live.'

'Deputy manager,' Mabel cuts in, her reproach at her grand-mother's mistake sharp and unforgiving. It conveys a note of annoyance that is well beyond her years.

Helena suppresses the sigh she feels rising in her gut. Now isn't the time for scolding, or for lectures about forgiveness and tolerance and how mortgages and bills need to be paid by adults who are forced to work their fingers to the bone. She refuses to believe that Vanessa is mean to her children. Having a temper is one thing; being deliberately cruel is another thing entirely. Instead she takes a deep breath and grips the steering wheel, trying to conserve what little energy she has before it leaches out of her like water spraying from a sieve. Today is going to be a long one. Too little sleep and too many tasks ahead of her.

'Okay, *deputy manager*, but it's still a very demanding job. Maybe when she picks you up from Josie's house tonight, you can try giving her a hug? Maybe you can help keep your rooms clean and tidy as well? Then perhaps she won't feel so tired all the time and she won't be so grumpy. Just a thought.'

A rapid glance in the rear-view mirror reflects two sets of mournful eyes in the back seat. Helena knows deep down that she is underplaying her daughter's temper, but she has to do what she can to lighten the moment. To reinforce the belief that Mabel and Noah are loved unconditionally. Eager to lighten the moment, Helena turns on the music and they all sing along to the dulcet tones of George Ezra, their previous remarks forgotten by the time they pull up outside the school gates.

'Josie is collecting you tonight and then Mummy will pick you up.'

'What about you, Grandma? Where will you be?'

This again. Helena needs to work – wants to work. She can't be everywhere. Josie is a childminder who charges reasonable rates; a patient reliable woman. She is practically part of the family.

'I have a job, my darlings, you know that. I'm going straight there after I leave the school.'

It's not much, a part-time position in the main library in town, but her job helps keep her sane. Too many hours spent holed up in the house resulted in myriad sombre thoughts rattling around her unoccupied head. Ferrying children to and from school and doing little else addled her brain and so on a whim, she applied for the position of assistant at the library and landed the perfect job. A few hours a week and even fewer responsibilities. She has neither the energy nor the inclination to take on anything remotely taxing, doing just enough to fill up her mind. Just enough to stop the darkness from settling in. The managerial duties of a large busy office environment that she once embraced and loved would now faze and overwhelm her. Another person. Another life.

'Come on, time to get moving.'

They part after a flurry of kisses, accompanied by murmurs and queries about bookbags and PE kits. Helena watches her grandchildren skip through the gates, a small wave of anxiety sliding over her skin at the sight of their retreating figures. She shivers, shakes off that unwanted oppressive feeling and blows them a kiss. Noah's eyes sparkle as he catches it in his tiny little fist. He slips the kiss into his top pocket with chubby semi-dextrous fingers. Horses gallop across her chest as both small bodies round the corner and disappear out of sight. They are safe, they are fine. Their mother is fine. Helena is fine. Never been better. So why, she thinks mournfully, does she feel so out of sorts, as if something monumental is about to happen? Not dread as such and certainly not the level of grief and anxiety she endured after Gavin's death, but there is something there. Like an oil slick slowly seeping beneath her skin and bleeding into her veins, poisoning her from the inside out. A headache threatens, streaks of pain shooting up the back of her skull. It feels as if talons have become hooked into her brain, their long claws gaining purchase, refusing to shift, like a guest who has outstayed their welcome. Her thoughts turn to Rachel.

Rachel.

Her other daughter. Her youngest child. Everything is always about Rachel. No matter how much Helena tries to get on with her own life, she is always there. Rachel is the darkness in Helena's thoughts. She is the thing that hangs over Helena day after day, her problems bloating and discolouring Helena's mind. Rachel is anything but fine, yet nothing Helena says or does can turn things around for her. She has tried. God knows she has tried. The worry and burden of Rachel is something that is always present, incessantly tapping away at her brain until her entire body aches with the effort of containing her worries and constant sense of unease. It's a difficult balancing act, living her life, being a good mother and loving grandmother while Rachel is out there, unloved and unkempt. Destroying her own life.

Helena takes a shuddering breath, erasing those final notions. Rachel is anything but unloved. She is loved as much as any other member of the family and yet their existences are so very different, her daughter's thinking and lifestyle choices beyond Helena's comprehension. She often wonders how and when the descent started. She shakes her head. That is a question for another time, the whole concept too wieldy and too complex to be picked apart while she is driving and short of time.

Traffic is unusually heavy with sirens and flashing blue lights that snake around her vehicle as she heads into town. Her journey is a stop-start effort for over half of the way. By the time she arrives at the library and bursts through the door, a tangle of limbs and bags, the ominous feeling has dissipated, its dead-weight presence already erased from her memory by the stress of navigating her way through innumerable emergency vehicles and finding a parking space that wasn't on the other side of town and didn't result in a twenty-minute walk to work.

Entering the library is a mood-lightening experience. She once described it to a friend as a spiritually cleansing moment, whatever woes she had before opening the doors evaporating and vanishing into the ether. Coming here doesn't feel like a job. She can't explain the sensation and doesn't particularly want to. Giving it solid form may result in it receding, and Helena can't risk such a thing happening. She cannot survive without this place. Her grandchildren are the love of her life. This place is her sanctuary. There is room enough for all of them.

Barbara is sitting scrolling through her phone when Helena enters the staffroom and hangs up her bag and coat.

'Morning, Barb.'

'God, I'm not sure it is.'

Close in age, Helena and Barbara share common ground when it comes to most things, often reminiscing about their childhoods and school years. Their children are also of a similar age, Barbara's daughters only a year younger than Helena's. She and Barbara often socialise outside of work and Helena considers her a good friend, but there are times when Barbara's propensity for dramatising the most mundane of situations can be maddening. After an evening of disturbed sleep, Helena isn't certain she is up to listening to her colleague's latest melodramatic outpouring which almost always boils down to a smidgen of a story she has built upon until it resembles a grisly episode of a soap opera. The original kernel of truth regularly gets lost amidst the fabrications and embellishments that have been carefully crafted around it.

'Well, we're here and the weather is being kind. No howling wind and the sun is about to make an appearance. Oh, and I managed to get a parking space without having to drive halfway around town twice over, so it's all good.' Her smile feels forced. Her attempt at being buoyant is actually an insult to Barbara's intelligence and already guilt is pricking at her. It's the midnight callouts. And Rachel. Thoughts of her youngest daughter regularly drain her of energy and patience. Everything is always about Rachel.

Barbara glances up at her, eyes veiled with sadness. 'They've found a body, Helena. Another one.'

Ice floods her veins, a wash of freezing liquid that frosts her skin and weakens her legs. A pain takes hold in her abdomen as she lowers herself into the chair next to Barbara, who glances up from her screen, her expression wounded and helpless.

'She was discovered close to town. Next to the supermarket. No further details released.'

'Her?' Helena says, her voice low and gravelly. 'So we know it's a female?'

'Not as yet, but the report is pointing towards it, using the same language as the last time. They've even used the phrase "another body", as if they're linked.'

The knot in Helena's gut tightens. This is the second body discovered in as many months. The plethora of emergency vehicles in town on the journey in, all those blue lights and screaming sirens, and somebody's family member lying close by, flesh cold, limbs solid. She wonders how long they have been there for, waiting to be found.

Razor-sharp wire cuts at her throat, her words sounding forced and strangulated. She tries to remain positive, to block out all unpalatable thoughts even though a voice in her head is screaming at her to wake up to the realities of what is happening in her hometown. 'It might not be the same as last time, Barb. The back of the supermarket is a haven for drug users. Maybe—'

'And that other young woman is still missing. The one we spoke about last week. Remember? She's been missing for months and months now.'

Helena does remember. How could she forget? The conversation she had with Barbara left a deadened sensation deep in the pit of her stomach. Photos of a young smiling female on every news site, her healthy complexion and toothy grin staring out at readers. Her name is Maisie Anderson, a healthcare assistant at the local hospital and at one time in the past, a carer at the nursing home where Vanessa works. The name Oak Meadow Care Home had jumped out at Helena when she first read about her disappearance, each letter, each syllable twisting her innards with fear. She had spoken to Vanessa about it, with her daughter claiming she barely remembered Maisie.

'She was only there a month or so. We sometimes use staff from agencies. She probably worked for one of them.'

And that was that. A young woman, missing and forgotten. Dismissed and discarded as if she never existed.

A wave of cold air brushes over Helena's face and neck. She wraps her arms around herself and shivers, lowering her chin to her chest for warmth and comfort. It's all too close to home for her liking, these ghastly findings, each body located just a few miles from where she works and just a short drive from her home. A young woman who lived in her neighbourhood vanishing without a trace. Any death or disappearance pains her, but the nearness of these grisly findings has more of an impact. Selfish, she knows, to think only of how such atrocities affect her and her family, but isn't that how most people feel when they hear about murder and missing people? Self-preservation for family elbows its way in, pushing aside social niceties. She thinks then of her daughter, Rachel. Her proximity to where the bodies have been discovered. Her vulnerability. She also turns her thoughts to the plight of those poor women and what they must have gone through. How their parents and families are coping. And then she thinks of how she would cope if anything happened to either of her girls. Rachel, however, is closer to where the bodies were found. Rachel is the one who worries her the most. There is something about her lifestyle that doesn't quite fit or make sense, like a missing piece of a puzzle. Helena still can't fathom how her youngest daughter ended up living on the streets as a homeless addict. At what point did things begin to spiral out of control? A sharp knife slices at her gut. She blots out those thoughts, biting and gnawing at the inside of her mouth as if she is attempting to inflict some sort of punishment for being a bad mother. Helena tastes blood and winces, before dragging her fingers over her scalp, pulling at small knots and tangles in her dark curly hair.

'Well, all we can do is wait to find out what the cause of death was. Might not be what we're thinking.'

'Or it might.'

The unspoken hangs between them – the fact that the other girl was brutally murdered. If this is the same, then two murders equals a serial killer.

As much as Helena knows that her friend is right, the need for drama at the expense of somebody's loved one before the facts and details have been released makes her uncomfortable. She is overcome by a compulsion to leave the room.

'Well, as a mother and grandmother, I would rather wait to find out from the experts what happened than speculate. Anyway,' she says, her voice brisk, denoting an element of enthusiasm that she doesn't feel after hearing this piece of news, 'haven't we got the local primary school in today?'

If Barbara detects her friend's deliberate attempts to avoid becoming engaged in conversation, she doesn't show it, smiling widely and slapping her hands on her knees before rising out of her seat. Dressed in her usual attire of crisply ironed black trousers and a white blouse, Barbara smooths down her clothes and pushes a strand of blonde hair behind her ear.

'Yes, you're right. How could I forget? Hope it's not that Year 4 boy again. The one from last week who had his finger stuffed up his right nostril for a good five minutes before selecting a book and handing it over to me with a flourish.' Her sigh is deep, her breath smelling faintly of toothpaste and coffee as it wafts towards Helena. Barbara gives her a wide smile, placing a hand on Helena's shoulder, and suddenly everything is back to how it was.

'Come on, partner.' Barbara's voice brims with sensitivity and humour. 'Let's try to forget what's happening in the big wide world and focus on our own goings-on in this place. I'll go and open up if you turn on the computers. Bring on those snotty-nosed, sticky-fingered children.'

Helena feels the warmth of her friend's smile, the solidity of her touch, and laughs, hoping she is right in her thinking and that everything is going to turn out just fine.

4

HELENA

Even when school visits go awry, even when children tear pages out of books and leave dirty fingerprints on shelves and desks; even when their teacher spends the entire time sitting in the corner staring at her phone while Helena helps pupils choose their books, she still loves these days. The noise, the hustle and bustle. The complaints and the whines, the laughter and the broad smiles. They are a part of real life. This isn't any old office job, a position that involves punching numbers into a computer in some cold clinical environment, or sending and receiving emails from people she's never met and likely never will. She is helping to guide and shape the next generation, keep them on track and steer them in the right direction. Books are a way to educate and enlighten. As crass and clichéd as it sounds, she does actually believe it.

'Angus, don't forget your bag!' The touch of the boy's soft skin against hers as he clasps the handle of his bookbag between his fingers is enough to force a lump up into Helena's throat.

She swallows, silently remonstrating with herself for allowing her emotions to get the better of her. She is tired, that's all it is. Tired and overwrought, Rachel and the discovery of another dead female all preying on her mind, weakening her usual steely resolve to not allow the problems of the world get to her. And then there is her mother to think about. A visit is long overdue. The thought of it hangs over her, a huge clock that ticks away in her brain, counting down until she is once again forced to step foot into her mother's stinking domain. Angus is clearly a loved child – clean, well fed. Happy. Not all little ones have the upbringing she did. Her fingers tremble when she rubs at her eyes. And not all younger people will take the right path in life even if their parents do the best they can for them. Some individuals have a self-destruct button, their finger permanently poised over it, ready to push.

Rachel.

No matter how easy the day, how high the sun is as it shines down on her, heating up her face and filling her with hope, Rachel is always there in Helena's mind – her face, her hunched body. Her addiction.

'She takes after me.' Sylvie chipped in when she discovered the plight of her youngest granddaughter, as if she and Rachel were part of an exclusive club. A fraternity known only to those who lived it, their minds and hearts aligned and angled towards complete annihilation. 'She'll be just fine. Stop worrying. That's your problem, Helena,' Sylvie had said as she tapped a cigarette out of the packet and slid it between her pursed painted lips. 'You're always trying to control things. Let the lass be. She's happy as she is.'

Helena had wanted to ask how her mother knew about Rachel's state of mind since she hadn't seen either of her grandchildren for over two years, but hadn't the energy to go there. Arguments with her mother were pointless, like trying to reason with an angry bull. Their previous encounter, a quarrel about the untidiness and turmoil of her mother's home, left her feeling physically exhausted and mentally drained. With limited time and energy she has to pick her battles carefully, and on that occasion she chose to back away and leave things be.

Lunchtime is a rushed affair, her food unfinished as a stream of elderly people file in, books clutched in their hands. They spend the next hour slowly perusing the shelves while her sandwich curls at the corners, the ham turning a sickly shade of green.

At 4 p.m., while the sun dips below the distant hills, Helena tidies the front desk and locks up. She heads to the staffroom to collect her things. It's been a long yet satisfying day. Plenty going on, lots to keep her occupied. A constant stream of tasks to stop her mind from wandering to places she would rather not visit.

Only as she leaves and makes her way to the car park does she find her thoughts being dragged back to those dead bodies and to the missing girl, Maisie Anderson. A world of displaced individuals; that, she thinks sadly, is the environment in which we live. A world where people disappear without explanation, then reappear in sinister and often murderous circumstances. Poor displaced Rachel. She oftens wonders if she could have done more, said more. Loved her more. Done something – *anything* – to stop the rot from setting in. Was her childhood so fractured that she felt a need to harm herself the way she does? Helena cannot count the number of nights she has lain in bed, trying to pinpoint the exact moment when it all fell apart. The truth, as she sees it, is that there is no one single defining moment. It's an accumulation of smaller things, moments that sometimes appear so small and insignificant they slip beneath the radar, unseen and unspoken.

The sharp chill of the setting sun is an immediate sensation that clings to her flesh, skittering over her face and settling in her bones. Helena stares across at the final vestiges of the shimmering golden hue as it sinks behind the hills, a misty orange orb flanked by a swathe of clouds the colour of gunmetal. She turns on the car radio and listens intently, the recently discovered body now headline news. The details are patchy with no gender or age given, no cause of death. But she knows. Everyone knows. Sometimes, the unexpressed is more voluble than spoken words spoken could ever be.

The last time she saw Rachel, Helena gave her a pay-as-you-go phone with money already on it, and a pre-paid card for a local café. No cash. She learnt that one the hard way, finding her youngest daughter asleep in an alley surrounded by empty bottles only days after stuffing £100 into her grimy unwashed palm. If only there were handbooks for parents like Helena; manuals with solid advice on how to rescue adult children from the grip of an addiction. She discovered very early on in life that the magazines and websites designed for parental assistance existed only for middle-class families whose greatest problems involved children who failed to make it to their first choice at university, or new mothers whose babies weren't sleeping through the night or fully weaned onto solids by eight months of age. Being the parent of an alcoholic drug user is a solitary journey, a path she must walk alone. With no husband or parents around to help, she has had to dig deep over the years, be resourceful and learn by her mistakes, because the one big lesson she has learnt since Rachel's life fell apart is that you can't help people who don't want to be helped. Rachel is her own person with her own mind. And what a strong mind it is too, claiming always that she is happy as she is, that she chose her current life and doesn't want to change. Her last parting shot to Helena just a few weeks ago was that she doesn't want to be like her mother or her sister.

'You always preferred her to me anyway. I hope the two of you are very happy together.'

Those words cut deep. It wasn't true. *Isn't* true. As a child, Rachel had been such an easy happy girl, asking for little, helping out whenever she could, whereas Vanessa had been more demanding. Unruly even. Gavin's unexpected premature death from a heart attack had had a bigger effect on Vanessa than it had on her sister. Surely Rachel could see that? And yet even as Helena tried to wrestle with those thoughts, convincing herself that Rachel was speaking through a blur of alcohol, her daughter's memory of that time hazy, she began to wonder if there was an element of truth to Rachel's words. Was her younger daughter neglected, her needs ignored and pushed aside? Was Helena partly to blame for Rachel's current lifestyle? Or was that statement simply a way of lashing out, blaming anybody but herself for her choices and less than salubrious lifestyle? Trying to tease out the separate strands of her life and examine them was like trying to catch the wind.

Helena stares at the clock on the dashboard. Home is calling, and yet her home is a cold empty place. Nobody there to greet her as she steps though the door. No welcoming cooking smells. No husband or partner to take her coat and tell her that her meal will be ready in ten minutes. There have been a few loose dalliances over the years, a few dinner dates and one intimate and less than memorable overnight encounter that left her feeling disorientated and out of sorts, but nobody who has meant anything to her. Nobody who could ever replace Gavin. Both her daughters were, and still are, her life. Until one of them suddenly wasn't.

A dead body found in town. Close to where Rachel hangs out. Helena turns the key in the ignition and swings the car out of the car park, heading towards the back of the supermarket.

She has to know. She has to catch sight of her youngest daughter. Even if she finds Rachel lying unconscious in a gutter, at least she will know she isn't dead. And as always, Helena will try to persuade her to come home, to have a bath and sleep in a comfortable warm bed, and as always, Rachel will refuse, possibly even swear and hurl abuse at her, but it won't matter because at least Helena will know that her beloved daughter is still alive. Just.

* * *

'Thought I'd croaked, didn't you?'

Rachel's mouth is curled up into a snarl, revealing a row of rotten incisors that are peppered with dirt and plaque. One of her front teeth is cracked and as Rachel opens her mouth, Helena can see a wedge of darkness where a row of molars should be. She looks away, her eyes directed over Rachel's shoulder. As a child, she was taught to brush her teeth and not eat sugar and was taken for regular check-ups at the dentist. Helena did everything she could to keep her daughter safe and healthy. And now look at her; at what she has become.

Tiny bolts of electricity needle Helena's skin. Sweat is pasted across her brow despite the plunging temperature. One of the people she was once so close to is now a stranger, their conversation slow and strained. The proximity of her daughter is a painful thing to bear. She has visions of scooping Rachel up in her arms, holding her malnourished scrawny body close to her own and bundling her off to the car to take her home. Once again, she wishes she could pinpoint the exact moment Rachel's life went into decline, but it's all a jumble of events in her head, the timeline and images disjointed and out of sync.

Even asking how she is keeping is pointless and marginally

insulting. Besides, such a simple statement would result in a volley of sarcastic comments being fired her way. Her daughter is an addict; she isn't an idiot. Always bright and sharp, even now she is able to read Helena's thoughts, to pre-empt everything that comes out of her mouth, which means that on the rare occasions they do meet, Helena has to tread carefully, thinking long and hard about what to say. It's like stepping into no-man's land, picking her way around the shrapnel of Rachel's existence. Working out how best to avoid confrontation. The simplest of greetings can result in the most painful of encounters.

'The body was found over there behind the bins if you're interested.'

Rachel points a filthy finger at a large building across the road then sits down on a rickety bench that barely shifts beneath her skeletal frame.

'Here, I got you this,' Helena whispers, every word she utters choking her, each syllable sticking in her throat like glue.

She refuses to cry. Tears bite at the back of her eyelids. A painful lump is wedged in her throat. Her daughter shouldn't be here. She should be at home with Helena. Or living a productive life in her own place. Rachel has a brain and could have been anything. Teacher, accountant, engineer. And yet here she is, hanging around the centre of the town, spending night-times in a hostel with strangers who all have their own demons to battle.

Helena hands over another pre-paid card for a local café. Dark eyes follow Helena's movements, suspicion and distrust leaking out of every pore until eventually after a torturous few seconds where the world falls into a lull, Rachel leans forward and snatches it out of her mother's hand, stuffing the card in her pocket as if it is contraband.

'You can always come home with me, Rachel. It's not safe around here. This is the second body that's been found. The police are already looking for somebody in connection with the first death, stating that it's suspicious.' The words pour out of her. She is unable to stop them. She doesn't want to. Saying nothing is tantamount to condoning Rachel's choices.

A sniff, eyes darting everywhere but at her mother. 'Yeah, this one might be different. Besides, the first one could have been a domestic incident. Usually is. Some bloke stalking his partner, then getting too handy with his fists when jealousy gets the better of him. Usual dickhead stuff.' She spits out the final few words, venom oozing from her, coating every inch of her skin until she is untouchable. Contaminated goods.

'Rachel, you are still vulnerable hanging around this part of town. Please, *please* consider my offer, and come home with me.'

Helena already knows what her answer will be but makes the request anyway. She cannot leave her daughter here without at least trying to do the right thing by her.

'Nah, I'm good. You get yourself off to spend time with your other daughter. Your favourite child.'

And there it is again. The accusation that she was neglected, that Vanessa was treated differently. That Vanessa was loved more than Rachel was or is. It's not true, and those words sting; they are like missiles, each one carefully designed to maim and wound. The suggestion that Helena favours one of her children over the other is preposterous and completely false. She refuses to consider it or speak about such a thing. It's the drink talking, the drugs and the malnutrition and the freezing temperatures all coming together like a perfect storm and skewing her thinking. There are no favourites in their family. Never have been and never will be. She loves all of her children and grandchildren equally, despite their flaws and obvious hostility towards her.

'Where are you staying tonight?'

She follows Rachel's eyes towards the block of flats beyond

the railway bridge and nods. Trying to persuade her again is futile. She can try next time they meet. And she will make sure they do. She will now make a point of driving here on a regular basis in order to keep an eye on Rachel's welfare. With a possible killer roaming the streets, her daughter needs her more than ever. Whether she realises it or not.

5

ALEX

Twenty Years Prior

By the time Monday arrived, the incident had been pushed aside. Alex's weekend had been one long round of drunken tirades from his mother; school and its many problems were relegated to the far reaches of his mind. And anyway, he could see that Oscar's wounds were all but healed, the incident now forgotten. Alex had already heard whispers in the playground about something serious that was going on in school. That would take precedence. Whatever it was, it would surely be more important than scraped knees and a stupid stolen pencil case.

Miss Lathaway remained seated at her desk as they took the register. No strolling about the classroom making idle chitchat, asking how everyone's weekend had been. He always dreaded that; having to hide his snarl, to lie and fudge his way through it to save losing face in front of the other children. His weekends were always the same – an endless stream of stomach-churning screaming matches interspersed with the occasional beating.

Alex watched Miss Lathaway. Her face was paler than usual, like a ghost. As if all her blood had been drained away. He had once read about how people turn white if they bleed to death. That was how Miss Lathaway looked; like she was slowly dying at her desk. Maybe she was. Maybe something bad had happened to her when she wasn't at school and she didn't have long left to live. Maybe that was what all the whispers in the playground were about.

Except it wasn't. At 10 a.m., the whole school was summoned into an assembly. The large hall was packed to the rafters as Mr Bradley, the headteacher, announced to everyone the sudden death of Mrs Gibson, the school secretary. They all sat dumbfounded and confused while staff dipped their heads, fighting back tears. Alex kept his eyes glued to Miss Lathaway, who looked as if she was about to slide off her chair onto the floor. He had seen her and Mrs Gibson go off together at lunchtime. They were probably friends. Maybe that was why Miss Lathaway looked ill and why her hands were shaking as she took the register in class. Maybe she now wanted to pass away as well.

People dying had always fascinated Alex. He once asked his mum what it felt like to die and was rewarded with a slap to the back of his head. He guessed that people losing their lives hurt more than just being hit, so it must be really bad because some of the times his mum beat him, it hurt so much he wished he would die.

The march back to class after assembly was done in silence. Alex felt a buzzing sensation take hold in his chest as two girls walked up to Miss Lathaway's desk and handed her a piece of paper. 'We miss Mrs Gibson,' they said in unison. Miss Lathaway glanced up from the papers that were strewn across her desk. Alex watched his teacher's eyes go glassy, like she was about to cry. Her bottom lip wobbled and she bit at it, as if she was trying to stop it from falling off. 'We've written a poem for her.'

The buzzing and vibrating in his chest expanded as he observed it all, like a bird trying to fly up his throat to escape. He tried to swallow it down but it just kept fluttering and fluttering. He had to let it out, to watch it fly away and soar up into the sky.

'Thank you. This is really thoughtful and beautifully written,' Miss Lathaway said, her voice sounding as if she were standing far away when she hadn't actually moved at all.

The girls returned to their seats, a sea of faces following their movements. Time slowed down and the noise in the classroom became a muted hush, even the most boisterous of pupils aware that today was not the time for bad behaviour or loud voices.

Except for one. He couldn't help it. He had tried to gulp down the trapped bird but it was too difficult. Better to free it, to let it out and then see what happened afterwards. Sometimes he had to make the bad things happen to allow the good things into his life. It didn't always work but there was that one time when he told his other teacher about his mother slapping him. He knew he shouldn't have said anything but after he had spoken, the teacher let him stay in at playtime and gave him a bag of sweets, so it was definitely worth it on that occasion.

Amidst the silence and watchful gaze of the rest of the pupils, Alex raised his hand, the insistent wiggle of his fingers catching Miss Lathaway's eye. His breath concertinaed in his chest, excitement bubbling and sizzling in his veins as her eyes narrowed and focused in on him.

'Yes, Alex,' she said quietly, her voice half soothing and half angry. He had no idea why she sounded that way. He was about to try to help, to let the other children know what had happened. Because in that assembly nobody explained to them how or why Mrs Gibson had died. And he wanted to know.

These things mattered to him. Death was important. Exciting even. 'What is it?' she said with a sigh. 'What do you need?'

His voice was a shrill rasp when he replied, like a high-pitched squeak even though he was trying to sound older and authoritative. As if what he was about to say was the most important question anyone had ever asked. 'How did Mrs Gibson die?' he said, his voice echoing around the room. 'Was she stabbed? Or was she shot?'

He raised two fingers and pointed them at her face, mimicking the sound of a gun being fired. Laughter bubbled up his throat, pulsing at his neck. He tried to stop it but couldn't. The laughter always had a habit of spilling out when it shouldn't. He didn't know why. It was just how it was.

Miss Lathaway took a rattling breath, her hand pressed to her chest as if her heart was about to fall out. Maybe it was. Maybe she was so sad that she had to push really hard to keep everything in place. That was another thing he had read about – that when people are upset about somebody dying, their hearts crack open inside their chest and they too can pass away. Maybe Miss Lathaway would also die. Maybe he was right and that was definitely why she was so pale and her hands were shaking.

'No, Alex, Mrs Gibson wasn't stabbed and nobody shot her.' Her teeth were gritted together. He could see her jaw pulsing as if she also had something trapped in her neck.

Alex thought perhaps Miss Lathaway now hated him for saying it. He felt certain she would like to drag him out of the classroom and scream in his face that he was a repulsive little shit. Just like his mother often did.

Except that didn't happen. Instead, her voice softened as she spoke. 'We don't know how she died just yet but we need to be respectful and not speak about such things. Now, it's time to get on with our work. I'd like these spelling sheets to be completed in the next five minutes.'

Alex was undeterred. He didn't want the conversation to be over. He liked it when his teacher spoke to him, her eyes locking with his. But it wasn't always easy, working out what he should and shouldn't say, and sometimes the wrong words fell out of his mouth. Like now. He swung around and pointed at the other pupils, fired up by all the attention. It made him warm and happy inside, seeing their faces turned in his direction, their eyes focused on him. Like a roaring fire flickering deep inside his belly.

'Bet you've never seen a dead body, have you? I have,' he said, his voice rising in pitch and volume. 'My nan died right in front me. She fell backwards, her mouth and eyes staying open even after she'd stopped breathing. Her skin went black and she hit the floor with a bang. And then there was this other time when me and my friends were by the stream and—'

'Alex, sit down! Now!'

The nice Miss Lathaway was gone. He had made her disappear with his words. Her big angry voice ricocheted off every wall. Alex slumped into his seat, resentment at her command crinkling his skin and making his stomach ache. The scrape of a nearby chair echoed loudly, the boy next to him edging away as if Alex were toxic waste. And now he had done something else that was stupid – he had made the other children hate him more than they did already. He pretended to not care. Easier that way. Even though he cared a lot. So much that his tummy would hurt every morning on the way to school at the thought of standing alone in the playground while all the other children played football and hide-and-seek.

Alex glanced at the clock then over at his teacher, who was still staring at him. He knew what came next. She would ask him to stay back for a few minutes after the others had all left. He didn't mind. He had something to show her. Something exciting. And then she would feel sorry for shouting at him. She might even want to be his friend.

* * *

Later, after the bell had sounded, after the rest of the class had filed out, their eyes lowered as they passed by him, she placed a hand on his shoulder, bending down to whisper in his ear. Requesting he stay back for a few seconds to chat about Mrs Gibson.

He nodded. This was his moment. A glow of sharp interest spread over his skin at the mention of Mrs Gibson. Miss Lathaway was about to tell him how she died. Excitement fluttered in his chest, making him warm and dizzy. He actually really liked Miss Lathaway. He just wished she would like him back.

'You know, it's always best to be kind to people, Alex. To think carefully before we speak so we don't frighten or upset anybody. I don't want to hear you say anything like that ever again. Do you hear me?'

Her words were like a pickaxe to his soul, gouging at his insides over and over. He had been tricked. This conversation wasn't about Mrs Gibson. It was about him. Him and his behaviour. His loose mouth and the stupid thoughts that rattled around his brain, banging against his skull until it hurt. He needed to do something to make it up to her. To make her like him. Because he so desperately wanted her on his side.

'I am kind to people, Miss Lathaway,' Alex chirruped, his smile stretching across his face as he spoke. 'Not like my dad. He once hit a man and went to jail for it. He said he'd like to hit my other teacher for shouting at me all the time but I told him not to. Not that it matters now as he left us and he's never coming back. Here,' he said glibly, opening his bag and reaching in. 'I got this for you. It's a present from me to you. Do you like it?'

He watched, bemused, as a shriek erupted out of her throat, her legs turning to liquid when she tried to stumble back from the dark red bundle that lay in the boy's cupped palm.

'It was dying anyway, Miss, so I put it out of its misery and killed it with a rock. It was funny watching it twitch about before it died. Made me laugh a lot.'

She stared down at the dead sparrow. Alex waited for her to do something. To *say* something. It was a good thing he had done, putting it to sleep, killing it and showing it to her. How could she not see that? Why did grown-ups always do the opposite to what he expected? He'd hoped for smiles and sympathy and yet her face was white like snow. She shook her head again and again as if it was vibrating, her hair bouncing around her face like candyfloss every time she moved.

When she did finally say something, her voice sounded like somebody was choking her, their big fat fingers curled around her neck until her eyes bulged and she couldn't breathe properly. Like one of those people in the horror movies that he watched when his mum fell asleep in the chair, too drunk to notice.

'Go home, Alex Broadwood,' she hissed, her eyes fixed on his, the darkness in them confusing and scaring him in equal measure. 'Go home and take that bird with you, and hear me when I say, never ever lift a finger to anybody or anything ever again!'

6

PRESENT DAY

I used to scream at the books I read that contained women like me. I would holler at females in films; weak, insipid creatures who made bad decisions resulting in them living as I do now. Frustration at their ineptitude making my teeth itch. And yet here I am, being held captive in a strange environment, slumped on a hard wooden floor. Hands tied tightly, the rope cutting into my flesh. A strip of fabric pulled around my face. My backside aches, fiery flames running up and down my spine. And then there is my surroundings. The photographs. The clothes draped over a chair. The perfume he sometimes sprays around the room – cheap and cloying. I have no idea who the woman in the photographs is. I do know him though. Not that it matters. He has never spoken about our association and clearly doesn't care that I have recognised him, making no attempt to disguise himself. And that scares me more than being held captive. It suggests two scenarios, both of which leave a sour taste in my mouth. He is either going to keep me here indefinitely. No chance of release. Or at some point, he is going to kill me.

The fact I am still alive and not already dead in a ditch mystifies me. I am tied up in what I presume is his house. Keeping me here serves no real purpose. He feeds me. He allows me to go to the bath-room for my ablutions, the length of thick rope that usually binds me removed while he waits outside. He doesn't beat me. God forbid he hasn't made any kind of assault on me, sexual or otherwise. Aside from my initial capture where he hit me and dragged me into his car, he has shown no violence towards me, which begs the question – why the fuck am I here?

His dialogue is brief. If I had to choose a word to describe his behaviour towards me, I would use the word dull. Emotionless. Much like this room. There have been a few times when I have made requests and irked him, his lip curling in response. Like the time I felt the familiar dull ache start up in my lower abdomen. By the time I dared to speak up and ask for sanitary towels and tampons, blood had begun to seep through my jeans. He had let out a roar and clenched his fists. I braced myself, closing my eyes, waiting for the hit. But it didn't come. He left the room, slamming the door behind him, returning a short while later with a carrier bag slung over his arm.

'I'll put them in the bathroom,' he said.

And then he untied my hands and I half limped, half hopped across the landing, following him to the bathroom. A pair of clean trousers and some underwear was waiting for me when I got there. And a pack of sanitary pads.

The sanitary products are always there now, stacked in the bath-room cabinet. I use the word bathroom loosely. The window has been covered over with a piece of wood that is nailed in place. Banging on it while screaming for help is pointless. The same goes for trying to escape. I know because I once tried it, using my bare hands to try and prise the wood away from the frame. My nails broke, some ripping away from my fingers, and my hands bled, splinters becoming embedded deep into the fleshy tips. He calmly kicked in the door when he became aware of my efforts, his face expressionless, his movements calm and robotic. With a firm grip, he led me back to the room, making sure the rope around my wrists was tied as firmly as possible until it almost cut off my circulation. Since that time, he leaves the door open, standing guard while I shower and use the toilet.

The bathroom is always spotlessly clean. Clinical even, the smell of bleach omnipresent. My eyes sting from the fumes when I set foot in there and do what I need to do. Showering. That's another thing he encourages. And when I do shower, it is always a shock. Already, I can feel muscle wastage from a lack of movement. Running my hands over my torso and limbs, I am appalled by the slackness of my flesh. Bones jutting out where muscle and sinew should be.

The house is quiet. He has a job, leaving every day and returning hours later slightly dishevelled, his collar unbuttoned, tie pulled to one side, his hair limp looking. So for now, I will sit and wait, whiling away the hours, working out ways in which to get out of this god-awful place before he finally tires of me and takes a knife to my throat.

7

HELENA

A criminal investigation is underway after a body was discovered in an alleyway close to the centre of Nunborough-on-Tees. A heavy police presence was visible in town as the area was sealed off and the forensic investigators called in.

Police have asked for anybody who was in the area on Monday evening to come forward with any information they may have.

More to follow.

The tremble in Helena's fingers as she reads the headline and brief account of the grisly find causes her to drop her phone. It skitters across the floor and lands underneath the sofa. Knees cracking as she bends, she arches her spine feline style to retrieve it.

She is cold, her flesh puckering at the thought of those words. She knew there was a body. Of course she did. A second body. No obvious links to the other dead woman. So far. And yet reading it, seeing it written there in black and white, feels like a punch to the gut. A curled fist slamming into her intestines with force. That headline has made it real, given the whole thing solid form.

Her breath comes in gasps, the air in the room suddenly thin, difficult to inhale. No matter how hard she tries, she cannot stop the images that flood her brain – bloated dead bodies lying on the cold wet ground, unseeing eyes staring up at a dark starless sky. Somebody's loved one. Somebody's child. We are all somebody's child. A mother somewhere is grieving for her baby.

Rachel.

And Vanessa. Both of her girls. Each vulnerable in their own special way. She thinks of Rachel roaming the streets at night, cavorting with unsavoury people. And then Vanessa making midnight dashes to the care home to tend to an emergency. Parking up in a dark area and walking alone to her office.

Hands still quivering, Helena struggles to open the bottle of wine she so desperately craves. Two unsuccessful attempts result in her letting out a growl of frustration and tossing the corkscrew into the sink. She doesn't need the wine anyway. Alcohol isn't the answer, she knows that. It's simply a salve for her current woes. A balm for her worries. Ignoring the local news won't solve anything either. She would rather know. With a daughter who lives on the street and another who works unsociable hours, she would rather know.

Time and again she has asked herself how it came to this, how her youngest daughter ended up living on the streets, and tonight is no different. And once again, like every other time, she cannot find an answer, the reasons for her daughter's downfall as elusive as the pot of gold at the end of a rainbow. Pinning Rachel down and asking why she ended up this way is like trying to snatch at shadows. Which is why Helena internalises her worries, spending night after night raking over the past, picking at specific days and events, trying to find one solid single reason why her youngest daughter has ended up in the gutter. Her job and her grandchildren often keep her mind occupied, stopping the obvious from slithering in, but tonight there will be no callouts, no midnight dashes to the other side of the village. Tonight her mind is free to wander down the dark damp alleyways of her memories, to stagger into those hidden misty places and fall down never-ending rabbit holes, coming up with rash answers that will exacerbate her anxiety and add to her low mood.

Tea or coffee; either is better than alcohol. Wine makes her sleeping pattern erratic, her dreams feverish and full of fear and angst. How can she possibly lecture her daughter about the ills of addictive substances if she herself sits night after night, wine glass in hand, consuming enough to fell a small horse?

The buzz of her phone drags her thoughts back to the present. She is reluctant to check it, knowing that once she gets hooked into reading messages, she will end up scrolling social media and perusing local news sites for titbits of information.

Eyes tapered, she picks it up and scans the screen, her flesh puckering as she reads the message, each word like a knife to her heart.

Your daughter is a fucking lunatic!

It's an unknown number and Helena's first reaction is to block it, but her curiosity is piqued, her nerves rattling and shaking.

Fingers poised over the keys, she thinks of a hundred

different things to say and in the end types the simplest of messages.

> Who is this?

Before a reply comes through, the phone rings again, Vanessa's name appearing on the screen.

'Vanessa? Everything okay?'

'Yes, of course. Why wouldn't it be?'

A pain travels up and down Helena's chest, lodging beneath her breastbone at the sound of her daughter's usual efficient brusque tone. Helena feels lightheaded; devoid of energy. A noisy swallow and then a sigh as she tugs at a strand of hair that hangs over her eye, pulling it out by the root and throwing it on the floor as if it is poisonous.

'Nothing. I just wasn't expecting to hear from you, that's all.' A clamminess pastes itself to Helena's forehead and neck. She shouldn't have replied to that message and now she itches to block it. Easier than getting drawn into something unpalatable. Besides, it might be one of those dreadful spam messages, designed to lure in nervous unsuspecting parents who end up passing over credit card details to perfect strangers. She is not one of those people. She's stronger than that. Savvy and worldly wise, more so than your average middle-aged female. She has had to be. And yet a part of her knows that this isn't the case, that such messages are almost always designed to pull at latent fears and heartstrings, make the recipient feel worried about the safety of their child or children. The message she has just received didn't have that type of emotive pull to it. It was an insult. No requests for personal information. No fabricated situations that require immediate assistance and a whole load of cash.

Your daughter is a fucking lunatic...

'Sorry. Ignore me. I'm just a bit tired and wasn't expecting a call from you.'

'I just wanted to let you know that it's parental consultations at the school next week. It's Wednesday afternoon at 2 p.m. You don't have to go if you're busy?' Vanessa says, her voice now a drawl. 'Or tired.'

A stifled sound escapes from Helena's throat, a heady combination of relief and annoyance at her daughter's thinly disguised sarcasm expanding in her abdomen. 'Yes, no problem at all. Wednesday is my day off. I'll look forward to it. Always nice to hear how my little cherubs are doing.'

Helena stops, takes a juddering breath, aware she is gabbling. If Vanessa hears her agitated tone, she does an excellent job of ignoring it.

'Right, thanks, Mum. Hopefully I'll be there as well. All depends how the day goes. Wednesdays are always tricky for me.'

Helena wants to reply that every day is tricky for her, her work taking precedence over her children, then sucks in a lungful of air and bats that uncharitable thought away. Vanessa is a single parent. It's the most difficult job in the world. What she needs is help, not a barrage of disparaging remarks from those closest to her.

'Well, if you don't get there, I'll bring Noah and Mabel home with me rather than them having to wave me off and go with Josie.'

'Ah, that's great, Mum, thanks. I'll let Josie know. Might save me a few quid if I give her plenty of notice.'

Helena ends the call on a positive note, a certain lightness taking hold, as if her body is pumped full of air. She checks her phone and on seeing no reply to her earlier message, blocks the number and slumps back on the sofa, the lightness short-lived as the previous feeling of doom returns and settles on her, pinning her to the couch. Try as she might, she cannot erase that message from her brain.

Perhaps it was one of Rachel's acquaintances. Some of them have mobile phones despite being homeless. She refers to them as acquaintances because they are definitely not friends. Just a gathering of people who spend their days wandering aimlessly around town before laying their heads down in the same hostel at night. Disparate souls with nowhere to call home. A friend wouldn't allow someone to live as Rachel does. They would intervene and help.

So would a decent parent.

Helena forces away that thought and swallows down the lump in her throat, refusing to weep for a daughter who rejects all offers of assistance. She has tried, God knows she has tried. And she won't ever stop trying, because she is her mother and that is what mothers do. Good ones, that is. Not people like Helena's own mum, the woman who couldn't care less whether Helena and her family live or die.

She wonders for how long Rachel will occupy space in her head, elbowing her way into Helena's thoughts day and night and taking up residence there until there isn't any room left for anything or anybody else. Grandchildren and the library are a reprieve, another avenue in her life. A place that is Rachel free. But even then, she is there, standing in the shadows, biding her time and readying herself for the moment when Helena's mind isn't occupied, and that is when she steps forward, her youngest daughter's many problems and insecurities back under the spotlight.

Rachel's mental deterioration has been so nuanced, so subtle, that Helena finds it impossible to pin down to one single event. Although there was that one time when she and Vanessa were younger. That day when they went off to play in the woods. If Helena was forced to admit it, then maybe, just maybe, it was around that time when Rachel's mental health dipped. Not a sudden noticeable collapse. More of a gradual downturn.

She shakes her head, unconvinced by her own thoughts. Perhaps she is putting too much thought into it, wildly grasping at events and incidents to explain why her youngest daughter took such a rutted and crooked path through life.

Flattened by exhaustion, Helena climbs the stairs, showers and clambers into bed, the trials of the day weighing heavily on her, the text message still niggling at her. It's the lack of control that scares her the most; she knows nothing of Rachel's life apart from the fact it is a difficult one. When they were children, Helena could manipulate and control her girls and their movements, make sure they were safe, warm and well fed. Parents have to relinquish that responsibility as their children grow and mature. They have to accept the life choices their offspring make no matter how unpleasant or unacceptable they may seem.

She rubs at her arms to invite warmth onto her flesh and slides down under the duvet. Sleep comes quickly, Helena soon drifting off into a deep slumber, her parental responsibilities and anxieties about her children melting away like ice at the first signs of spring.

8

ALEX

Twenty Years Prior

Alex kept his head lowered, his eyes following the trickle of amber liquid that traversed and pooled over the tiled floor. He observed with a sense of humiliation how it seeped through the cracks, the small rivulets of urine forming a puddle at his feet. Shame consumed him. He looked at anything other than up at her, his own mother. He kept his eyes fixed on the kitchen door, noticing how it hung to one side, the hinges held on by one solitary screw. He stared at the grime in the corners of the floor. And the buckle of the large belt that swayed close to where he stood, the leather strap clenched between his mother's bony fingers.

'Clean it up.' Her voice rang around the room. 'Get a cloth, boy, and clean up this mess.'

Alex scrambled to his feet, scurrying upstairs where he grabbed at a piece of mould-ridden fabric that was slung over a radiator. Anything for a quiet life. Anything to avoid another beating.

Her eyes followed his movements, narrowed in anger. 'Not

that. Get a flannel from the bathroom. Useless, you are. Friggin' useless waste of space. No wonder your father left us, having to put up with you every single day.'

Taking the stairs two at a time, he came back, a frayed filthy face cloth hanging from his fingers. Already stained, its putrid smell reminded him of the dead bird he had kept in his school-bag. He wasn't sure why he did that, keep its bloodied feathery body for so long until the decay set in. Sometimes it just happened, a need to hit and hurt and lash out at anything and anybody overtaking him. Making him do things. Bad unspeakable things. It disgusted others, all that blood, but not him. He tried to suppress the joy he felt after seeing the looks on the faces of the other children in his class when he regaled them with the tale of how he killed the bird and then showed it to their teacher, but in the end he couldn't control the laughter that bubbled up his throat. He wasn't like the others. He knew that. The sight of somebody or something in distress lit up his senses, setting off a furnace somewhere deep in his belly. Once, Tara Holywell had fallen and banged her chin on the playground and was so badly injured she had to go to hospital. Alex had tried to stop it, his loud guffawing as she limped back into the class-room, blood dripping off her face in long scarlet streaks, but it came out of nowhere. He could still recall the collective looks of dismay from the other kids, how they turned away from him, widening the gap between them. Cutting him off completely. But the more isolated he became, the more he felt the need to impress them, to try to win back their friendship. And so the cycle of doing things – terrible things – was impossible to break.

Even at his tender age, Alex could see the differences, how they all skipped into school every morning in their shiny new shoes and fashionable clean clothes, bags slung over their shoulders that contained things he could only ever dream of owning. A treasure trove to a desperate impoverished boy. Sometimes standing apart on his own had its advantages. He was able to observe them from afar, study their behaviour, watch their movements and discover their weaknesses. Being different, being the poor deprived boy in class, had its benefits. What doesn't kill you makes you stronger.

'Now mop up that mess or you'll feel the weight of this belt on your back, my lad.'

Alex scrubbed and wiped. It wasn't a punishment. He would rather live in a clean house than a dirty one. If only his mother felt the same way. Being surrounded by dust and filth made him edgy and restless and sapped him of energy. So he dabbed and mopped until the flannel was saturated and the puddle on the floor was almost dry. The kick she gave him as he got to his feet knocked him back down again. He held on to the face cloth, unwilling to risk dropping it and his minor transgression being used as another excuse to hit him. Anything but that belt. The memory of it as it came down across his bare behind the last time she used it made him wince.

'Get up. Wash your hands and clean that flannel. You stink to high heaven. And change your piss-stained clothes. You're nothing but a big baby.'

He skulked away, tiptoeing around her, avoiding squeaky floorboards. Trying to make himself invisible. Unseen and unheard. Anything could trigger a beating. Anything and nothing. There were no rules. Just an unstable woman with loose fists and a heavy belt. It was all he had known. Since his dad had left, things had deteriorated. It was bad before. Now everything had turned to shit.

He could smell her breath as he passed, the stench of alcohol and cigarettes trailing in his wake. Alex had once tried a slug of the vodka she drank but it made his throat burn. The cigarettes were easier. He quite liked them and often stole a few from her packet when she was asleep. She was always too drunk to notice. Or too stupid. As far as he could tell, one was the same as the other.

Upstairs, he stripped off his trousers and underwear, the smell of urine causing him to gag. The general filth in the house masked most of the odour. Still, he knew his clothes needed washing. Sitting in urine-soaked trousers would repulse him. Unlike his mother, he knew how to take care of himself. How to stay clean and keep up appearances as best he could. It was all he had, his looks and razor-sharp reflexes. Everything else about him was warped and off-kilter, his dark thoughts bent out of shape.

In the bathroom, he filled the tub with hot water and rubbed at the fabric with a bar of soap, sloshing the items in the water and repeating the process until the smell dissipated and the yellow watermark vanished. Then he wrung each item out and laid them over the side of the bath to dry. Standing at the sink, Alex washed himself. It felt good to sluice the grime off his skin. Therapeutic even. Each consecutive wash and rinse took him further away from the house and further away from her. One day he would be a grown man; he could put all of this behind him and take charge of his own life. He would do things he had only ever dreamed of. He would buy his own house and car and work in a top office job, driving there in a slick expensive suit and shiny patent leather shoes. But for now, he had to endure the beatings, try to control his bladder and keep his fear in place when she wielded that belt and shrieked at him, doling out threats with a glint in her eye that told him she meant every word.

Clean and mildly invigorated, he opened his wardrobe doors and pulled out joggers and an old sweatshirt, dust motes swirling as he yanked them off the hanger. Dressing quickly, he lay down on his bed and stared at the ceiling. It isn't true that children are like their parents. He knew that he would find a way to break free of all of this. Like a caged bird, he would flap his wings and learn to fly, fleeing this rotten stinking place and leaving it far behind him.

9

PRESENT DAY

It's months, not weeks, that I've been kept here. My periods have helped me keep an idea of time, my body as regular as clockwork despite my horrendous living conditions. Despite being holed up in a shithole of a room with sporadic visits from a madman. I'm given regular meals and fluid, but the lack of movement is taking its toll. While he is out of the house, I try to rotate my shoulders and flex my legs, but it isn't the same as being able to get up and walk about. I have a sore on my lower back and my skin is pale and flaky. A lack of natural light has resulted in pasty flesh and dull, dry hair. It's been a long time since I have looked in a mirror. He isn't stupid or careless enough to leave one in the bathroom. No sharp objects. Nothing I can use to jab him in the throat and watch him bleed out before making a hasty retreat and finding a way out of this makeshift prison.

The house is quiet, the distant chirrup of birdsong a welcome sound that cannot be deadened by bricks and glass and blackout blinds. Sometimes, when he is in a good mood, he opens the curtains a fraction. Just enough to allow a sliver of daylight in, but not enough for me to see out. He may be deranged but he isn't an idiot. Control is his thing, his defining feature. Control of the house, control of any speck of dirt that dares to creep its way into the place. Control of me.

I think of my life outside these four walls, and wonder if people are still out searching for me or if they have assumed I have disappeared of my own volition and don't want to be found. It happens. People go missing all the time. Their faces appear on the television, online and in local newspapers, but after a few months, people tire of it. They grow weary of being bombarded with news updates and so the police and the press move on, find a new story to feast on, the carcass of the missing pecked dry. That's all I am now. A pile of dry bones slumped on a floor in a house that is definitely not a home.

My chest convulses as I swallow down a sob. I refuse to stay here. I need to find a way out of this place, but he is making it almost impossible for me to find a route out. There is a world outside this room and I need to get back to it. I have a family, friends. A job. I have a life and I want to live it, not sit here day after day while it passes me by.

The first few weeks here were the worst. I allowed my mind to think about the most awful outcomes, visualising my own demise. Wondering where he would dump my body after slitting my throat or bashing me over the head with a heavy object. The most depressing thing about having lots of time to think is the fact that my brain led me down the darkest of paths, never allowing the light to filter in. It's a lonely rutted lane, littered with potholes and traps. Littered with dead-ends and monsters that lie in wait. But then as time has passed, I've come to realise that he needs me. For how long, I don't know, but he needs me to satisfy some weird ghastly urge that he has. Perhaps he enjoys to dominate, to be the one with all the power. Or maybe I'm putting too much thought into this and he is simply unhinged. I do have some thoughts, and they are this – I am a replacement for the woman in the photographs. There is a resemblance. I have had enough time to think about it and although his answers aren't forthcoming whenever I ask, there is a flicker of something in his eyes each time I mention her.

A dart of dread whizzes up my spine at the sound of the key in the lock, my notions curtailed. It's him. He has no visitors. Nobody ever calls or knocks. No doorbells ringing or loud knocks from below that could help set me free. I'm alone here. I long for a cold caller to rap at the door or for a neighbour to call around unannounced asking to borrow a cup of sugar. But it's not going to happen. I know that now. I've been here long enough to realise that this is only going to end one way. That perhaps one day I will be the one whose face is plastered around this room, and another poor unsuspecting female will take my place.

A creak on the stairs turns my blood to sand. I sit up, attempting to remain alert. Waiting for him to appear in the doorway. Making sure that today isn't the day when his brain has splintered beyond recognition and he enters this room, a hammer in his hand, his face twisted with malice.

'Hello,' he says, his tone sickly sweet. Sweeter than I've ever known him to be. 'I've brought you a present.'

A sparkle of something is thrown at my feet, his smile crooked as he waits for me to respond. I nod and lean forwards as far I can, feigning interest in the small silver bracelet that has landed on the floor next to my foot.

'I realise you can't thank me, but I hope you'll like it.'

And with that he is gone, his body vanishing out of sight, leaving me alone once more. I stare at the tiny bracelet that I can now see is splattered with crimson streaks. I know what it is and I know now that I'm not the only one. This is proof. There are others out there. Other women who haven't been as fortunate as I have. I wouldn't consider myself privileged or lucky but I'm here, breathing. I'm still alive.

Although for how long is another matter.

10

ALEX

Fifteen Years Prior

Derek Roper was the most putrid of all the teachers. His lessons always brought out the worst in Alex. The young lad could see the resentment and displeasure in old Roper's eyes, his sour expression and downturned mouth; clearly retirement couldn't come soon enough for him. Roper was old school, a dinosaur, his teaching methods antiquated and out of touch. Alex thought that even the simple task of driving to work every morning robbed him of energy. He looked like a guy who was running on empty before the day had even begun. Sometimes he was hauled in to man the behaviour unit, a place where other teachers, when things became riotous, dumped the most difficult of pupils. Alex had only been there once or twice. It was a room full of testosterone-fuelled teenagers who hated school with every fibre of their being. Alex identified with that particular sentiment, always counting down the days until the end of term. He guessed old Roper felt the same way. You could see it in him; he no longer had the drive or the enthusiasm he used to have as he entered the classroom and prepared for the day ahead. Rumour had it that he was once the best teacher ever, but now, the buzz and the adrenaline that purportedly surged through him was no longer present. It was clear even to the dimmest of pupils that Roper's eagerness for teaching dissipated a long time ago. Probably once the behaviour of pupils deteriorated with fewer and fewer sanctions available for teachers to keep order. No more being able to wield a cane to keep everyone in line. No more beating kids until they were black and blue. Poor Roper was left helpless and tongue-tied, groups of teenagers milling around him, firing insults his way with no holds barred.

Ever had sex with a horse, sir?

What's it like to be the oldest, ugliest fuck in the school?

Every day brought a new insult. Alex recalled one time when Roper had shrieked at them that their shock tactics and behaviour were lower than a snake's belly. They had rolled with laughter, Alex included. Roper obviously kidded himself that he was hardened to the abusive remarks, but Alex could see that they still stung, each barbed comment forcing his face into a scowl, his eyes becoming dull and desperate. His expression stricken and ghost like.

Alex watched as Roper's car entered the car park and ground to a halt. Standing behind the bushes, Alex waited, staring over at the school, a square sprawling edifice with few, if any, architecturally attractive features. It never failed to repulse him. Even the staff hated it. It was obvious by the way they carried on, shouting at the kids and leaving as soon as the bell sounded, each of them becoming jammed in the door as they headed out to the car park in a large unruly huddle. In many ways they were worse than the pupils. Disenchanted and desperate to get home every evening. Each of them forced together every day. Yet each of them always alone.

Roper stopped as he clambered out of his car, Alex silently observing from afar. The old guy stared up at the building. Like everyone else, he was probably wondering which uneducated swine drew up the plans for such an eyesore.

Ninety-seven days. That was all that was left of his working life. He had talked endlessly about his retirement. Ninety-seven days was also all that was left of Alex's time at this school. They were leaving together, their sentences served. Alex suppressed a snigger. Did Roper really have enough energy to stagger to that finishing line? He looked half dead as it was. Did the old man really have it in him to see it to the end? All he had to do was let the insults slide off him like liquid mercury and keep his anger in check. Alex imagined Roper being pushed too far and then losing his temper and subsequently his pension. Rumour had it that he had been dragged into the head's office last week over the Gallantree incident. Apparently, Paul Gallantree, a particularly argumentative student, had complained to the headteacher about old Roper's foul language after Gallantree had tried to stab another pupil with a sharpened pencil as she passed by in the corridor. Alex had watched as Gallantree had snarled and shrugged his shoulders when spoken to about the incident, calling the other pupil a bitch when asked to apologise. Gallantree was right about that. She was a bitch. A proper stuck-up little slut. But Roper didn't see it that way and had let his rage unravel, calling Gallantree a grotesque little bastard. With hindsight, Roper should have let it go, but it did provide some much-needed entertainment on an otherwise dull day. Alex imagined the telling off he got in the office, declaring that he was sorry about his language and having to suck up to the headteacher because he wanted to keep his pension, thinking that he had worked too long and hard to let some acne-riddled youth take it from him.

The best ideas always came when Alex wasn't planning them. In his peripheral vision, he could see the outline of Roper as he made his way through the main doors of the school. It was over half an hour until the bell was due to ring. Plenty of time to do what he needed to do. Plenty of time to wreak just enough havoc and make sure Roper's final days in this school would be memorable. He darted behind the bush and back onto the main path that led into the schoolyard where gangs of pupils were beginning to gather. Striding past, Alex headed towards the door, his mind homed in on the task in hand. Stabbing other pupils with pencils and swearing at teachers was primary school stuff, acts of defiance that an eight-year-old could achieve. He was better than that. Bigger and smarter. His misdemeanours would be the talk of the school. He would make sure of it.

* * *

Every lesson always started the same way. Roper leaning down to open his briefcase, murmuring about the smell of old leather and how it gave him such pleasure. Alex imagined it was one of the few things, if not the only thing, that gave him satisfaction during his working hours. Sad, really, that that was all the old guy had going for him, nostalgic recollections of those first few heady years of teaching hitting him in the solar plexus every time he smelt an old briefcase. He once told the class that the dim memory of becoming a teacher was now a glowing unreachable thing, like a distant star that died many eons ago but continued to shine. It had made Alex's toes curl, listening to him rattle on like that, wondering why somebody didn't tell him that he was making a complete tit of himself, acting like a fucking poet in front of thirty teenagers who couldn't give a shit about him or his teaching career and how it had slowly gone down the pan.

Alex slid into his seat, watching as the rest of the class barged their way in and slumped into chairs. All of them crammed together in one small space. Thirty resentful teenagers shoehorned into primitive squalid surroundings. With a leaking roof, rotten windows and shabby textbooks, even Roper had declared on more than one occasion that kids deserved better. Not that any of it mattered any more. They were all due to leave. And it couldn't come soon enough.

Alex felt Roper's eyes land on him as he scanned the room, waiting for everyone to sit down. He knew that his teacher thought of him as a brooding individual with a predilection for harming animals, and on occasion, teenage girls. He was right. That was one thing the old guy had going for him. He was accurate when it came to sussing people out. Alex rarely mixed with his peers, preferring his own company. He found the other kids immature and lacking in intelligence. He was a lone wolf, the boys giving him a wide berth and the girls snarling and curling their lips in disgust as he passed them in the corridors or outside in the yard. Alex wasn't ugly and he knew it. If anything he thought himself fairly good-looking. No acne, no stinking hairy armpits disguised by endless sprays of cheap deodorant. And yet girls his age ignored him. He wasn't bothered. It was their loss. He was on the countdown to freedom. Soon this crumbling building and all the people in it would be a dim and distant memory.

Roper lifted out his large textbook, slamming it on his desk, its heft enough to cut through the noise and gain everyone's attention. Alex reckoned he loved doing it, the power of the ensuing silence bolstering his fragile ego.

Why do I have to learn about this Shakespeare guy when all I

wanna do is train to be a plumber? Somebody had shouted it at
Roper last week when he asked them about how Shakespeare
presented the inevitability of fate in *Romeo and Juliet*.

The answer to the lad's question had dried up in Roper's
mouth. That was because there weren't any replies that made
sense. Even Alex could see as Roper had tried to speak that he
was struggling to come up with anything to persuade everyone
that studying a writer who croaked over four hundred years ago
was a decent way to pass the time. The old man might have
loved the classics but watching him trying to pass on that
passion to a room full of angry listeners was like watching somebody place their head in the mouth of a hungry lion. The
ensuing growls of furious teenagers as they had hurled insults
his way, reduced him to a gibbering anxiety-riddled wreck. By
the time they'd left the room later that afternoon, it was obvious
that Roper was close to tears, his face pale, his hands white as he
gripped the desk like a man about to pass out.

This morning, however, they took notice of his demands for
silence and sat quietly, heads lowered, pens and pencils poised
and ready. Even Alex.

It was amazing how keeping track of time was usually Alex's
forte, each second a minute, each minute an hour, but not today.
Today's lesson passed quickly and without incident, the silence
broken only by a few sighs and murmurs. And then the slow
rhythmic sobbing of a girl at the back of the classroom, Louise
Harker's hiccupping cries cutting through the whispers, her
moaning and weeping becoming too loud and energetic to
ignore. Alex felt his pulse soar, flames licking through his veins.
This was his moment, his turn to shine. One whisper before
class was all it took, and now that whisper had taken hold and
was doing the work for him.

He saw Roper glance up from the page he was studying,

glasses perched on the end of his nose, eyes scanning the room for clues as to what was going on.

'It's him, sir.' Sarah Finley's whisper cut through the cries and moans. She swung around and stared at Alex. His eyes rested on her chest then slowly moved up to her face. He smiled at her. She was pretty, but not stunning. Her eyes were narrowed, lips set in a grimace as she spat out the next sentence, her voice a near shriek. 'He's telling everyone that he followed Louise into the toilets and has got something in his bag as evidence.'

Sarah Finley was both correct and incorrect with her assumption. He had told one person, not everyone. One person was all that was needed to spread a rumour in this school. Bystanders clung on to anything of interest and spread it around like candy. It was all so easy, so very easy and simple. He knew how to play people, how to lure in and shock the unassuming. And this was without even trying.

A ripple of disgust and accompanying lassitude slid around the room. Alex could sense it – the apprehension and revulsion. And yet there was something else there too; interest and curiosity. No matter how revolting the crime, people were always willing to watch and listen, to suck up every last morsel of a disgusting story. Like ravenous creatures, they sat and waited, hoping to feast on the misery of others.

Roper's eyes were upon him. Alex knew that the teacher had a choice: either disregard the whole occurrence and carry on with his reading, hoping the girl's tears dried up, or do something about it. There was only ten minutes left. Watching the cogs whir in Roper's brain was the most fun Alex had had in weeks. He guessed that Roper could shush the weeping girl, hoping she would stop, all the while praying for the sound of the bell so the sudden rush to the door would drown out her cries and she would no longer be his problem. Or he could step into the lion's den, ask Alex to explain his story and empty his bag.

Alex made a point of looking up at the clock behind Roper's desk. Only nine minutes left now. Nine minutes of growing mutters and seedy insults being thrown about. His blood sizzled. Could Roper manage it? Was he able to keep a lid on the growing fracas? Stop it from spilling over into an explosive unmanageable mess? Alex coughed in an attempt to conceal a bout of uncontrollable laughter. The growing situation was comedy gold. Better than he could ever have hoped for.

'It's the smell, sir. It stinks round here. And it's coming from that freak's bag,' Sarah Finley hissed as she pointed at Alex, her face creased with disgust.

A loud protracted sigh from Roper, as if what was unfolding was the worst thing that had ever happened to him. Alex felt sure far worse events had taken place in this classroom. A tic took hold in the old guy's neck, a small pulse that juddered repeatedly beneath the thin flesh of his throat, knocking and hammering to be released. Alex had seen it before, how Roper's little nervous twitches appeared when stuff like this happened. He wanted to feel some sympathy for the old man, but it just wouldn't come. It was Roper's job to manage the behaviour in class, to stop things like this from happening, and he failed so often that maybe he deserved to feel nervous and out of sorts. So no, if he was being perfectly honest, he didn't feel any pity for the struggling teacher. What he actually felt was hatred and irritation at Roper's ineptitude and lackadaisical attitude.

Then as if propelled by an invisible force, Roper stood and strode up to Alex's desk, placing his hands firmly on the surface and leaning over, doing what he could to block the view of those around him. Alex sat, unmoving, his face a mask of passivity. Rheumy blue eyes met his, Roper's stare an unnerving thing to behold. Alex felt his features being studied and remained still. Unmoving and unmoved. Whilst other young males of his age struggled with hygiene and eruptions of acne, Alex was aware that he had the complexion of alabaster and the perfectly sculpted features of a budding handsome young man. He wasn't egotistical. It's just how it was.

Sweat bloomed under Roper's armpits, tiny beads of perspiration lining his neck and arcing his hairline as Alex continued to sit, spine rigid, his eyes following Roper's every movement. Alex was loving this, waiting for the moment when his teacher finally realised what was happening. Because Sarah Finley was indeed correct with her assertions. If only the old fart would hurry up and get this thing over with. Alex wanted the big reveal, to feel the warmth of the moment when everything unravelled and Roper fell apart in spectacular fashion at his feet.

Scooping up the satchel from the floor, Alex smiled as Roper opened it and snapped it shut again, the sight inside clearly roiling his guts. It was a used sanitary product. Alex had spent the last hour praying his plan would come to fruition. And now it had. If only the rest of the class could see inside that bag. That would be climatic, his defining moment. Still, at least Roper got an eyeful. He now knew what sort of dark thoughts roamed inside Alex's head. For some reason, that revelation made him giddy, excitement gripping him, swelling in his chest and warming him through.

'You,' the teacher hissed, his teeth clamped together. 'Stay here at the end of the lesson. Don't you dare move from that chair.'

Alex smiled. He had won. The rest of the class wouldn't see his trophy but at least old Roper had got to study it close up. That was enough to thrill him, to send a tingle of euphoria up and down his spine.

With the handle of the satchel hanging loosely from one finger, Roper marched back to his desk, flinging the bag underneath his chair with a loud smack. Alex would put money on the fact that his teacher thought this little exploit was a new low, that Roper was sifting through all the things he had seen and heard from delinquents over the years in his head, ranking them in order and slotting Alex's escapade at the top. Or at least he hoped so. Sneaking into the female toilets unseen and unheard was no mean feat. He did it because he felt compelled to, because some people deserved to feel shocked. There was also another reason behind his little stunt. He didn't do it to humiliate Lisa or Louise or whatever her name was. He did it because he enjoyed it. He felt exhilarated sneaking into a place where he shouldn't have been. It thrilled and excited him. And the worst part of it was that he didn't care who knew it.

11

HELENA

The pride that any mother should feel at hearing their child's teacher heap praise upon her offspring is woefully absent. In contrast, Helena soaks up the teacher's words, each one floating and dancing in her abdomen, shafts of warm light glowing deep in her soul, while Vanessa sits, stony-faced, smiling only occasionally, shaking her head and giving a grunt of approval when asked if she has any questions.

Helena can sense her urgency, her daughter's overriding compulsion to check her phone for missed calls and messages. Vanessa was reading her phone when they met outside the school gates, and continued to check it as they waited in line to speak to Noah and Mabel's teachers.

'Work again?' she had asked when the silence between them became too much to bear. Vanessa's eyes roved over the screen, her finger quickly scrolling and replying to what felt like a hundred calls and messages.

'What? Sorry, yes. It's been a busy week.'

'Aren't they all?' Helena had replied, her voice a low drawl.

The sarcasm was lost on her eldest child, Vanessa's eyes already fixed once again on her mobile.

'Well, aren't we the proud Mummy and Grandma,' Helena says as they stride into the large hall where Noah and Mabel are happily playing under the watchful eye of the teaching assistant.

'Did we do well?' Mabel asks, her eyes glittering with hope and anticipation.

'Of course you did well!' Helena says, her faux jollity a way of overcompensating for their mother's low mood and truculent disposition. 'Didn't they, Mummy?'

She turns, hoping to force Vanessa out of her sullen temper, and is relieved when she finally cracks a smile and manages to ruffle Mabel's hair and blow Noah a kiss.

'Of course they did! We expect nothing less, do we?'

It's not much, thinks Helena, given how glowing their teachers' feedback was, but it's better than nothing. Better than a gloomy countenance and displaying more interest in her phone than her own children.

'How about we all go to Grandma's house for tea? Come on,' Helena says quickly before Vanessa has a chance to decline, protesting she is too busy or is waiting for a callout or any other number of excuses she can think of. 'Let's get going. Shall we have pizza or would you prefer slug sandwiches? Or how about crocodile pie?'

Both children make the usual faces, disgust and laughter merging into one big happy bubble of noise.

'Come on, then. Let's get going. Race you to the car!'

The three of them leave Vanessa behind, the screech of laughter billowing in a cloud of happiness above their heads as they run on chubby unsteady legs towards Helena's vehicle. Helena turns, resigned to Vanessa's reluctance to join in. She watches her slumped figure, wondering what is going on in her daughter's head. Sometimes it's easier to give in to Vanessa's moods than to cajole and fight. Another battle for another day. Right now they are going to enjoy the moment and maybe, just maybe, it will remind Vanessa of how lucky she is to have two delightful children who shine in every way possible, lighting up the lives of everyone they meet.

'Jump in,' Helena says softly, ruffling their hair as they slide into their respective seats, delight emanating from their small features. She straps them in and stares at them both long and hard, their natural joy and smiling faces never ceasing to enchant her. Just when she thinks she can't love them any more than she already does, her feelings swell and grow once more. 'Come on,' she sighs softly, her voice a calming sound amidst a shriek of children's laughter. 'Let's go and celebrate.'

It's morning, and memories of the previous evening float in her mind – the effervescent presence of her grandchildren, the lift she felt as she watched them tuck into pizza whilst sitting at her kitchen table. She felt buoyant, giddy even. As long as Mabel and Noah were with her, she was able to keep thoughts of Rachel at bay. Vanessa's mood lightened as the evening passed, her previous reticence to join in the celebration, gradually disappearing. They even embraced as Vanessa bundled up the children and stood at the doorway. Helena could swear she saw tears brimming in her daughter's eyes after they hugged, but the mood was fragile, a soap bubble too delicate and frail to catch. Another time. She'll wait until things are a little less shaky between them, Vanessa's work schedule not as gruelling, and then she will ask. This is the problem with taking on managerial duties; it leaves very little time for family life. For the small, seemingly insignificant things that count for an awful lot.

Right now, there are other matters afoot, things that are rocking Helena's small world, the ground beneath her feet feeling unsteady, as if everything is about to rip open and swallow her whole.

Grief and shock tighten around her throat as she watches the news on the television. News about the two dead women. It hammers at her temples with such ferocity she feels dizzy and marginally sick. They are both somebody's daughter. Somebody's child. She cannot imagine how it would feel to lose either of her girls.

Police are asking everyone to be vigilant and to report any unusual sightings in and around the area of Nunborough and beyond.

It's unthinkable that these things have happened so close to home. So close to where her youngest daughter spends her time. Helena will go again today to speak with Rachel, try to convince her to come home. To be warm and dry. To be safe. She cannot fathom why Rachel is so averse to the idea. Why she would rather spend her time roaming the streets with strangers whose sole aim is to drink themselves to death, or to pump their bodies full of drugs. What is wrong with home comforts and being surrounded by a loving family?

The police haven't used the phrase 'serial killer' yet but it's there, hidden between the lines of each broadcast and newspaper report. Two suspicious deaths. Two young women whose bodies were found close to one another only months apart. And another still missing.

She stares out of the window, watching the hustle and bustle of passers-by as they scurry along the pavement and climb into cars, all in a rush to get to work on time. Two dreadful deaths and yet the world keeps on turning. Somewhere close by, two families are grieving and another searches for their daughter while everyone else plans their days – conducting meetings, speaking to customers, carrying out all manner of mundane activities while somebody somewhere weeps for the dead.

Already the conspiracy theories have begun to circulate online, armchair detectives and psychologists putting in their two penn'orth, claiming to know who the murderer is, why they did what they did to those poor women. Suddenly everyone is an expert without any knowledge or formal training.

And then, of course, comes the dissection of the lives of the victims, people questioning why they were out alone at night, as if they are somehow to blame for their own demise. As if they are to blame for some maniac sneaking up behind them with ill intent and a heavy weapon.

What sort of woman walks the streets on her own in the early hours?

One type, that's who. And we all know who they are and what they're up to!

Maybe if they were home at that hour, this would never have happened.

Disgusted, Helena snaps her laptop closed. People and their comments repulse her. She hopes they never have to suffer the trauma of losing a loved one. Never have to spend night after night worrying and mourning, grief scooping out their insides and carving a huge hole in their hearts. Losing Rachel to the streets was as bad as losing Gavin, like having a limb removed. If it takes every last breath she has, she will convince her youngest daughter to come home. Helena cannot rest, knowing her offspring lives and operates in close proximity to where those murders took place. She will make it her mission to bring her child home, and if it means dragging her kicking and screaming into the car, then that's what she will do. It's called tough love, a phrase she once thought silly and trite, an excuse for parents to mistreat their own children, but now she knows it as doing what is necessary to make sure your offspring stays alive.

Breakfast is a bite of cold toast that sticks to the roof of her mouth, and a swig of cold coffee. Mabel and Noah are standing at the gate when she screeches up outside Vanessa's house and hurls herself out of the car.

'You're late, Grandma. Mummy said you've made her late for work.'

'And us for school,' Noah adds as he bends down and scoops up a handful of gravel. He spreads his fingers and lets it fall through the gaps, his eyes bright with interest as it lands in a small pile at his feet.

'I know, I know. Sorry,' she says, her breath a series of small hurried gasps. 'I got caught up doing things.'

'Doing what?' Mabel asks, her mouth set into a pout.

Reading ghastly stories about the murder of two women in our hometown.

Helena leans down and pulls up Mabel's collar, their noses almost touching. 'Well, if I'm not mistaken, it's somebody's birthday in a few weeks so I had to do some secret stuff. But obviously I can't say any more than that.' It's a perfect excuse to keep the real reason for being late to herself. Children should never be privy to such horrid details. The world is a scary place filled with damaged people. Protecting her family is her main aim in this frightening journey called life.

Mabel lets out an excited squeal, her feet shifting about as she jumps up and down. Then a sudden change in her mood, a downward sloping mouth, the pout exaggerated, her eyes downcast.

'Mummy says she might be at work on my birthday.'

A vice tightens around Helena's skull. Work again. Vanessa

had promised to put in a holiday request for it. She'll speak with her later; Helena feels sure her daughter's birthday is something Vanessa should prioritise. Evening shifts have already cut into their family time. Would it really hurt her to use one day's holiday in order to be there for her child on her birthday?

'I'm sure she'll be there. We'll sort it later.'

'Sort what later?' Vanessa appears at the door, the groove on her forehead deep enough to excavate Roman ruins.

'Nothing. We need to get moving. I've made you all late!'

Vanessa smiles and Helena takes a juddering breath. She had expected a frosty reception for her tardiness and is relieved to instead be greeted with a mellow daughter. Mornings are tricky; Helena knows that all too well. Getting two youngsters up and ready and out of the door is an ordeal, especially for a single parent. After Innes, Vanessa's partner left, Helena expected her daughter to fall into a slump, and admittedly there were times when things were difficult, but their lives are back on an even keel, the structure of the day helping to hold everything together.

'I'll collect them from yours at 6 p.m. as usual,' Vanessa says, her mind already focused on locking up the house and rummaging in her bag for her phone.

There are times when Helena would like to chat, to ask her daughter about so many things – her job and how it's going, whether or not she has a current partner, the fact she needs to take care in town on her night shifts after the recent deaths. Where the father of her grandchildren is right now...

The time is never right, their encounters brief and hurried. She wonders what sort of a man would walk out and cut off all contact with his own children. She and Vanessa weren't as close at that time, Helena's memories of Vanessa and Innes's relationship hazy and distorted. The children were toddlers, and Helena's attempts to help and intervene were ignored. She was kept at arm's length, her contact strictly limited to picking up and dropping off the children at nursery. Often, she was kept at the door, not even stepping over the threshold let alone being offered a cup of tea or a biscuit. So she was only too happy when Vanessa began turning to her for assistance after Innes left. Their relationship turned a corner and began to blossom and she was glad to be carried along in the slipstream of Vanessa's newfound happiness, questioning little and helping out wherever she could. And now that initial happiness is waning, Vanessa becoming sullen and unreachable again. And it hurts. God it stings, but Helena is terrified of things going back to how they used to be, so she says nothing. Her eldest daughter is back in Helena's orbit. She can't afford to lose her again. She has learnt to take things slowly, only approaching certain subjects when absolutely necessary. Only saying things that Vanessa wants to hear. And whether that is the right thing to do is anybody's guess but her options are limited, their connection brittle and easily shattered. Their relationship is a rickety structure built on pillars of sand. Digging deeper foundations to keep everything safe will take time, but Helena knows that it will be worth the wait.

'Okay, see you later.'

Her daughter has already moved off and is halfway into the driver's seat, Helena's words lost to the growing autumn breeze.

'Come on, you two. Let's get you to school. Don't want to be late, do we?'

'No, otherwise we'll get into trouble and Mummy will smack us again.'

Helena's heart jumps up her throat. It may not be against the law, but in her world, smacking is forbidden. She never hit her own children and is horrified at the thought of her daughter using such brutal methods to discipline her own youngsters.

'I'm sure that isn't the case at all. Mummy is just super busy with her job. And sometimes when we're busy, we all get a bit grumpy.'

'It is the case,' Mabel pipes up. 'She smacked Noah the day before yesterday because he didn't eat all his supper.'

Ice spikes Helena's spine, a rod of it spearing her backbone. Above them, the sun makes a sudden dramatic appearance, its amber hue illuminating Mabel's soft features and stretching over Noah's head. His hair is the colour of spun gold. Such innocence and beauty streaked and darkened by the mention of unwarranted violence. Her stomach churns and her face flashes hot and cold.

Noah is a quiet boy, gentle and unassuming. Mabel must be exaggerating. Always prone to drama and embellishing stories, she has taken a seed of an event and it has grown in her mind, taking root until it no longer resembles what actually took place. Helena convinces herself of this because the alternative is too terrible to contemplate. Vanessa has a temper; she knows that. But would she really let her anger unspool in front of her children? Would she hit them so hard it could be considered abuse? The thought of it makes Helena nauseous, her head buzzing with dread. This is why she needs to stay close, to help out and keep everything on an even keel, especially the delicate equilibrium of her daughter's finely tuned personality. Not that she is a monster – far from it. But she is under pressure. She has a busy job, a lot of responsibility, and it is a fact that the most even tempered of people with the hardest of shells can sometimes crack.

'Right, enough now.' The clap of Helena's hands as she

chivvies them into her car echoes in the crisp morning air. 'No more idle chitchat or we really will be late for school.'

'Yep,' Mabel replies, mimicking her grandma's sing-song timbre. 'Or it will just be another reason for Mummy to get angry. And we don't like it when she gets angry, do we, Noah?'

Helena suppresses a deep sigh and leans in to strap both children into their seats. A twinge pulses at her temple, the threat of a headache banging in her skull. Hearing about Vanessa's temper is all the more reason to step in and help. She can't be there all the time but she can intervene and assist, perhaps have the children stay over at hers one night a week. That way, Vanessa gets a break. A break from work and a break from Mabel and Noah who, although delightful, are also demanding simply because they are children. Catering to the whims of small people is draining, and Helena should know. She was once in Vanessa's shoes. The fact she never once raised a finger to her own daughters lingers in her brain. She pushes that thought away. Everyone reacts differently to stressful situations. Helena is a calm person and Vanessa isn't. That's all it is. She isn't a cruel mother or a child abuser, just a woman under a lot of strain.

'I'm picking you up tonight, so how about fish and chips for tea?'

An excited squeal pierces her eardrum, Noah clapping his hands while his sister watches bemused.

'I don't like fish. You know that, Grandma.'

'Yes, I know, and as usual, I will get you sausage and chips.'

'With gravy,' Noah shouts, a small bubble of saliva escaping from his mouth and bursting in the air in a tiny wet explosion before vanishing into the ether.

'With gravy,' Helena chimes before slamming the door shut and climbing in the front, relieved to have moved the conversation along.

She will speak with Vanessa later that evening. If time and her daughter's tight schedule allows. It's the stress of the job. The higher salary is enticing but is it really worth the extra tension it is putting on their family? All of Helena's thoughts and efforts have for so long been focused on Rachel that perhaps she has neglected Vanessa's needs, missed some vital signs that she is struggling and needs extra help. Guilt almost swallows her whole. It is so difficult dividing her time equally between Rachel, Vanessa and the grandchildren that there are days when she feels close to despair. Here she is judging her adult daughter for being a less than effective parent when she herself is missing important signs that her own child is in need of help. Neglect takes many forms and maybe Helena is as guilty as Vanessa, pouring all her efforts into Rachel, who bats it away while Vanessa is desperate and refuses to ask her own mother for assistance.

'Right, munchkins. Let's get you to school.'

She turns on the engine and they swing right at the end of the road and merge into the line of traffic that stretches out of the village and onto the main road, Helena feeling that she has turned a corner and things are about to improve.

12

HELENA

'All I'm asking is that you give it some thought, Rachel.' It's difficult to not scream at her daughter. Helena has to stop herself from yelling that Rachel needs to take a long hard look at her life choices, at how miserable her existence is and how everything she does and says has a ripple effect on their family, her actions and the decisions she makes spreading much further than her own little social circle.

'Don't need to. Quite happy as I am, thanks very much.' She stares off over Helena's shoulder, doing what she can to avoid eye contact with her mother.

Helena's chest vibrates with the effort of containing the roar she can feel building in her throat. She decides to resort to emotional blackmail, unashamedly using her own grandchildren as bait. 'What about your niece and nephew? When was the last time you saw them? I met with their teacher only yesterday and they are both doing so well at school. Mabel is quite the little scientist and Noah is the next Monet. His drawings are something to behold.' Helena stops and takes a rattling breath. 'It's Mabel's birthday in a few weeks. They ask about you all the time.'

This isn't strictly true. It's been over a year since the children have seen their aunt Rachel, perhaps even longer, and the memory of her is fading fast in their tender little minds.

Rachel shrinks into herself, curling up on the park bench, knees tucked under her chin.

This is it, thinks Helena. This is how she has to approach Rachel from now on. Use the children as a means of getting her daughter back home. She can see by Rachel's pained expression as she stares off into the distance that she has hit a nerve. Somewhere deep down in her ravaged core, in the very heart of her, she must miss them. Even if she doesn't wish to see Helena, she must at least have an urge to make contact with her young niece and nephew.

'I can arrange a visit. I can't bring them here, but we can meet at my house. I can pick you up and—'

Rachel's voice is whiplash sharp, a crack in the surrounding silence. 'I know exactly what you're doing, Mother. I'm not fucking stupid, you know.'

The ground tilts and sways beneath Helena's feet. She was so close; she can't rupture this moment. And yet already, she can feel it slipping away. She has to do something, *say something* to get it back.

'Maybe we can go somewhere neutral? A café close by?'

No response. Helena feels certain Rachel can hear the pounding of her heart, is able to see how it's thrashing wildly in her chest. She swallows and tugs her jacket tighter around her shoulders, pulling up her collar against the cold wind. Then she notices Rachel's thin, ragged coat, a now threadbare reminder of a time when she had a job, money. The means to look after herself. A time when she was able to buy her own clothes and live in a place that was warm and dry and had food in the cupboards.

'Maybe. Will have to think about it.'

It's difficult to suppress the sigh that Helena feels rising up her gullet. Rachel is making this as difficult as possible, her reactions and answers as erratic and unpredictable as the breeze that circles and buffets them.

'Well, every day that you hesitate and delay is a day closer to the children forgetting about you altogether.'

She can feel the hardness of Rachel's stare, the way her eyes travel over Helena's features, searching for *something*. She has tried it all with her daughter and has very little left. Her tank is almost empty. And yet she cannot stop with this fight. She won't. It will take a grave illness to put a halt to Helena's visits here, for her to cease with the incessant pleas for Rachel to change her ways and accept help. In the past she has brought leaflets with contact numbers and addresses printed on that Rachel could call for support, all of which were probably discarded as soon as she walked away; torn up by her daughter or thrown in the gutter. But she rested slightly easier at night knowing that at least she had tried.

'Next week, maybe? Somewhere near here.' Rachel's voice is barely more than a whisper, as if saying those words and making a connection has pained her, exposing parts of her soul she would rather remained hidden.

Hope blossoms and unfurls in Helena's veins. It's a start. A loose promise that may not be kept, but it's more than she has had in over a year.

'Tomorrow I'll bring you a voucher for some new clothes. Maybe get yourself some new jeans and a warm jacket?' She stares down at Rachel's old trainers, the once white fabric now grey, caked with mud and dirt. 'And perhaps some new shoes or boots?'

Rachel nods and smiles, and Helena feels as if her heart is on fire, a sudden warmth fluttering and flowing through her body.

They part, Rachel slinking away down a damp alley while Helena heads back to the small car park on the other side of town, stopping and leaning against a wall to catch her breath as she puts as much distance as she can between herself and the place Rachel calls home. The park and neighbouring shuttered shops and dank alleyways are tinged with a depressing air that seeps into Helena's pores, poisoning her thoughts and staining her dreams. Tomorrow before she goes to work, she will come back and bring a voucher so her daughter can buy herself some new clothes and be presentable for her niece and nephew. It's a small step and yet at the same time, a huge leap; more than she had hoped for. They have come a long way in less than an hour.

The air smells sweeter, the crisp leaves on the trees a vivid array of eye-catching gold and sepia, small insignificant items that mellow and lift Helena's mood as she clears her thoughts in readiness for the morning. She is a step closer. It feels like it has been a perilous journey, strewn with dead-ends and potholes, but at long last, her daughter is nearly home.

The day and evening pass in an uneventful blur, a buzz present in Helena's veins every time she thinks about Rachel. This could be it, she thinks as she feeds the children and hands them over to Vanessa who, once again, is in a screaming hurry with no time to converse, no time to answer questions about the well-being of her children or to explain to Helena where Innes is and why he took off when he did. One problem at a time. Instead, she focuses on getting Rachel back home. A pulse of something resembling happiness throbs beneath her skin, expanding and glowing inside her. This could be it. This could be the moment when they reunite as a family and everything goes back to how it used to be. Her two daughters, both sisters, back together once more.

* * *

She rises early and leaves the house imbued with a sense of positivity. The radio is still intent on broadcasting as much as they can about the murders, gleaning information from people about the victims via a phone-in. Interview after interview filled with despicable gossip and hyperbolic nonsense designed to shock and lure in more listeners. For the first time in a long time, Helena is relieved, excited even, to arrive in the town centre, pulling up in a space and hurrying through the car park, flinching at shadows, her skin puckering at the dim echo of distant footsteps. Thoughts of a serial killer puncturing her buoyant mood.

A brisk breeze pushes at her back, the morning air clean and fresh. A good day to turn things around. She thinks of what possibly lies ahead, how to control the conversation, keep calm. Be the voice of reason.

The voucher she buys from a large department store in town is more than enough to make sure Rachel has some decent warm clothes to wear. Clutching it in her palm, Helena picks up her pace. Today is going to be a busy one. And yet she has to make sure she gives everything she has, dig deep into her reserves and pluck out every bit of enthusiasm and energy that is in there; keep smiling, nodding and being the people pleaser that she is in order to make sure her daughter complies with her wishes.

Rachel is in her usual place, seated on the bench near the local park, a spread of foliage behind her. The uninformed could be forgiven for thinking she is a commuter or somebody simply resting and preparing and taking stock before commencing with the rest of her day, but upon closer inspection, they would soon realise that something is awry, her gaunt features and pallid complexion a sign that her life isn't a parallel of their own. Her ragged clothing is an obvious indicator that she is homeless. This, thinks Helena as she approaches, is the problem. Her younger daughter excels at covering up and concealing her thoughts and way of life. Which is why Helena finds it so diffi-cult to climb inside Rachel's head and work out how and why she has ended up in this pit of despair. She is an enigma. A mystery, even to her own mother.

Helena's gaze travels over Rachel. At least she is cleaner than yesterday, her hair brushed and tied up, strawberry-blonde curls springing free out of the tight band. Always petite, Rachel now looks much younger than her actual years, her skinny face and body adding to her juvenile appearance. Helena doesn't want to think about how thin she is beneath those baggy clothes. How malnourished and unhealthy her daughter is after living on the streets for the past few years. She is here and for now, that is enough. One step at a time.

Helena sits next to her, the voucher exchanging hands in a swift moment, just long enough for her to detect Rachel's embarrassment. This is painful for her – a grown woman accepting charity from her own mother. Today is the first time Helena has sensed this from her daughter. Overcome with emotion, and before Rachel can resist, Helena leans forward and embraces her youngest child. She jumps back almost immedi-ately as if burnt. Shock courses through her, her arms flapping wildly, an inescapable pounding in her head that bashes and thumps at the base of her skull.

'What the hell, Rachel?'

Helena reaches over and pulls a knife out of her daughter's back pocket, the size and heft of it enough to make her feel faint. The jagged gleaming edge enough to terrify her, to make her want to turn and run at top speed in the opposite direction. Despite the biting-cold weather, beads of perspiration coat her chest and neck, heat prickling at her scalp.

'What the fuck are you doing?' Rachel's mouth is wide with panic. She takes a quick glance around before staring intently at her mother, eyes tapered, pupils dark with menace and undisguised fury. 'Give it back, Mum. Please!' Her voice is a growl, her lips set into a grimace.

Stronger and more able bodied, Helena holds on to the knife, moving her arm back, resisting Rachel's attempts to retrieve the dangerous-looking weapon. She holds it aloft, the sharpened edge glinting in the early morning sunshine, and then realising her mistake, lowers it, tucking it out of sight beneath her bag even though they are completely alone.

Tension stretches between them, the atmosphere thick and heavy with unspoken accusations. A solid wall of dead air that separates them. Helena wants to speak, to undo the sudden damage to their gently developing relationship, but the words won't come.

'A knife?' she finally manages to splutter, two small words that tumble out, accompanied by a series of gasps. 'Why have you got a knife, Rachel? *This* knife? I mean, *why*? Just why?'

Shame snakes through her as certain thoughts and images filter into her brain. She tries to blot them out, tell herself it's not possible. Her daughter is many things, but a murderer she is not. Details of how those two women died hasn't been released. Strangulation, blunt-force trauma. There are any number of ways in which those females could have been killed. Rachel is tiny. Practically emaciated. It's simply not possible. And yet the words 'serial killer' refuse to exit her brain.

'For fuck's sake, Mum. I need it for protection. You've seen where I live. Now give it back or this deal is off. No knife, no meetup with the kids.' She is hissing, yellowed teeth clamped together, bared like a feral animal that has been cornered by a hungry predator.

Helena can feel the heat of her daughter's distress, adrenaline pumping through her, making her twitchy and on edge. Although still alone, they are in a public space. Anybody could walk past, emerging from behind the bushes at any given moment. Avoiding a confrontation is paramount. Nerves screaming, her hands bone cold, Helena reaches beneath her bag and reluctantly passes the knife over. It's then that she notices it – the silver ring that Rachel is wearing, incongruous against her drab clothing and filthy, bitten fingernails.

Helena points at it, fear of what she is about to be told clogging up her lungs and obstructing her windpipe. Stopping her from being able to breathe properly. 'Where did you get *that*?'

Any items of value that Rachel once had have all since been sold or pawned to feed her addiction. Colour floods her daughter's pale cheeks, a sudden spread of pink that reaches the tips of her ears. She snatches her hand away, slipping the knife into her back pocket.

'Found it. People lose stuff all the time. Keep your eyes lowered to the ground and you'll be surprised what you can find, what some people throw away. More money than sense.'

A hole opens up inside Helena's chest. Air rushes in, leaving her feeling cold and empty and scared. More than scared. For the first time in a long time, Helena is terrified. This isn't normal behaviour. Rachel's mental decline is becoming more noticeable. There once was a time when she spoke clearly, still had some ethics and values that mirrored Helena's. But not any more. They are now like strangers, a vast chasm opening up between them that is stretching and widening by the day.

Helena glances at her watch. She had hoped for longer with her daughter, but things have turned sour, her original plans for coffee and a long talk about Rachel's future now crooked and seemingly out of reach.

'Don't bring that *thing* with you next week when we meet up with the children.' Her eyes flick to Rachel's back pocket where the jagged blade sits. 'You do know it's against the law to carry a weapon around, don't you?'

Rachel's low sarcastic guffaw floats away out of earshot as Helena picks up her pace and heads back to her car.

13

ALEX

Fifteen Years Prior

She was doing it intentionally. That much was obvious. The way she brushed past him, the sly looks and deliberate pout. The tinkling of her laughter that trailed after him as he left the room. All calculated attempts to rile and humiliate him. They were all the same, those girls with their painted faces and nails, their push-up bras and bare midriffs; school shirts tied in the middle to reveal as much flesh as possible. Skirts hitched high, resembling a belt rather than a piece of clothing. Out to tease. Doing what they could to arouse him before darting away. Alex felt a twinge of desire, the musky scent of her perfume when she passed him in the corridor alerting his senses. It soon turned to revulsion, images of his own mother catapulting into his brain, his body softening in response to his own internal battle. He hated them all, the girls in his school. Girls and women everywhere. Wanted and hated them in equal measure.

'Freak.'

The echo of her insult slammed into him, knocking all the air out of his lungs.

'Slut.' His response was a mutter, barely a whisper and yet a deep howl in his head.

She wasn't worth the trouble. Shouting would just exacerbate the problem, make everyone think even less of him. Best to stay on his own, keep his thoughts tucked away, concealed from the rest of the world. They wouldn't understand. None of them ever did.

The walk home gave him time to think, to clear his head after old Roper had rattled his cage about the grisly find in his bag. Staying back after everyone else had left, Roper had let his mouth fly, telling Alex what a lowlife piece of scum he was. It didn't bother him too much. He had suffered worse. Was about to suffer far worse once he stepped through his own front door. Whether or not Roper had made a phone call to his mother was irrelevant. Things rarely changed behind the doors of 21 Elder Terrace. Trouble or no trouble. Good or bad. They all merged into one big fucking nightmare inside that house.

He stood at the end of the road, steeling himself, staring at their dilapidated house in the distance, trying to determine whether she was having a good day. Or whether a brooding darkness had been unleashed in his absence. Open curtains indicated a positive mood. Drawn curtains meant trouble.

Moving closer, he could see the shadows of the murky fabric that covered the window. Black, the colour of death. The colour of his skin after she used to beat him. He became adept at hiding those bruises over the years, but he was older now. Stronger. The violence wasn't as frequent. But it was still there, her mood a simmering cauldron of blistering acid that bubbled and spat at anybody who came near. It was the threat of it that he hated, the fact she would catch him unawares. The fact he was often now close to hitting her back. One punch; that was all it would take. And then what? It wasn't the killing that scared him. It was what came next. The aftermath. The inevitable punishment for finally sticking up for himself. For declaring that after years of torture and violence, enough was enough.

The smell hit him as he stepped inside the house – stale cigarettes and unwashed clothes. Stinking bedrooms and a mouldy damp bathroom. He couldn't remember the last time the house was cleaned. The place was a shithole. It had always been a shithole and it had taken him years to realise it. As a younger child, he assumed everyone lived as they did. A rare visit to the house of a classmate was an eye-opener with a kitchen floor so clean it shone like glass, and parents who smiled and joked and asked questions about their day. Parents who hugged and laughed and fucking well cared.

That was way back though, before the decay really took hold, before he stood out as the class freak, the one they all despised. It didn't bother him so much, being alone. Easier to be alone than to put on an act. Besides, he pretty much despised them in return.

'Where've you been?' The shriek of her voice, the pitch and timbre of it, ragged and hardened after decades of cigarettes and neat vodka, puckered his skin.

He remembered as a young child wishing his mother could be like the other mothers with their recently combed hair and fresh-looking complexions. Their new clothes and the habit they had of standing around the school gate, chatting and smiling. Being pleasant and convivial. Being normal.

'Why would I want to mix with that lot?' she had sneered when Alex asked the question. 'Gang of judgemental little bitches is what they are, with their trendy clothes and clacking mouths.'

He had spent the evening locked in his room that night after asking, his stomach rumbling, throat desert dry. At 1 a.m., she unlocked the door and passed in a stale sandwich and a glass of lukewarm milk. He made sure to thank her, reassure her that he wouldn't say anything like that ever again, that he would keep his probing questions to himself. He learned the rules at a young age, survival instincts taking over. Keeping him safe and alive.

Turned out his mother was right. For all of her faults, she was astute enough to know those types of women for what they were. Spiteful hypercritical sluts, each and every one of them.

'Stayed back to revise in the library.'

They both knew it was a lie but she went with it anyway. Easier than poking around the detritus of his day. It was all unnecessary business. She didn't care and he wasn't about to tell.

'They've been here again, Alex.'

It pained him to ask, but he knew all too well the ramifications if he didn't.

'What did they want?'

'They said if I don't pay them by next Monday, they'll be back and will put the windows through.'

Anxiety ballooned in his chest. 'How much this time?'

'Two hundred pounds.'

She sat hunched, eyes glazed. Alex strode towards her, lifted his hand and struck her hard across the face.

It was like slapping a skeleton, the feeling of brittle bone beneath the flesh of her cheek still thrumming against his palm. If she was shocked or distressed by the hit, she concealed it, staring up at him, a dead-eyed expression on her face, mouth set in a thin line. God, he hated her. Why was she so fucking pathetic? Why were all women like her? Desperate, needy, whining creatures who, without a second thought, would suck the lifeblood out of everyone around them.

'I haven't got the money, Alex.'

She was stating the obvious. Of course she didn't have the money to pay them. Any cash she had went on booze, or up her nose.

'I'll sort it, Mum.'

'You'll have to, otherwise we'll be up shit creek without a paddle.'

He gritted his teeth, his jaw aching with the effort of clamping it together. Her favourite phrase, used time and time again. He hated the way she sat there, hopeless and helpless, creating problems for others to fix. And that cackle. He loathed the cackle. He loathed that almost as much as he loathed her.

Later, when she was sleeping, her thin frame slumped in the chair, he crept out of the house, hat pulled down, hood tied tight around his face. He knew where to go, how to seek out the vulnerable people. Not stupid helpless people like his mother. Not sad sick folk who had no idea how to make it through each day. It was the ones who thought themselves sensible and safe and above being robbed. The ones who left themselves exposed. They had no idea of how to stay protected or how to avoid people like Alex, thinking that their status and wealth would protect them. Those were his type of people. The ones he sought out on his late-night prowls. It was laughable and so very easy. And better than that – they were everywhere. He would get the cash they needed with ease and maybe even a little extra for his efforts. He'd done it before and would have to do it again at some point. Each time became easier, his skills honed, his nerves a little less frayed. If anything, it gave him a buzz, seeing the look of terror in their eyes as he snatched handbags and purses out of their grasp, the ensuing wrangle illuminating his senses, setting off a fire deep in his abdomen. He dared himself to think that he didn't do it for the money, that terrifying those women made him feel alive, opening up a bottomless well deep within his body that had been inert for too long. And there was a reason why he always chose women. Men fought back and he wasn't stupid enough to risk losing, always opting for the easiest route to getting that cash. But more than that, females deserved it, with their sly manipulative ways and devious thoughts. With their provocative clothing and made-up faces that masked the evil beneath. So although tinged with anger whenever his mother did this to him, her needs overshadowing his, it also set off something else, releasing something inside of him that had been suppressed for too long. A Pandora's box of latent desires and urges. And once the lid was fully opened, allowing the depths of his dark yearnings to escape, he knew there would be no putting them back.

14

PRESENT DAY

The light is fading. I can tell by the shifting shadows in the room, the way everything is slowly suffused with a wash of grey. Soon he will be back up, allowing me to relieve my bursting bladder, bringing me food and a drink before helping me to clamber onto the bed where I spend each and every evening.

Many images, all of them stomach-churning, have rumbled through my brain since he unceremoniously dumped that bracelet at my feet, its silvery glint catching my eye. It's all about keeping me in line, letting me know how dangerous he is. My one attempt to escape was futile. With arms and feet tightly tied, and my mouth gagged with a strip of coarse fabric, finding a way out of this place feels impossible. The only time my gag is removed is when I eat and drink, and screaming isn't an option because he holds a knife in his hand. He doesn't brandish it or press it close to me, keeping it instead, gripped by his side, and he hasn't ever threatened me with it, but it's there as a warning. Just like this bloodstained bracelet. Everything he does is carried out with cold, clinical precision. Laced with simmering menace.

A familiar creak cuts into my thoughts. The sound of the door being opened. I pull myself out of my dark reverie and look up to see him standing there, his silhouette reminding me of the night I was taken. The night when I left work after a twelve-hour shift, tired and marginally dazed. My senses were dulled by exhaustion and I didn't hear him approach me, didn't see his car parked over by the bushes next to the Parkway. By the time I noticed the figure to the side of me, it was too late. His hand was clamped over my mouth, my arms pulled tightly behind my back. Terror had ripped at my gut. It felt like a waking dream. A hideous nightmare. I had decided to walk home from the hospital after my shift ended and thought that a stroll on a clear balmy night would help wake me up and revitalise me. How wrong I was. The warmth of the evening coupled with a long gruelling shift clouded my thoughts, making me oblivious to my surroundings. I'm not to blame for what happened. Don't think for one minute that I am saying victims should be held accountable. He is a monster, for fuck's sake. I'm simply furious that I was caught at all. Caught and bundled into the boot of his car and driven here to a place that was a twenty-minute or so drive from where he assaulted me. He's clever though. He may have driven round in circles to fool me. I might be holed up in a house a stone's throw from the hospital. Or I could be in a house in Stokesley, South Bank or Stockton to name just a few of the many towns in the northeast of England. My location is a mystery. I could be anywhere.

'Time for your shower.'

He pulls me up to my feet and I hobble alongside him to the bathroom. Once we get there, he unties me and pushes me inside, standing in the doorway with that knife in his hand. A pile of freshly laundered clothes sits neatly on the floor.

'Usual routine. Leave your dirty things on the floor and put those on once you're clean and dry.'

I squat on the toilet, his presence a thing that still repulses me. Even after all this time, after all these months, although he turns away, refusing to watch, the fact he is there at all while I carry out intimate bodily functions that should be conducted privately condenses my stomach into a tight, painful knot.

While I am relieving myself, I think of all the ways I can get out of this place – running at him and pushing him down the stairs, pretending to faint and then grabbing the knife when he bends down to check on me. A hundred different ideas, and yet I am still here, still tied and bound, because deep down, I know that he is bigger and stronger than I am and he would win.

The shower is hot and I spend longer in there than usual, my mind ticking over, brimming with possibilities, all of them, on the face of it, impossible. I am tired, wasting away. He is a force to be reckoned with. Physically, I am no match for him. Mentally, he is also sharp. But then so am I. My days spent in this place have allowed me time to think, to delve into the darkest reaches of my brain, plucking out ideas. Ways in which I can survive this ordeal and get home to my family, my friends. My life. It's not as if he even watches me while I am showering. He shows no obvious signs of arousal or excitement. This whole thing is a fucking mystery. I have pondered over it day after day, night after night, and have come to the conclusion that he gets his kicks by exerting control. Control over somebody who is smaller and weaker than he is. Not a six-foot muscle-bound giant of a man, as that would prove how pathetic and feeble and inadequate he really is when they fight back and beat him senseless. No, he chose me because it makes him feel powerful, when in fact he is no more than a puny defective monster whose brain isn't wired up properly.

'Hurry up. Get dry and get dressed.' His voice is brusque, an edge of impatience setting in.

I step out and it's while I'm getting dry that I notice it – the towel rail is loose, the metal edge coming away from the wall. It's not much of a weapon but after so long being held captive in this place, it feels like a golden opportunity. Not right now though. I'm tired, my limbs aching after a day spent slumped on the floor. Mornings are easier, my body not as sore, the mattress helping to alleviate the pain that always settles in during the waking hours.

As soon as I'm dressed, he is beside me, tying the rope around my wrists as tightly as he can. I want to lean forwards, to roar into his face that he is a fucking maniac, to tell him that I hate him and that one day I will get out of this place and then everyone will know what he has done. But I don't, because timing is everything. When I do fight back, I will have only one chance and I'll need to get it right, to wrench that knife out of his hand and plunge it deep into his chest before bolting down the stairs and out of the door.

But for now, I will have to be content with going back into that room. I will have a few sips of water before my gag is reapplied, then I will climb into the bed and let sleep take me away to a dark place where none of this horror exists.

15

HELENA

'Hi, Mum. Me again. I wasn't expecting this one, but I really need to go.'

The phone falls out of Helena's grasp, her dexterity diminished by grogginess and tiredness. She is unbelievably fatigued after trying to get through to Rachel, bone-achingly tired by her attempts to try to persuade her youngest daughter to change her life trajectory and right now, she is tired of this; these midnight dashes to Vanessa's house. It's only been just over a week since the last one. They are becoming far too frequent. It's as if her daughters are working in unison to push Helena to the brink of exhaustion. Frustration at her own inability to say no grips her. The fine line between helping out and being taken for granted is so blurred she no longer knows where it begins and ends. Only hours ago, she was thinking that maybe she had neglected Vanessa and now here she is, thinking all kinds of terrible thoughts about how selfish her daughter is and how much Helena would love to curl up and go back to sleep.

Grit sits behind her eyelids, marring her vision. The thought of getting up and driving at this hour is enough to make her want to close her eyes and rest for an age. And yet she knows that is out of the question. A multitude of thoughts swirl around her head; dangerous notions of how she could ignore the call, see how Vanessa manages without her. See if she can find somebody else who will jump to attention and babysit at this hour, see if she can find anybody who will do her bidding the minute Vanessa snaps her fingers. Thoughts of how she could just let Rachel get on with things, no matter how unacceptable her choices are. Right now, it feels as if her daughters are controlling her life. They are adults and yet here she is, still caring for them, doing exactly as they ask. They tell her to jump while she asks how high.

And then she thinks of Vanessa, out on her own in the early hours and the fact that two bodies have been found with another still missing, and guilt pricks at her.

Her gaze reluctantly shifts to the bedside clock, as if seeing the time will make this real, the illuminous green digits burning into her brain like a branding iron – 12.02 a.m.

'I'm on my way.'

The words she really wants to say but knows she never will, about how tired Helena is, how these midnight dashes simply aren't sustainable, how she knows so little about Vanessa's life despite seeing her so often, all remain in her head. Easier to say nothing than say the wrong thing and risk upsetting somebody who she knows has a temper and is resistant to any form of scrutiny. Vanessa perceives any probing as criticism and all questions have to be carefully crafted to avoid confrontation. It's just how she is, how she has always been. Helena knows this and suddenly realises that for all of her life, she has managed her daughter's moods to avoid any possible clashes. So rather than lie there and feel sorry herself and this impossible situation, she gets up, because she is the one who has caused this, by pandering to somebody who refuses to, or is unable to, have insight into their own behaviour. She didn't neglect Vanessa, she spoiled her.

She dresses and slides into her car. All the way there, Helena rakes over the conversation she will need to have with Vanessa at some point about how frequent these callouts are becoming and how she needs to take care. It won't be easy, Vanessa interpreting each sentence as a barbed comment, but Helena is truly frightened for her daughters. Vanessa might be feisty, but she isn't immune to being attacked by a psychopath. The streets are no longer safe. The care home where she works is on the outskirts of town, not so far from the murders, and for months now, the staff have been asking for lights in the car park as it is surrounded by dense woodland. At this juncture, nobody knows where the deaths are taking place. Whoever is carrying out these atrocities could be transporting the bodies and dumping them in town. Details released by the police have been scant, leaving everyone to make up their own theories, doing what they can to advise their daughters and sisters, and keep their families safe.

A pounding sensation thrums in Helena's head. She lets out a trembling sigh, knowing that she needs to stop this. This level of anxiety is intolerable. It's eating away at her sanity and upsetting the stability of her finely balanced life. And yet how is she supposed to settle when she has two daughters who are out in the dead of night when a murderer is at large?

The house is in darkness when she pulls up outside Vanessa's, save for a dim light in the hallway.

'Thanks, Mum. Sorry, got to go.'

Helena tries to take hold of Vanessa's arm as they pass on the front path, but she is too quick for her, Vanessa yanking herself free and climbing into her car. Always evasive. Always too damn busy to stop and chat. The night is still, too quiet to call her back, to tell her daughter that this is untenable. Dangerous even. Tomorrow. They will speak in the morning and come to an arrangement. It's been a trying week and Helena is tired. Her ability to assist will only stretch so far. She will feel differently in the morning, she is sure of it. Dappled sunlight, warmth and clear skies above, and all will be well again.

And yet, a murderer is still at large. A clear warm day won't lessen the threat or detract from the truth of the matter – that somebody somewhere knows what happened to those poor women.

The mattress groans when she climbs in, images of glinting blades and Rachel's pinched sunken frame filling every space in her head as she closes her eyes. It takes her over an hour to unwind and shut off her mind to the dramas of the day. Sleep is an escape, the only respite she has from her troubles, imagined or otherwise. As the darkness descends, she welcomes it, bending to its will and allowing herself to be carried off into oblivion.

* * *

Small wet bullets hit the window, the rhythmic pattering of rain rousing her from a deep slumber. She drags herself up and wakes the children, stopping briefly to glance in Vanessa's room. Her daughter is curled up foetus-like under the duvet. Helena pulls the door to and heads downstairs with Noah and Mabel in tow, their feet a tired low shuffle as they take a seat at the kitchen table.

'Who's that out there?' Noah points a small chubby finger to the window.

Helena's eyes shift to the back lawn, a flicker of a movement at the edge of her vision sizzling her blood. It's early. The side gate has a padlock on it. Nobody can get in.

'There's no-one out there. Eat your breakfast. We don't want to be late.'

Her voice sounds disembodied, the words she utters echoing in her head. Her legs are like liquid as she moves closer to the window, pulling the blinds to one side to get a closer look. Relief crackles in and around her. She laughs and turns to face the children.

'Definitely nobody out there. I think we're a bit tired and misty-eyed this morning.'

That part is true. She is still weary, jumping at shadows, every nerve ending ablaze. She takes a rattling breath and makes breakfast, gulping down a mouthful of hot coffee to rouse herself. Her plans to have a conversation with Vanessa will have to wait until another time. Anyway, Helena is in work this morning. It's going to be a busy one with an author event planned first thing and another school visit in the afternoon. Besides, Vanessa getting called out was unexpected. These things happen. Emergencies in a nursing home are common. She also has a memory of Vanessa telling her many months ago that the manager is on long-term sick so the staffing situation is tricky to manage, a depletion of people resulting in everyone being leaned on. Her thoughts last night were instigated by fear and fatigue. As predicted, things seem clearer, easier to bear this morning. They'll get through this. They always do.

By the time she bundles the children into the car, her energy levels have been restored. Three cups of coffee have helped point her in the right direction of the day and given her just about enough energy to tackle whatever it may bring.

The laughter of her grandchildren as they skip down the footpath into school is enough to banish any persistent doubts she has about being called out in the early hours of the morning. Last night was an anomaly. She was tired, her thinking skewed. Her family need her and she needs them, and that is all she has to think about. Everything else is just detritus; insignificant issues that clutter up her life and draw her focus away from the important stuff. She would still like to bring up the subject of safety, and how she hopes Vanessa is being vigilant. She fears it's too late for Rachel, who will bat away all her mother's attempts to bring her home, but she can chip away at her other daughter and hopefully make her aware of the possible dangers that lurk in the most unsuspecting of places.

Traffic moves freely on the drive into town. Helena avoids turning on the radio. She knows as much about the murders as she is able to handle. Every local station is squeezing the story dry until there is nothing left but pips and a curl of desiccated skin.

Helena parks up and walks into a hushed environment, Cassandra, the head librarian, sitting at her desk, eyes lowered, a hand draped across her forehead.

'Everything okay, Cass?'

A closer look tells her that it isn't. Helena can feel it, the solemnity of the place, the way Cass is sitting hunched over her computer. Her ashen pallor and stricken expression. Something is wrong. Very wrong. A pulse starts up in Helena's neck, a rapid beating that makes her unsteady on her feet. The parquet flooring swirls beneath her, each tile eddying and whirling. She places a hand onto the edge of the main desk, its cold surface an assault against her burning flesh.

Cass shakes her head, a lone tear spilling down her cheek onto her collar. 'It's Barbara.'

A bubble of air becomes lodged in Helena's gullet. She swallows and on instinct, places a hand across her breastbone as if to still her thrashing heart. She thinks of Barbara's own weakened arteries, the stroke she suffered a few years back. The long journey she had to get back to being healthy again. Helena thinks of all of these things, her head swimming with a thousand different possibilities, but isn't prepared for what comes next.

'Barbara? No, please, surely...?'

'Not that,' Cass says quietly. 'Not Barbara. It's her daughter, Francesca. She's been found dead.'

The slightly swirling room gains traction, increasing to a speeding carousel. This isn't right. It can't be. A vice clamps itself around her temple, squeezing tighter and tighter until her vision attenuates and she is forced to stagger to a nearby chair, her body folding into it like a marionette with its strings severed.

'But she's only in her late twenties! How? I mean what on earth could cause—'

Cassandra runs her hand through her hair, shaking her head. She turns to face Helena, her face wet and streaked with mascara. 'They think she's been murdered. They found her body close to where the others were found in town.'

Helena can't contain the shriek. Tears threaten to fall, burning the back of her eyes. This isn't right. It can't be. The memory of the conversation she and Barbara had only a few days ago about the discovery of a body punctures her brain, the sharpness of it enough to make her cry out. A hot arrow of pain slices through her thoughts.

'What are we going to do, Cass? We can't close the library. We've got so much to do, and yet...'

They sit in silence, anything they attempt to say feeling pointless, a hollow ring to it. Nothing they say can make any of this go away. Barbara's daughter is dead. Helena stares at her hands. What is the protocol in this type of situation? Is there anything written in the library's staff handbook or the policy and procedures manual for situations such as this one? She doubts it. This is unprecedented. An emergency of sorts. Closing the library feels like the right thing to do; they are a small close-knit team, and yet they have members and authors and local schools who are due to visit in just over an hour.

'There's nothing we can do. We're here now. We've got to carry on as normal.'

Grief. That invisible emotion again. Helena stands up, the room still rotating as she heads to the staffroom. She goes through the motions, putting her lunch in the fridge, hanging up her coat and placing her handbag in a locker. The whole thing feels surreal, as if she will wake up and thank God such a fucking awful nightmare is over. Except it isn't. It's happening. This is real. Francesca has been found dead. She has probably been murdered. Poor Barbara has lost her daughter in the most horrific way imaginable. All the time Helena has been worrying about her own daughters while Barbara has had to go and identify the body of her firstborn child. Her beautiful baby girl, lying cold and alone in a morgue somewhere.

Eyes glassy with tears, Helena stands and heads out of the staffroom, doing what she can to summon up enough strength to face the trials and tribulations of the day ahead, the safety of her own daughters filling every available space in her head.

16

ALEX

Twelve Years Prior

'I'm off out. Got to get to work. See you later.'

The slamming of the door echoed around him, the frame shuddering from the force as he left the house, refusing to wait for her reply. There was little point. She was so far gone these days she rarely spoke, her brain struggling to cope with the most basic of tasks.

It was an alien sensation, going out to a job like the others. Except Alex wasn't like the others, and he knew it. Leaving school, getting a job at the local car showroom as a salesman, being his own man. Those were the things that bolstered him. Gave him an air of confidence. Made him think he could do whatever he wanted. The sensation of being independent set off a furnace deep in his gut. By day he was a salesman, still honing his skills and learning his trade, by night a young man, able to afford a few beers, smart clothes. Maybe one day, his own vehicle. And yet still certain feelings crowded his brain. Feelings he felt sure others didn't have. He had dreams of hurting people, his body responding and twitching, everything sparking and coming to life as he watched his victims in his mind's eye, faces contorted in terror as they struggled and gasped for breath beneath the pressure of his large hands.

It was an easy, forgetful journey into work. Commuters getting on and off the bus. People either reading newspapers, eyes glued to their phones or staring out of the window. He watched them, intrigued. Wondering if they had the same thoughts rumbling through their heads. Thoughts of how he would love to take a sharp blade and push it hard into the stomach of the woman who was continually tapping her foot, or thoughts of how he wanted to pick up a heavy object and slam it into the head of the female next to him who kept shuffling away from him as if he were polluted.

It was a relief to disembark and reach the showroom, his mind now firmly fixed on the day ahead, wondering how many customers would walk through that door and actually make a purchase.

'Busy day ahead?' Letitia, the receptionist, was standing behind the desk, smoothing down her pleated skirt. Always in first. No matter how early he arrived, she was always there before him. Standing behind her desk. Waiting. It was as if she knew how to rile him without even opening her mouth.

She had nice legs though. Alex liked that about her. Sometimes when she wasn't looking, he would watch her, noticing her little quirks and idiosyncratic ways. Like how she tapped the pen against her teeth when she was concentrating. Or how she ran her fingers through her hair when she was nervous, twiddling with the long strands, wrapping them around her pale slim fingers. He had thought about asking her out for a drink, maybe even a meal, but never managed to follow through with it. Girls like Letitia didn't socialise with guys like Alex. Because beneath her carefully applied make-up and expensive perfume, she was just like the rest of them. *Women.* They were all alike; cunning, wily. Thoughtless and callous.

'Always busy,' he replied, doing his utmost to sound casual. Unperturbed by her question even though his heart was pounding madly at the sound of her voice.

It was best he kept his distance, keeping the small talk to a minimum. The one time he let down his guard, she slithered in like a snake, voice sibilant as she hissed a line of sarcastic comments. Trying to belittle him. Asking him about possible girlfriends. About his private life and pastimes. Was it any wonder he hated women like Letitia? They did nothing to help themselves, throwing out razor-sharp comments and wearing scanty alluring clothing to attract attention. Could they not see what they were doing? Leaving themselves open to harm and destruction. Because one day, their behaviour would come back and bite them. He would make sure of it.

'Do you fancy a drink after work?' He could feel her eyes on him, was able to smell her sweet breath as she sat close by in the tiny staffroom, asking the question he didn't want to hear. He had to be careful here, make sure he didn't walk into a trap. Then it came, the sucker punch. He needn't have worried. It wasn't that sort of request. As if the likes of Letitia would ever show an interest in him. Despite having a fairly handsome face, he knew that females like Letitia could see his true intentions. It was as if they were able to peer inside his head, these women. See him for who he really was. 'Joy from the office is leaving next week and she said she didn't want a proper formal leaving do, so we thought we could maybe all just call into The Wheatsheaf on the way home from work tonight? All a bit last minute I know, but we couldn't have her leaving us without doing something for her, could we?'

He wasn't sure whether to feel relieved or angry. Not a date then. Just a casual afterthought. All morning, he had tried to avoid Letitia, skirting past her desk and skulking around the showroom behind a sea of cars. That was where he did his thinking, watching out for potential customers, working out his sales pitch and spiel. And now he was stuck here in a small, dank area that passed off as a staffroom, thinking up a million reasons why he couldn't attend.

'Sure. Why not?' The words were out before he could stop them, his brain responding before he had a chance to think it through.

Eagerness and lust had got the better of him. What he really wanted to do was get up and leave, tell Letitia that he didn't mix with her type – all lip gloss and tease – but instead found himself being drawn into the conversation, carried along by her undisguised zeal and eagerness. By the sweet smell of her happiness and the delicate whiff of her perfume.

The coffee was lukewarm as he gulped it down, his sandwich dry and tasteless. A quick glance at his watch told him he had been sitting there for long enough. He had work to do. Cars to sell. Money to be earned. And yet the aroma of her musky perfume, her close proximity, the way she looked at him...

No.

He couldn't do it. Alex stood, pulling on his jacket, making sure his shirt was free of creases, his jacket and trousers as clean and straight as they could be. The smack of his heels on the hard flooring rang out as he left the room, as if to accentuate his despondency and feelings of relegation. Always the afterthought. Never the main man.

Later that day, she strode up to him, her eyes locked on his. It had been a quiet afternoon, no sales and an empty showroom. With his fists shoved deep into his trouser pockets, he half turned away, his mood too low to speak with her again. This was why females like Letitia pissed him off. They didn't know when to stop, none of them ever knowing when to take a step back and disengage. They knew so little and yet gave off an air of self-assurance that was breathtakingly arrogant.

'Will we see you there tonight then, Alex?' Her body was turned at an angle, her head leaning to one side as she tried once again to catch his eye.

He could see her in his peripheral vision, her crooked stance, hip and leg jutting forward to give of an air of seduction. Her sickly-sweet smile. And a trail of that perfume again as it crept closer to him. That powerful intoxicating fragrance that was specially designed to lure in unsuspecting admirers. Like a Venus flytrap, she would snap if he got too close. She would draw him in, all the while doing what she could to break him, and then he would be forced to do things that should never be done to another living soul. Things that regularly haunted his thoughts. His dreams. His every waking moment.

'Yes, of course. I'll see you there.'

Already the idea was taking shape in his mind, the image in his brain making his blood pump faster and his heart race, thundering through his system, igniting parts of his body that he would rather remained dormant. His sudden arousal disgusted and humiliated him. For all he was now a grown man, able to work and earn money and live his life the way he had always wished, there were still certain things in his life that were beyond his control.

'Great. We'll see you there then. We're meeting in the bar at the far end next to the open fireplace.'

Her footsteps were a cold clinical echo, the tip-tap of stiletto-toes against marble a loud crack as she strode back to her desk and scooped up her jacket, shivering and shrugging it over her shoulders. Sometimes, those who appeared friendly and open were the ones with the darkest of intentions. And Letitia was without doubt one of those people. An iron fist in a velvet glove.

He knew that if he were to sidle up to her in the pub, she would loosen up, her tongue freed by the alcohol, her mind sharpened and ready to attack. She would sip at her wine, talons at the ready, and she would belittle him, making cutting remarks about his dress sense, his inability to understand her subtle humour. His lack of girlfriends. So no, he wouldn't be meeting them there. He would send his apologies after taking a bogus phone call, feign illness or tiredness. Maybe even use his mother as an excuse.

She is disabled and needs lots of care.

It's not an ideal set-up living as we do but it is what it is and whether I like it or not, she is my priority. Sorry to have missed it. Maybe next time.

And then he would finally pluck up the courage to tap into those grisly images that have been festering in his head for so long he can't recall a time when they weren't present, and at long last he would make them a reality.

17

PRESENT DAY

Turning over to alleviate the aches and pains is the most difficult thing. Everything is tied so damn tightly, my arms wrenched halfway up my back. Even the gag on my mouth is stretched and stiff, the knot of the fabric that keeps it in place an uncomfortable lump at the back of my head.

The room is dark and silent. I have slept briefly, but am now lying here wide awake, trying to work out how I'm going to get out of this room and this house. One chance. That's all I will get. And it has to be in the next day or so. He isn't stupid. He will soon spot the defective chrome towel rail and mend it before I have a chance to pull it off the wall and use it as a weapon. Already I have images in my mind of me bringing it down on his head over and over and over, the weight of it enough to crush his skull into a dozen different pieces. It's not an ideal weapon, but it's old fashioned and made of metal and it's the only thing I've got to hand.

I'm being fanciful, I know that. I will be lucky to get two hits in before he turns on me. That's why I have to get it right first time, be as precise as he is. To deal with a monster, you have to think like one. I can do that. I've watched him, seen how he operates, how he thinks and moves. He's clever, astute and strong, but he isn't invincible.

A creak from one of the rooms next door cuts into my thoughts, stilling my blood. I wait, a breath suspended in my chest, wondering if he is up and about. I hold my breath and count the seconds – ten, eleven, twelve.

Nothing. Just the howl of silence that reminds me of how alone I am. Separated from the outside world. An owl hoots in the distance. Then a car rumbles past. And then I am plunged back into a void of nothingness where time loses all meaning.

I struggle about and manage to sit up in bed, the surrounding darkness gradually losing its opacity as my eyes adjust. I glance at the photos of the woman who resembles me that are pinned to every wall. This shrine is a prison and I need to get out of it. The only way that will happen is if I carry out my plans with the meticulous precision of a stealth bomber. Be as he is – cold, detached, and accurate.

Tomorrow is when I will strike. It's now or never, and never isn't something I am willing to let happen. I'm not going to be like the woman in the photos, whoever she is. I'm willing to bet she is dead, and I am also willing to bet that he is the one who killed her.

I lie down and close my eyes, inviting sleep to take me. Beckoning it so I can put my plans into motion. I need rest. I need every bit of strength I can muster in order to fight off my captor. My eyes flutter, before closing completely. It comes quickly, that soft transition into a cocoon of welcome darkness, and when I wake the next day, a thin watery stream of light pooling on the floor beside me, I will know that my time has come.

18

HELENA

Somehow, the press have discovered where Barbara lives. Helena pulls up outside her friend's house, parking her car as close to the driveway as she can. She lowers her head, trying to avoid the flashes of cameras and the shouts and barrage of questions from nearby reporters. It's like a horror film, faces leering in at the driver's side window, police officers wrestling with them, pulling them back, arms fanned out to form a barrier. Helena doesn't know which is worse – the armchair commentators who think themselves qualified psychologists and hardened journalists, posting vile comments online, or the real culprits who make their living by feeding off the misery of others; standing outside their homes, waiting for titbits of information, stopping passers-by and neighbours and pumping them for details about the family and the victim. Doing what they can to glean as much information as possible out of strangers in order to fill that white page and sell more papers to swell their coffers. That's what it's all about – not compassion or humanity or kindness in times of distress. It's about cold hard cash. And it sickens Helena. She has no idea how they sleep at night.

She slides out of her car, suppressing the urge to scream at them all to fuck off. Lecherous individuals, that's what they are. Abhorrent bottom feeders who thrive on the outlandish and the unthinkable.

Keeping her head dipped, she runs up the path to a half-open door that is manned by Barbara's sister, who hurriedly ushers her inside. Helena decided at lunchtime that at some point she had to undertake the difficult task of contacting her friend. Ignoring Barbara felt like the wrong thing to do – cold and heartless. She was ready for a knockback, to be told that they as a family needed to time to come to terms with their loss, but instead she received a heartfelt reply asking her to call round. And now here she is, feeling at a loss as to what she should say or do.

Before she can even open her mouth to offer her condolences, she is gently steered into the living room where Barbara sits slumped on the sofa, eyes downcast.

'She's just seen the doctor who has given her some sedatives. We're trying to persuade her to sleep for a little while.' Barbara's sister gives Helena a thin smile and cocks her head slightly to indicate her obvious feelings of anxiety and helplessness at the sheer gravity of the situation.

'I can't sleep!' In uncharacteristic fashion, Barbara raises her eyes and bellows at everyone. 'How am I supposed to sleep when my baby girl has been killed?'

Helena's throat closes up. She asks God to forgive her for wishing she were elsewhere. Anywhere but here, in the middle of this hideous situation. There is nothing she can do or say to make any of it better. It will never be better. Helena knows that. And Barbara knows that she knows. But worse than that, Helena finds herself feeling thankful that her own daughters are still alive. It is a terrible thought to have in her head – heavy and cumbersome and angular – and she wishes it would leave, but it sits there, refusing to dislodge itself, leaving Helena feeling so guilty she wants to cry.

'Take a seat.' She is lowered onto an armchair, gentle hands guiding her. 'I'll go and make some tea.'

A heavy silence descends. Helena flicks her gaze between Barbara and her husband, Jem. They are sitting side by side, an ocean of grief separating them. In the kitchen, the clatter and scrape of crockery cuts into the quiet, allowing Helena time to formulate what it is she wants to say.

She swallows, taps at her chest with splayed fingers. A bubble of air is lodged in her throat and her head pounds. Simple reflex actions now feel forced and artificial, as if every breath is an onerous undertaking.

Eventually, she speaks, her voice ghostly and disembodied.

'Barbara, I am so, so sorry. There isn't anything I can say to make any of this go away but I want you to know that I'm always here for you.'

She feels breathless with the effort of it. Fingers laced together, she hopes it is enough because she doesn't think she has anything in reserve. Grief and shock have robbed her of her usual strength and vigour.

Jem replies, his voice husky. 'Thank you, Helena. It means a lot.'

A cup of tea is placed in her hand. Barbara's sister, Suzanne, leans forward, half turning away from her sister and brother-in-law, her gaze firmly locked onto Helena's face. 'Poor Barbara and Jem. And poor Rhoda. She was on holiday in Greece and is on her way back as we speak. It's taken her ages to try to arrange a flight due to the strikes at the airport.' Suzanne clears her throat and smiles again, standing up to face her sister. 'Everything is such an awful mess.'

Helena stares up at her, the whole situation hazy and surreal. She thinks of Rhoda, Francesca's sister, only a few years separating them. It must feel like losing a limb. She grasps her cup until her fingers ache, unsure what else to do. A young woman has been brutally murdered and here they are, drinking cups of fucking tea.

They all sit, fingers curled around steaming pieces of porcelain, gazes lowered, each of them too afraid to catch the eye of the other. After a few seconds, the silence is broken, Barbara's voice abrasive and dripping with spite, the sound of it frosting Helena's flesh.

'We spoke about this the other week, didn't we, Helena? I said another woman had been murdered. And you dismissed it. Do you remember?'

Helena does remember. All too well. Cold water swills through her veins. She shivers, her foot tapping nervously. Steadying her breathing, hoping what she is about to say is enough, Helena clears her throat and speaks.

'Barbara, all I can say is that I spoke without thinking. You were right, and I was wrong to dismiss your concerns.' She swallows down the hiccupping sob that threatens to rise up and explode out of her. This is awful, worse than she ever imagined. She is way out of her comfort zone here. Well out of her depth. Treading on treacherous waters, possibly about to lose a good friend because of her loose mouth and judgemental curt manner.

'Yes, you were wrong. And now my daughter is dead.'

Barbara's wailing fills the room. Helena can hardly breathe. In seconds, she is by her friend's side, pulling her close and wrapping her arms around her. She waits for a rebuff, to be told to get out of the house and never return, and is overwhelmed with relief and gratitude when Barbara leans closer, weeping into her chest.

'Oh God, Helena, what am I going to do? Francesca is dead. My baby girl has been murdered and I'm never going to see her again. What the hell am I going to do?'

* * *

Exhaustion presses down on Helena like a lead weight as she crawls into her car. She takes a shuddering breath, trying to drum up enough energy to drive home, focus on the road and not collapse beneath the sheer heft of the fatigue that clings to her like lichen. She and Barbara had sat together after her friend's rush of anger had subsided, their tears mingling until she felt sure they would both become dried out husks. By the time she left with promises of a return visit as soon as Barbara was up to it, Helena could barely walk in a straight line, her vision blurry and distorted, her limbs wooden with devastation and horror.

The road is clear of reporters, only one policeman standing guard outside the house. He gives her a curt nod as she drives past, her freezing fingers clasped around the steering wheel. Once again, her thoughts turn to her own daughters and their safety. Why is parenting so bloody difficult? She had imagined that caring for babies was always going to be the most trying part of motherhood, but she's finding it increasingly tricky to switch off and let them get on with their own lives now that they are both adults. Her feelings oscillate between feeling stifled by their constant demands to wanting them both by her side. Rachel with her rapidly deteriorating health and living circumstances, and Vanessa with her demanding job and midnight dashes, both of them giving her cause for concern in vastly different ways. She rubs at her eyes with the back of her hand and navigates her way through the streets, bypassing the town centre as she heads to the A66 and back home where a hot bath and her soft bed beckons. One thing she feels sure of as she pulls up outside her home is how she will now act in the presence of her two daughters. It's time she got a grip, stopped being so soft and accommodating, pandering to their needs. No more feelings of helplessness. No more tiptoeing around their moods and ever-changing reactions to the simplest of statements. She will be the strong-willed mother she should always have been to stop them becoming the next victim of the psychopath that currently stalks the streets of their hometown. Whether it be shouting or yelling or nagging at them incessantly, she will do what it takes to make sure her daughters are safe and don't end up on a cold slab in a morgue next to Francesca.

19

ALEX

Twelve Years Prior

'Such a pity you can't make it, Alex. Maybe next time?' Letitia was standing with Joy, their eyes wide with faux shock at his admission that he wouldn't be able to attend the leaving get-together after all. Family emergency. It happened. His mother was frail and ill. She always came first. It was just how it was.

He gave them a cursory nod and turned away, the sight of both females enough to set off something inside him that he always kept hidden, a twisting of his stomach. A series of unspeakable thoughts. Neither of them would miss his presence at the gathering. He had spent all of his life on the periphery. He was a marginalised man. It didn't matter. None of it mattered at all. His own company was something he had always preferred. They may have been making all the right noises, saying the right things to show their disappointment and concern at his sudden turnabout, but they knew a lie when they saw one. Both women were just like his mother – needy, spineless, selfish. Most females were.

No, not most. All.

He had seen it so often, how they paraded about, showing off swathes of flesh, taunting people. Inviting trouble. And then crying like babies when it came their way. He was willing to bet that Letitia had a change of clothes under her desk in readiness for tonight's bash. She would sashay her way into the bar, all tits and legs. Maybe even a bit of bare midriff exposed as she turned heads and commandeered the room.

The twinge of desire he felt at that thought was enough to make him pick up his coat and backpack that contained everything he needed, and head for the door. Usually he was one of the last to leave, locking up and making sure the alarm was set. A showroom full of cars in an area that could only be described as a slum was too much of a temptation for many. But tonight, he was the first to make a hasty exit, doing what he could to dampen his ardour, his own desires sickening and infuriating him. That he couldn't control them only fuelled his anger. Making him hate Letitia even more.

The walk out of town sharpened his senses, giving him the courage to do what needed to be done. Using his mother as an excuse for not attending the leaving party painted him in a better light. He could use his role as her carer to his advantage. She did have her uses after all. Sometimes being worthless was the most worthy thing of all.

Although he was better off than he had ever been in his life, money was still an issue, his commission-based salary leaving little left for luxuries. It was two bus rides to get to the place he wanted to be and then a brisk half-mile walk down a deserted country lane. He wasn't so stupid as to hop off at the bus stop next to the pub and have witnesses who could testify to his whereabouts. He was smarter than that. He may not have stayed on at college and acquired the necessary qualifications to prove his intelligence, but he had a good brain and could think quickly, using clear-headed logic and common sense. His teachers were wrong. All those highly qualified people who had spent years at the chalkface. They thought themselves experts in their field and yet they were unable to see him for who he really was. He was just another kid that they couldn't wait to see the back of. Another useless, badly behaved lad who once he had left school was forgotten, replaced by another and then another. Because they were all out there – people like him. So many rudderless teenagers, wading through life with no clue of how to behave. How to function in a burgeoning society. So many like him. But not quite the same. He was different. Unique. Maybe his teachers couldn't see who he really was, but he knew what his trajectory through life was going to be. He had ambitions, things he wanted to do. Not just another poverty-stricken kid from a shit home and a shit family; he was going places. Some-how, he would make a name for himself.

By the time he rounded the corner and spotted the pub in the distance, his body was vibrating with excitement, bolts of electricity pulsing through him.

A small wooded area next to the car park provided plenty of cover. He crouched next to a tangle of weeds and checked his watch. His timing was perfect. In a few minutes they would all arrive, spilling out of cars, all superficial excitement and fake laughter. All gloss and vapid chatter.

Seconds ticked by, turning into minutes. The temperature dipped as the sun set over the hills beyond the roof of the pub. Patient and fired up by the prospect of what lay ahead, he waited, his mind ruminating the possibilities of what the night could hold. What he was about to do. The satisfaction he would gain from it.

The distant rumble of an engine curtailed his musings. Alex

watched, a breath suspended in his chest as his colleagues pulled up in the car park, each of them clambering out of a vehicle in an excited frenzy before heading inside. No sign of Letitia yet. Refusing to be left behind, she would soon pull up, driving the new car her dad had bought for her. His skin prickled at that thought. She reeked of privilege and self-importance. Some people didn't know they were born.

It only took a few minutes of crouching and waiting, trying to stem his excitement and racing pulse, and suddenly there she was, stepping out of her little Ford Fiesta. Letitia. All tits and bare legs. All make-up and curls, and exposed midriff. Christ, she was so fucking predictable. Funny how she thought herself clever yet had no idea what was coming next. She was oblivious to the fact that he was waiting for her here, crouched and concealed behind the overgrowth in the near darkness. Not so intelligent after all. Just another errant young woman who thought herself above being harmed.

Leaves rustled as Alex crept out from behind the hedgerow, hood pulled up, scarf wrapped around his face, a tingle in his groin. She made it so easy. Too easy. Part of him wondered if she actually knew and was deliberately hanging around, pretending to adjust the strap of her handbag. Maybe she enjoyed it as much as he did; the chase. The moment prior to it all happening. It was a kind of dance they were doing; the way she moved to one side as if inviting him in, how he reached forward and clasped his hand over her mouth. The struggle as he dragged her into the bushes, her hands slapping at his, her nails clawing at him to try to release his grip. And then the final part, that sweet spot of the moment when he wrapped his fingers around her throat and pressed until his entire body shook with the force of it.

She fought back. Of course she did. He expected that. He

would have been mightily pissed off if she had just laid there and let him overpower her. The fun was in the fight. But he was stronger, heavier. And he was winning. Until the sound of another engine close by curtailed his plans. His fingers loosened from around her neck. Her head fell back, eyes fluttering. His breath came in short bursts as he stared down at her. He had two choices – finish this thing or leave her and run.

The vehicle growled to a halt. The sound of slamming doors, then voices. Hand pressed over her mouth, he waited, breath hot and sour against the fabric that covered his face. He couldn't risk it. They were only a couple of feet away. The slightest noise would alert them to his presence. He couldn't risk getting caught. This was just the beginning of his venture, his first foray into the murky world of proper violence and possible murder. This was a step up from snatching handbags and stealing money. It felt too good to risk losing it to a stupid error of judgement. This was typical of Letitia. Typical of women of her ilk, to make it go wrong. To ruin the moment. Fucking bitches, each and every one of them.

Retreating footsteps gave him a chance to leave. As quietly as he could, Alex lowered her limp, semi-conscious body to the ground, removing his hand from her mouth before covering her face and body with leaves and twigs. Then he stuffed wet foliage in her mouth to stop the moans and any possible screams once she got her strength back. He scrambled to his feet and picked up his bag before turning and making a hasty exit through the small woodland path that led back the way he came.

* * *

'Is that you, Alex?' Her voice was a whine. Child-like and

pleading. 'I'm thirsty and I'm hungry. You're late home. Where have you been?'

He closed the front door, the sound of his mother's voice rattling in his brain and jarring his nerves. A job half done. That was what she was. Letitia and his mother were both tasks he had yet to complete. Both of them needy individuals who bit at his brain, pecking and pecking until he couldn't stand it any longer, feeling as if he was going mad under the pressure.

'For fuck's sake, of course it's me. Who else is it going to be?' His voice, powerful and laced with unspent anger, echoed up the stairs.

He threw his hoodie over the newel post, then picked it back up and marched into the kitchen holding it aloft before dropping it into the bin along with his scarf and shirt. He would burn them later, tell his mother the fire was old wood and dead leaves from the garden. It wasn't as if she was able to get up and check anyway, but since she had come off the drink, her senses were heightened. Her curiosity sharpened. Suddenly she was eager to engage with the world around her. Pity she wasn't so keen a few years back when he was a kid and he needed her help.

'I need to use the toilet, Alex. Please help me.'

He took the stairs two at a time, the sound of her high-pitched demands scorching his skin like hot oil. Her bedroom door was exactly as he left it. She had stayed put all day, but he was definitely going to have to do something about her voice. At some point a passer-by would hear her shouts and cries, and he couldn't risk that happening.

'Come on then. Let's get you to the bathroom.'

She was a pitiful sight, her bony body slumped on the bed, the rope on her wrists and ankles cutting into her thin wrinkled skin. She had done it to herself, filling her body with toxins, pumping alcohol into her bloodstream for all those years. Making him keep her tied up like a prisoner in her own home. And this was the net result. She no longer drank or took drugs simply because she couldn't. He had put a stop to it. But the damage was already done. She was a wasted figure of a woman and he was at a loss as to what to do with her. Keeping her tied up seemed like the only solution. It wasn't ideal, but what else was he supposed to do to stop her killing herself and completely wrecking this house? It had begun as a punishment after a visit from a man with a machete, demanding money. Alex had decided that he could no longer live like that. So he dragged her upstairs and wrapped a piece of old rope around her wrists and ankles. A rage had burned at his core. He had planned to keep her like that for just a few days until she was clean, but with each passing day he realised it was easier to keep her tied up in one place than to allow her to roam from room to room, searching for drugs or booze and wrecking the recently cleaned house. She wouldn't have found any. He had tipped every last drop down the sink after tying her up. And as far as he knew, she didn't have any money for drugs. He ran a tight ship, her past transgressions too deeply embedded in his memory to risk giving her free rein. Besides, she might tell somebody about their current set-up. It would be viewed by outsiders as strange and cruel. But it worked for them. For him. She'd had her run of the house for all of his childhood. It was time for the balance of power to shift.

'Remember what I said. No screaming or I'll have to punish you.'

Her eyes were wide, full of fear. He smiled and felt himself relax a little. She was scared of him. That was good. No fighting back. Zero resistance. He was too tired for confrontation. It had been a long day. A busy one. The adrenaline of the attack had receded and he was slowly sliding into an abyss, exhaustion swamping him.

'There you go,' he said, freeing her and pushing her into the bathroom.

It was dark in there, the window nailed closed, a board covering it to block out all light. No chance of her escaping. He couldn't take any risks. One day she would thank him for it, but for now they had to build up a relationship, learn how to adapt to their current conditions.

'I'm sorry, son,' she murmured, her eyes staring up at him as she tried to meet his gaze. 'The bed. It needs a clean. You were gone for ages and I couldn't hold it.'

The movement of air wafted the stench his way – the strong tang of stale urine. The stain on her clothes was suddenly apparent, the dark patch on her jeans making him queasy. He kept his hands pressed to his sides. There had been enough violence for one day. He knew his limits, how far he could go. People did bad things, unacceptable things. They did them all the time. It was his job to inject some normality back into their lives. To make sure they knew right from wrong and behaved accordingly. He wouldn't hit his mother for her ghastly lapse in decorum because after all, he was her son and she was his mum. Unlike her behaviour towards him as a child on the occasions his bladder failed him. He recalled those beatings with startling clarity. He wouldn't do that. He would let it go this time. But she was going to have to be careful, be better. Because he didn't have the patience for such lapses and it was about time she realised it. Soon she would see that their set-up wasn't so bad after all. There was method in his madness. Order in his little world. Which was exactly how he liked it. All he was doing was trying to take care of her and keep her from harm while he held down a full-time job and ran this house. He was just a hardworking man trying to do the best by everyone. He wasn't a monster.

20

HELENA

Arranging contact with Rachel after their last disastrous meet-up was easier than she anticipated. Helena couldn't be certain, but she could have sworn she saw a flicker of excitement and compassion in her youngest daughter's eyes at the mention of Mabel and Noah. Getting her to leave the knife elsewhere was another matter with Rachel claiming she needed it for protection.

'Protection from who?' Helena had asked, her face set into a scowl. 'Two small children and your own mother?'

The ensuing silence where Rachel tapped her foot and bit at her lip felt as if it would never end. And then there was the matter of that damn ring. It sat incongruously on Rachel's bone-thin finger. Numerous accusatory thoughts about its provenance ran wild in Helena's head until she felt as if her skull would crack in half. Speaking to Rachel about it was pointless. Getting her to agree to a meet-up with the children was a huge step. She wasn't about to scare her off with a barrage of questions and thinly disguised allegations.

Vanessa's reaction to the meet-up had been less than enthusiastic, her lip curled into a snarl followed by a shrug of her shoulders and a slight shake of her head when Helena informed her eldest daughter of her plans. It's no more than she expected. Rachel and Vanessa have never been close; not as close as Helena would like. Playful and tolerant as children, they grew into very different people once they matured. Her memories of that time are hazy but Helena recalls Rachel always being on the periphery of Vanessa's life, doing what she could to break through her older sister's confident shell and never quite managing to succeed. Perhaps that's where her problems started. Living in the shadow of somebody who achieves without even trying must be soul-destroying. Gavin's premature death should have brought them together. If anything it drove them further apart, cutting through the thin worn cords that connected them like a knife through butter.

And now, even after all these years, their differences are still apparent. After Vanessa's look of disdain at the mention of taking the children to see Rachel, Helena had wanted to shout at her that she was lucky to have a sister. Despite Rachel's current problems, she was still her sibling. It wasn't Vanessa's duty to help Rachel but as a close relative, the least she can do is visit and listen. To be there for her. To make up for their fragmented childhood when Rachel constantly had to put up with the air of authority that Vanessa exuded, the balance of power always tipped in Vanessa's favour. Helena tries to rake further into their past, visions of them playing together forming in her mind; four small children from school always splashing about in the stream down by the woods. The name of the other girl will forever be etched in her mind for reasons she would rather not think about, reasons that haunted her for many, many years, but the boy's name eludes her. Always quiet and brooding, Helena felt duty bound to encourage her daughters to play with him. His homelife was dreadful and despite her own grief, her pity for him stretched to inviting him over and allowing him to play in their garden. Smiling rarely, he would watch from the sidelines as the girls frolicked and ran about, as if joining in was something he was unable to do. But then after that fateful day by the stream, Helena became more fearful for her girls, thinking always of their safety and making sure they stayed close to home, and the boy faded into oblivion. At that point, the world felt like a dangerous place. She almost laughs out loud at the irony. All these years later and nothing has changed. Her life has come full circle.

Death was all around them then, an omnipresent force, and it is back once more, their lives overshadowed by a killer who is stalking their town. All life, no matter how damaged, should be cherished. And Rachel is damaged. She knows that. But since when did damaged people suddenly become worthy of contempt?

The clang of the school bell drags her back to the present. Her gaze is fixed on the door where both children make their exit every day. She watches, eyes narrowed against the growing breeze, cold air biting at her face as she stands, fists slung in her pockets. Waiting for her grandchildren to appear and brighten her day. All around her, people chatter; parents, grandparents, childminders, older siblings, all waiting for the emergence of their child.

And suddenly they are there. She gives a wave when she sees Noah spill out with a group of youngsters, followed by Mabel, who is busy hoisting her satchel up over her shoulders.

They run towards her, small feet tapping on the pavement, lunch bags swinging in their hands.

'Come on, my darlings. We're going to see your aunt Rachel.' Noah's body feels as light as air when Helena scoops him up, her right arm holding him close to her chest while reaching her free arm down to hold on to Mabel's hand. These are the moments that make it all worthwhile, thinks Helena as she smiles, savouring the softness of Mabel's skin, the chubbiness of her fingers. The warmth of Noah's breath against her own flesh. All small experiences; tiny irreplaceable events that buoy her up. Fill her with gratitude and make her glad to be alive. These are the good times that help banish the bad thoughts from her mind.

She steers the children clear of the throng of parents at the school gate, manoeuvring and slaloming through a wall of bodies until they reach the car.

'Who's Aunt Rachel?' Noah cries, a small crease appearing between his eyes.

'It's Mummy's sister, silly.' Mabel's voice is a gentle harmonious sound, like the delicate chirrup of birdsong on a summer's day.

Helena thanks whichever deity is watching for her granddaughter's sunny disposition. There are times when the strain of the day is evident in Mabel's frown and manner as she exits the classroom, dismissing her brother's probing questions with a curl of her lip and a sharp putdown. But today her granddaughter is feeling positive, her face flushed with happiness.

'Look, Grandma,' she adds. 'I got Star of the Week.'

A shiny certificate is thrust under Helena's nose, an A5 piece of card covered with smiley faces and gold star stickers.

'Well, isn't that just amazing?' Noah's feet make a clattering sound on the pavement as Helena lowers him, placing him next to her legs in order to take the certificate from Mabel's hot little hand. She studies it closely before leaning forward to envelop her granddaughter in a solid warm hug.

Mabel melts in her arms and Helena feels a tightening

sensation in her chest, the strain of the past few weeks culmi-
nating in a moment of tearfulness that she manages to shake off
before either child notices.

'When we meet up with Aunt Rachel, after we've had our
main snack, maybe we can have a lovely treat as a reward?'

'But what will I get?' Noah's eyes are suddenly glassy with
unshed tears. 'I didn't get Star of the Week, so I won't be able to
have a treat, will I?'

'Oh, my darling.' Helena wraps her arm around him and
nestles him into her body. 'Of course you will.' She winks and
smiles. 'I didn't get a Star of the Week certificate either but you
and me and Mabel are all going to have some ice cream after
we've had our ham sandwiches.'

'I don't like ham sandwiches!' Mabel's voice slices through
the moment.

'Neither do I. I want cheese!'

Laughter erupts out of Helena's throat. Disagreements that
would usually make her tired and exasperated are now a
welcome distraction. It feels good to have some normality
injected into the moment, their squabbles a pleasant respite
from the things that plague her thoughts day after day. Hour
after hour. An endless carousel of darkness and foreboding.

'Come on, you two fussy little munchkins. Let's get to that
café and meet Aunt Rachel.'

The drive there is punctuated with laughter and questions
about why Aunt Rachel doesn't ever visit their house, whether
she likes ice cream or apple pie, and whether she prefers
ketchup on her food or mayonnaise. Helena listens, trying to not
focus on whether Rachel will turn up at all as promised, and if
she does, how clean, affable and approachable she will be. Children are astute creatures, especially Mabel, an observant young
girl who will immediately find flaws in Rachel's appearance if

she arrives unwashed, appearing at their table wearing ragged dirty clothes.

Turns out, her worries were unfounded. While she is busy taking off the children's coats and hanging them on the backs of their chairs, Rachel saunters through the door wearing a new jacket and shoes, and a pair of freshly laundered tailored trousers. She looks like a different person, her hair brushed and scraped back into a ponytail that swishes about as she walks in and quietly closes the door behind her. Helena glances over at her daughter, a spread of warmth soaring through her veins like the first rays of sunshine after a gruelling winter. She smiles and swallows down the lump that has surfaced in her throat, saving the tears that are threatening for later, when she is alone. This is an occasion she rarely experiences, but one that is taken for granted by many. She will remember every word, every look and every tinkle of laughter. Each and every smile she will cast to memory and store it in a special corner of her heart.

'Hi, everyone.' The sound of Rachel's voice, the way she makes a deliberate attempt to soften her features when smiling at Mabel and Noah, sends a tremble through Helena, her skin a heady combination of fire and ice as she watches her daughter's movements. They can do this. *She* can do it. Together, she and Rachel will make this thing work. It's the least they can do for the children. This is Rachel's moment to shine, to win over these small, smart people and make a lasting impression on them.

They spend the next ten minutes ordering food and drinks and chatting about the world in general. Noah sidles up next to Rachel, his legs touching hers, his gaze fixed on her face. He is mesmerised and fascinated by his aunt.

'You look like my mummy, except my mummy has a bigger face and body than you.'

Rachel laughs. Helena feels her head spin. Children; observant and brutally honest. She pulls at her collar, wishing she hadn't sat next to the heater, and finds herself talking incessantly about anything and everything from the children's school to the ever-changing weather. It's difficult to control her gabbling chatter and marginally neurotic behaviour in a bid to detract from Noah's comment. She hopes there isn't more to come. And yet, perhaps he should speak openly. He is a child and children speak freely without the confines of social expectations that hold adults back. Kids engage without any preamble. Maybe this is what Rachel needs – to be exposed to the brutalities and honesty of children's thoughts. To see the world through their eyes.

'Why don't you ever come to our house to visit us?' There is an edge to Mabel's voice. Something more than idle curiosity. A sharpness that stills Helena's blood.

'Maybe I will. From what I've been told by your grandma, your mum is always busy working.'

Helena can feel Rachel's eyes boring into the side of her head. Can detect the animosity at the mention of Vanessa. She wills this moment along, waiting for it to pass, for the atmosphere to lighten.

'We could come to your house to see you?' Noah watches Rachel intently, the innocence in his tone enough to reduce Helena to tears.

'Aunt Rachel's flat is too small, which is why we're all here!' She is aware that her energy and voice are excessive but can't seem to stop it. 'Right, children, it looks like our food is about to arrive.' Helena turns, watching as the waitress approaches their table, plates of sandwiches and bowls of fries balanced on each arm.

Rachel eats slowly, each mouthful clearly an effort. It's as she lifts her fork to her mouth that Helena sees it again. That damn ring. Not so incongruous now that Rachel is clean and less shabby, and yet Helena's eyes are still drawn to it. It's stolen, that much is obvious. Now isn't the time to speak or even think about it. Notions of Rachel attacking defenceless people and robbing them can wait until another day. She realises then that even these moments, these purportedly happy family times, will always be tainted. Until Rachel comes back home, nothing will ever feel right.

'Mabel, why don't you show Aunt Rachel your certificate?' Helena's voice sounds as if it is coming from somebody else.

She will say anything, do anything, to keep this meeting on track. To make sure it's as calm and peaceable as it can be. Happy memories. That's why they are here, to create joyful moments for the children to look back on.

The certificate is plucked from Mabel's bag and brandished in front of Rachel's face. To her credit, Rachel showers her niece with praise whilst also keeping Noah in the conversation.

'I'll bet you're ace in school as well, aren't you, little fella?'

The look of adulation on the faces of both children is enough to convince Helena that despite her fears and anxieties that have got her stomach squirming and roiling, arranging this get-together was the right thing to do. Rachel also looks settled and happy, a wash of colour lighting up her pale skin.

They eat in companionable silence until Noah announces he is finished and would like some ice cream. Helena orders dessert for the children and a coffee for herself and Rachel.

The puddings arrive in record time and Helena watches a river of pink sticky liquid run down Noah's hands and onto his arms as he tucks into his bowl of ice cream, each spoonful like liquid gold being ladled into his small willing mouth.

This is a blissful moment. The building of a new bridge that will help bring Helena back to her daughter. Perhaps even help

Rachel forge a connection to her elder sister. She reaches across and places a hand on her daughter's arm. Rachel doesn't flinch, doesn't pull away or frown. This is it, she thinks gleefully. They are on the road to recovery. This time next year, Rachel's current living conditions and lifestyle choices will be a thing of the past, a blip in their lives.

'Your phone is buzzing, Grandma.' Mabel nods to Helena's bag, a low vibrating noise audible above the sound of the nearby chatter and the clanks and whirring of the coffee machine behind them.

'Sorry,' she says quietly. 'I'll just check who it is. Won't be a minute.'

It's a message from Cassandra about work, but that isn't what catches her eye or traps a bubble of air in her chest, making it difficult for her to breathe properly. A news notification has appeared with a picture of one of the victims below the head-line. A smiling blonde-haired young woman, fresh-faced and relaxed, stares out at Helena. A holiday pose from a time when she was happy. Unaware of what awaited her. She is wearing a white T-shirt and knee-length navy shorts. A handbag is slung over her shoulder and on her finger is a ring. A silver band with a jade stone in the centre. The same ring that Rachel is wearing.

A pain shoots behind Helena's eye, forcing her to press the heel of her hand onto her forehead to relieve the dull throb that has set in there. She has two choices – scoop up the children and leave with no explanation, or sit this out and then confront Rachel later. Threaten her with the police, even. Ask her how she got that piece of jewellery. Rings don't fall off fingers. They are wrenched off. Stolen. Taken from dead people.

The room shrinks around her, swirling like a kaleidoscope, a wave of colours bursting inside her head. She thinks that she cannot stand or walk, yet knows that she must. It's imperative she appears normal for the sake of the children. Unperturbed by what she has just seen. Even though a hundred angry wasps are stinging and biting at her flesh.

'I'll go and pay the bill.' Helena tries to smile, trusting it looks genuine. Her face feels wooden, her smile a grimace. 'If you want to put on the children's coats for me, that would be a huge help.' Her eyes travel over Rachel, averting her gaze from her hands. Trying to avoid the glare of that jade ring. That fucking stupid stolen ring.

'I can put on my own coat.'

'So can I!'

Helena leaves her daughter to sort out the squabbles. It's the least Rachel can do given what she has put her mother through these past few years. What she continues to put her through day after day, week after week. Year after fucking year. It's endless, a never-ending warped merry-go-round of worry and sleepless nights and absolute blind panic.

Her hands are trembling as she pushes her credit card into the machine, her mind blank when she attempts to remember her PIN. She is too deep in shock to think clearly. Too horrified to function on any level. Cold air rushes into her lungs, her mouth a thin line of unease as she takes a long, sharp breath through her nose, exhaling slowly. Gradually as if in slow motion, the numbers come to her, sliding into her brain one after the other. Helena swallows; this is what happens in times of stress. This is what her own daughter has reduced her to. A gibbering wreck. A woman who dares to wonder if her own child is a murderer.

Shame blooms in her mind, dampening her clothes and hairline. A wedge of disgust at her own thoughts sticks in her throat. She doesn't want to have such thoughts lodged in her brain and yet cannot seem to shake them away. Thoughts that her daughter is possibly a murderer but also something else. A notion, a wish that is unholy and atrocious and something no mother should ever entertain. Helena fights back tears, disgusted at herself for daring to wish that her youngest daughter had never been born.

21

PRESENT DAY

It's dark, the usual chink of light from behind the thick curtains that tells me it's time to wake up, absent. I long for a clock or a watch. Anything that will help me keep track of time.

I lie for a while, shadows looming in my brain, my mind raking over the night he captured me. The night he stripped away my liberty and took control of my life. For what feels like the millionth time, I wonder if I could have done anything differently – walked another route, called for a cab to get home. Ridden a bike even. I would do anything to be able to turn back the clock and change things. But it's too late now. Going over it time and time again is pointless and exhausting. I need to focus all my energy on getting out of here.

I think of my family, my parents and my brothers. Are they still out there searching for me? Have the police got any leads? My phone was in my bag when he bundled me into his car. It was switched on. He has either dumped it somewhere or has smashed it and dropped it into the River Tees. I am willing to bet it was the latter.

Tears prick at my eyes. I don't want to be another missing person, my face plastered all over the internet, posters of me stuck to lamp-posts in the vain hope somebody will have seen what happened. These things nearly always end up going only one way. And that isn't the way I want this to end. People who escape these situations are few and far between; in fact, I can't think of one single case where somebody who mysteriously disappeared without a trace suddenly appears again, staggering into the nearest petrol station or shop begging for help. Those things only happen in films. And yet here I am, lying in this room, plotting and scheming. Actually believing I can make a bid for freedom after clattering him over the head with a metal towel rail. If it wasn't so serious, if my life didn't actually fucking depend on it. I would laugh till I cry.

Eyes still heavy with fatigue, I close them and pray for morning to arrive, the idea of getting out of here and making it home almost within reach.

* * *

'Wake up. Come on. It's late. You need to get up or you're going to make me late for work.'

His voice is a crack in the room, splintering the darkness in my brain into a hundred pieces. My head aches, the words he utters forcing me sideways into the day. I should have stayed awake, remained sharp and ready. As it is, I'm woozy, my thoughts fogged up, my vision blurred. How I manage to sleep when I am tied up is beyond me. Maybe I'm slowly dying. Maybe I'm already dead and all of this is an illusion. Maybe I'm in hell.

Limbs creaking, I shuffle around the bed, placing my feet on the floor to lever my body upwards. He stands at the doorway watching, observing my struggle, doing nothing to help. I would rather it stays that way. The thought of his hands pawing at me is enough to make me retch. Besides, the struggle is worth it. It's the only exercise I get, the only way I have of keeping some sort of muscle tone. I'm slack and thin but not quite at the point where I'm ready to collapse. My fight comes from within – I'm fuelled by hatred.

He steps forward and unties my feet, allowing me to walk with him to the bathroom, passing the photographs of the unidentified woman that are plastered over every wall. I keep my eyes lowered, refusing to look at the lady who resembles me. Refusing to wonder if I will be next, my face leering down at some poor unsuspecting female who has been snatched off the street and brought here to die while my body rots in a ditch somewhere.

As we approach the bathroom, I try to talk myself through what happens next, allowing myself to believe that this is it. That this is the part of my roughly hewn plan where I slam him across the side of his head with a length of metal and he collapses at my feet, blood gushing out of his temple.

'Get a shower,' he says gruffly. 'And don't be long.'

As usual, a pile of freshly laundered clothes sits on the floor. I glance at them, my brain screaming at me to look at the towel rail to make sure it is still loose. He places the knife at his feet, then unties my hands and removes the gag. The glint of the blade is enticing. I am usually repulsed by its size, disgusted and scared by the sheer heft of it, but this morning it holds a certain amount of appeal. Am I really brave enough to do this? To risk my life without any solid idea of how I will escape if I do actually manage to maim or injure him? I have no knowledge of my location or where he keeps the keys to any of the doors. It shouldn't matter. Telling myself I'm being cowardly and stalling for time, I turn on the taps and step out of my clothes. A hot shower might help wake me up, give me enough strength to see this thing through. It's small and insignificant, my level of preparation, but it's all I've got.

Ignoring his presence, I swallow down the disgust I feel for him and get washed, my chest hammering as I lather my body and rinse my hair. My body feels weak and wiry when I step out and rub myself *dry. It's as I lean forward to wrap my hair in the towel that I'm able to see it clearly. The rail is still loose, a sharp screw keeping it fixed into the wall. Fired up, I put on my clean clothes and pull the towel off my head to brush my hair.*

'It's coming out in clumps,' I say, my voice a whisper.

I make a play of grabbing large strands from the hairbrush and holding them in the palm of my hand. His disgust is palpable. Any mention of bodily functions or anything connected to ill health appals him. This I learnt a long time ago when I vomited on the floor and he rubbed so much bleach onto the wooden boards, my eyes stung. And yet he has no qualms about leaving me slumped and tied up in a stuffy dark room while he goes off to work every day. He is a mass of contradictions. A monstrous enigma.

'I need more exercise, to be walked and fed regularly otherwise my hair and skin will become diseased. See?' I hold out the ball of hair for him to look at. 'Next it will be skin rashes and scurvy.' He steps back as if stung. I hide my delight. I've unnerved him. Disgusted him even. Good. 'I've also got some sore spots on my back. Look.'

I swivel around and roll up my shirt, sensing him behind me as he moves forward again and bends to take a closer look. It feels as if my heart is going to beat its way out of my chest, my abdomen a huge expanding mass of thrumming blood. I have no idea if he is holding the knife or if it is on the floor. I suspect the former but from this angle it's impossible to get a proper look.

'Can't see anything. Your skin is clear.'

'I felt them as I was getting washed. You need to look closely.'

Using the wall to keep my balance, I place one hand on the tiles and the other on the towel rail, then I take a deep breath and I pull with all my might.

22

HELENA

It's been over a week since the meet up with Rachel and the children. A week of terror and turmoil and dread. Each day has bled into the next, Helena going through the motions, her routine and her job the thing that keeps everything together. Except that since the most recent murder, that isn't entirely true. Going to work has proven as difficult as staying at home, Barbara's absence another reminder of how awful things are, how crooked and bent out of shape everything has become. Every day that passes puts more distance between her and her youngest daughter. Upon waking the morning after the meet-up, she vowed to contact Rachel, but now a week later, it feels impossible to know where to start; what to say. How to broach the subject of her daughter's whereabouts on the evening that Simone Callaghan was killed. That's her name. Helena has made a point of remembering it; of speaking to Simone every day when she gets out of bed, when she drinks her coffee and makes the journey to work. She talks aloud to whomever may be listening, hoping for atonement, apologising for what her daughter may or may not have done. Apologising for Rachel's existence. But more importantly, a deep apology for not doing the right thing and going to the police. How does one do something like that? Where would she even start with such a fucking awful turn of events? And so she has done nothing. She has carried on with her life, her hideously messy, headache-inducing life that is spiralling out of control just as she dared to think that things were about to turn a corner.

Next week is the funeral of Barbara's daughter, Francesca. Another tragedy. Two friends thrown together in the most disturbing and harrowing of circumstances. Helena's blood runs cold as she thinks about the unthinkable. What if Rachel is somehow linked to Francesca's death? It's not impossible; she is wearing the ring of one of the murder victims.

Helena rubs at her eyes, wishing she could blank it all out. Take the coward's way out and pretend none of it is happening. Except it is, and the longer she leaves it, the harder it will be to speak to Rachel. Three women are dead and another is still missing. The police and the press are now openly talking about a serial killer. And Helena's daughter is wearing a piece of jewellery that belongs to one of the victims.

A pain darts through Helena's head, stopping behind her eyes. She feels sick and unsteady, and as she sits, pondering over what could have taken place, how she could have ever given birth to somebody who would do such terrible things, a streak of something resembling hope spears her thoughts. Rachel is emaciated. A tiny slip of a thing. She isn't strong enough to attack somebody. She is barely strong enough to walk in a straight line.

Yet she has a knife.

Even the smallest and weakest of women could overpower another female with a sharp serrated blade.

She swallows down a rush of bile that travels up her throat. This is a pointless endeavour. She is going round in circles and not coming up with any credible answers. If she reports her suspicions to the police, the rift between her and Rachel will grow even wider, the damage to their relationship irreparable. Even making an anonymous call would prove challenging. Phone calls can be traced. She feels trapped by her own inadequacy, backed into a corner with no means of escape.

Today, she is off work, the day stretching out ahead of her. Hour after hour of dark seething thoughts that refuse to leave her be. In the end, Helena leaves the confines of the house and walks until she reaches the small woodland area on the outskirts of town, guessing that she has probably covered three or four miles. Gripped by a sudden thirst, she decides to call into the nearby pub, a big old barn-style building aptly named The Wheatsheaf. Stopping to catch her breath, mildly ashamed of her poor levels of fitness, Helena decides that she will buy a glass of lemonade, sit in a quiet corner, and pretend that her life is normal when in truth, it is unspooling at lightning speed.

The place is quiet, only a handful of people milling about at the far end of the room. Behind the bar, a television catches her eye. She can't help but stare up at it as she places her order, her stomach clenching. It's the news, a glossy-faced solemn woman reading out the latest police press release about the murders. Helena wants to block it out but is drawn to it like a moth to a flame, the urge she has to listen to every word like a form of self-flagellation.

'Awful, isn't it?' A middle-aged woman behind the bar drops a lemon into Helena's drink and slides it across the surface towards her. 'Those poor women. Who would do such a thing? Mind you,' she continues without waiting for a reply, her arms wobbling as she vigorously dries a glass and places it on a high shelf, 'I recall there was once an attack here on a young girl. Quite a few years back. It was in the car park out back. She was lucky. She lived. Can't be the same fella who did it though. It was a good ten years back, maybe even longer.'

'Did you work here back then?'

The woman laughs and widens her eyes. 'Aye, I did. I'm the landlady here. Had this place for nearly twenty-five years. Just counting down to retirement now.' She winks and heads off to serve a customer at the other side of the bar.

The glass is refreshingly cold against Helena's burning flesh as she picks it up and takes a seat over near the small leaded window. Her heart is beating fast, the sound of it pounding in her ears and crashing against her skull.

Can't be the same fella who did it though...

Even the landlady presumes the perpetrator is a man. Perhaps it is. That's the most likely assumption. Maybe Helena is heading down the wrong path here. Maybe Rachel did actually find that ring. It could have fallen off in a struggle during the attack.

She takes a sip of her lemonade and places it on the table, the heat of her body not quite reaching her fingertips. She presses bone-cold trembling hands on her knees and shuts her eyes, wishing she could block out every negative thought and image. Wishing she could be somewhere else. *Somebody* else.

'Is this anybody's seat?'

A male voice from behind her, loud. Insistent. Helena opens her eyes, spins around to face him, trying to appear unperturbed by his sudden presence.

'No, feel free.' She sweeps her hand over the small barstool and attempts a smile. It feels alien, her mouth twitching in resistance. The skin on her face stretched to breaking point. She wonders if she will ever feel happy again.

A creak of wood as he drags it across the tiled floor to his table where a group of people are seated. Helena turns away, afraid they can see her thoughts, the dirty family secrets she is harbouring. The awful lies and depravities she is forced to hide from the rest of the world. Every worry is etched on her face; chiselled into the lines and grooves on her forehead, her misery evident in the dullness of her eyes and downturn of her mouth.

Nearby noise and chatter heightens her feelings of gloom, their laughter and the ease with which they interact with one another something that now feels out of her reach. Aside from her work colleagues, it's an age since she has been sociable and conversed without anger or an agenda. Most of her time is spent trying to pin Vanessa down in a bid to speak to her about the children or her gruelling callout rota, or talking endlessly at Rachel who rarely listens anyway. A wave of sadness hits her; sadness at what her life has become. She would give anything to see her two daughters happy and speaking to one another. To be like the people at the next table, laughing and chatting and comfortable in their own skin. Vanessa distanced herself from Rachel once her addiction took hold. When questioned by Helena about their rift, Vanessa shrugged off her behaviour, claiming she and Rachel had never been that close anyway. Helena suspects it's the embarrassment of having a homeless sister. Always the brusque, busy professional, Vanessa simply cannot understand why Rachel lives as she does. She once claimed that there is help for those who are willing to accept it and since that time, she has made a point of changing the subject whenever Rachel's name is mentioned, claiming that not everyone can be saved. Those words sent a ripple of dread through Helena, as if Vanessa was turning her back on her only sibling. It's a strange thing, given her career choice, but Helena finds it difficult to imagine Vanessa displaying compassion and empathy towards the residents in the care home she manages. She suspects it is Vanessa's efficiency and administrative skills that have got her thus far, and that is indeed something of which she is proud, but she would give anything to see a gentler side to her elder daughter, to see her stop and take a look around, to appreciate the things that she has and maybe, just maybe, spare a thought for those less fortunate than herself.

The lemonade is cold as she takes a sip, sending a chill down her throat and settling in the pit of her stomach. Loneliness. That is another issue in her life. Helena loves her grandchildren but it's at times like this that she misses having a partner. Somebody she can laugh with, cry with, sound off to. Somebody with whom she can share her worries about her daughters. Because it always comes back to her children. Every concern, every sleepless night – they always without a doubt involve her offspring.

She finishes her lemonade and stands, suddenly eager to be home. The walk hasn't alleviated any of her anxieties. If anything it has heightened them, her mind too crowded to sort out the fact from the fiction. Rachel is wearing a dead woman's ring. That is the only thing she knows to be true. And until she confronts her daughter and speaks openly about it, these rogue thoughts that are repeatedly jabbing at her brain are only going to multiply. She thinks of that text message – *Your daughter is a fucking lunatic* – and knows that she cannot put it off or leave it any longer. The sooner she meets with Rachel and asks her what she knows about its owner, the sooner she can decide whether or not to believe her. Only then can she set about helping her to get off the streets and back to a normal life. Until that time, Helena's life will be on hold, her existence a brooding hiatus where the air around her feels toxic and nothing and nobody else matters.

With a feeling of growing alarm that sits at the base of her stomach, Helena leaves the pub and makes the long, lonely trek back home.

23

ALEX

Twelve Years Prior

She was off work for over a month. When Letitia did finally come back, she arrived at her desk looking tired and dazed, and half the woman she once was. That pleased him. Not that he was able to show it. Alex's emotions were kept locked away in the farthest reaches of his mind. And only he held the key to those particular sentiments.

The police had already been into the showroom, arriving a few days after the attack. They interviewed everyone who had been at the pub that night but didn't speak with Alex because, as he explained to them, he had got the bus home to care for his ailing mother and didn't attend the leaving get-together. And they believed him. He had already primed his mum, planting the idea in her head that she was mistaken and that he hadn't been late in on that particular evening just in case they decided to call and question her. Not that she needed priming; although sharper than she had been in years, her brain was still addled by years of alcohol and drug use. By the time he had finished bamboozling her with his endless statements and questions, she no longer knew who she was, never mind where her son had been and what time he had arrived home.

Alex stood idly, basking in the rays of sun that filtered in through the showroom, the damage he had inflicted on Letitia all those weeks ago a heady reminder of his capabilities. The fading bruises on her neck – he had done that. The bags beneath her eyes from a lack of sleep – he had also done that. And the haunted expression on her face, the way she jumped and trembled whenever anybody came near – that was also down to him. Just the thought of being able to wield that sort of power, to impact somebody else's life and no longer be the underdog and the butt of everybody's jokes, gave him a warm stirring in his groin. He imagined her lying awake at night, jumping at shadows, terrified of every sound; the creaks and groans of a sleeping house sending ripples of fear over her flesh, forcing her to slide under the covers to escape it all. Such thoughts gave him greater pleasure than anything he had ever known. Part of him was worried that she would recognise him. The hood and scarf he wore that night to conceal his face didn't cover his eyes, but it was dark, they were hidden in the shadows, the shrubbery making it even more difficult to see anything. She didn't recognise him, he felt sure of it. He would know by now. The police would have questioned him. Besides, he grabbed her from behind. By the time he pulled her into the shrubbery and pressed one hand over her face and another round her neck, she was barely able to see anything.

'Good to see you back,' he said, attempting to keep his exhilaration under wraps. To come undone at this juncture would prove disastrous.

Seeing her fragility, how timid she had become since the incident, how every bit of confidence and arrogance that she'd once possessed had leached out of her, was such a delight. For so long, the way she walked, the things she said, the knack that she had of controlling every room she entered, had infuriated him. But now she had been reduced to a babbling wreck. A flimsy delicate version of the person she once was. Damaged and partially broken. And it was all because of him.

Letitia gave him a half-smile, a watery thin-lipped grin before she lowered her gaze and began rummaging in her hand-bag, producing a tissue to dab at her eyes.

'Thank you. It's good to be here. Nice to have some normality back in my life again.' Her voice was a whisper. She bit at her lip and picked up a pen, her hand poised over a pile of documents.

'Have the police made any progress with arresting anybody?' A dullness was evident in his tone as he tried to inject an air of nonchalance into his manner. Too much excitement would be harmful, too little compassion would make him appear cold and heartless. It was all about balance. Tipping those scales neither one way nor the other and remaining neutral. He could do that.

'No. They've interviewed quite a few people but so far, nothing.' Fresh tears bubbled out of her eyes and coursed down her cheeks. 'The investigation is being wound up in the next few weeks, so they may never find out who did it.'

Relief and excitement swelled in his gut. He had got away with it. The police and Letitia were all too stupid to work out that it was him. Hardly a brain cell between them. It took nothing at all to creep around the back of that car park and hide in the shadows. No effort required. Some people deserved to feel unhappy and vulnerable, leaving themselves exposed to danger. Letitia didn't know it but he had actually done her a favour. He was teaching her how to take care of herself and stay safe in an unsafe world. She had been taught a salutary lesson in remaining vigilant. Next time she may not be so lucky. Next time she may wind up dead.

'Well, you know where I am if you need any help with anything.' He gave her a meek smile, the one he had been practising in the mirror over the past few weeks. A half lift of his mouth, a tilt of his head. A sorrowful expression.

He wanted to get it right; just enough to reassure her that she was now in a secure place surrounded by people who wished her no harm. Her features were soft and welcoming. Trusting even. She wiped at her eyes and smiled back, giving him a small wave with pale trembling fingers, her once-painted talons now clipped short and bare of the garish colours she previously favoured.

Alex turned and made his way over to the showroom floor. God, this was so easy. Far less difficult than he'd imagined. Snatching purses from strangers was one thing, but being able to stand just feet away from someone he had attacked, someone he had come close to killing – the thrill of it elevated him to a level that he'd never thought possible. That familiar twinge in his groin still threatened. That was something he needed to learn to control. He had to dampen his ardour, save that sensation for when he got home and was alone with his thoughts.

It was a wonderful thing, a notion to treasure and mull over, knowing he had broken her. And yet she still had some way to go before she understood his true capabilities because people like Letitia were too dim to learn the most valuable of lessons. She needed to up her game, start looking over her shoulder and not frequent poorly lit places next to a patch of woodland where monsters could lurk. She was alive at least, and he hoped she was grateful for that small mercy.

24

PRESENT DAY

It doesn't come loose easily. But it does come loose. I am able to pull the towel rail away from the wall. It all happens so quickly. Before he can react, I am brandishing a length of chrome in my hand, my face twisted with rage, a roar exploding out of me that comes from deep in my gut. Months and months of unspent anger and fury pumping out of me in a hot sour rush.

With both hands clasped around the rail, I run at him, screaming and hollering, using everything I have to knock him to the ground. If I can't use the weapon, then I will use my body and the rail as a shield to push him over, hoping he topples backwards down the stairs.

The shock on his face, the sudden jolt of horror in his eyes, doesn't last long. He is momentarily stunned but before I can inflict any lasting damage on him, he raises his hands and comes back at me, his bulky frame casting a shadow over my diminutive body. I refuse to give up, however, my size no barrier to my bid for freedom. It is so close I can practically taste it. I'm not going to be the woman in the photographs. I am not going to allow this freak to keep me here any longer.

Wielding the heavy rail, I wave it about before bringing it down on his arm. He lets out a howl, the sound like the dying throes of an animal caught in a snare. He holds his arm tightly, fingers clasped around his bicep, a wave of anger rising up his neck and face in a sudden crimson flush. I need to hold my nerve, not be cowed by his crazed expression and his size.

'You fucking bitch!' His voice rings around the room, full of anger and incredulity, his pitch rising as he begins to move towards me. 'I've kept you safe and fucking warm and this is the thanks I get.' Spittle flies out of his mouth, a silver trail gathering in the cleft of his chin. 'I could have killed you. I should have killed you! And now look what you've done!'

A film of tears blurs my vision. He is trying to stop me in my tracks, to unnerve me. It won't happen. An empty threat, that's all it is. If he had wanted to kill me, he would have done it by now. Maybe he will after this episode. Maybe this will be the catalyst, his anger finally unleashed, the genie too big and too fiery to put back in the bottle. But not if I kill him first.

I don't say anything. I need to conserve all my strength, use every-thing I have to fight him off. The knife sits at his feet. I need that blade. Once again, I run at him, blind rage driving me on. The rail connects with his body, pushing him backwards. He falls over on his backside, scrambling about on the floor. But he doesn't stay there. Before I can do anything, he is back up and running at me, his body a huge wall of muscle and bone. I hold the metal rail as tightly as I can, using it to push him away, pressing it hard into his abdomen. Some-thing touches my bare foot, the skittering of metal cutting through the sound of our cries and the pounding and clashing of our limbs as we connect.

He stops, also aware that whoever gets to the knife first will have the advantage. We both bend down but he is faster than me. Stronger. Before I can run, I am being pushed up against the wall, the blade pressed hard against my throat.

'Drop the metal rail, you stupid cow. Drop it!'

I consider holding on to it but can feel the sharp, cold edge of the knife being pushed into the thin skin of my neck. The clang as the rail hits the tiled floor echoes around us. I've wasted this opportunity. It's probably the only chance I will get. Things will become much more difficult after this. If I survive, that is. Part of me no longer cares but then another part of me is screaming to escape, to get out of this godforsaken hellhole and run, and to keep on running until there is no breath left in my body, my lungs empty and deflated.

Fingers push at my back, a firm hand propelling me along the landing until we reach the bedroom where I have been held captive for so long now. The place where I will most likely die. That was probably my only chance, my one and only opportunity, and I've blown it. Suddenly everything looks bleak, a pall settling over me like a lead weight. And yet, still something lingers, a tiny streak of hope that colours my vision, telling me that this isn't the end. That I can try again. Be better, more resourceful. Stronger. Every second that passes convinces me that I'm not going to die. His grip on the knife has loosened, his hold on my arm as he leads me to the bed less rigid. He could have slit my throat in the bathroom, hauled me into the bathtub and watched me die. Except he didn't. I'm still here. Still breathing.

A flicker of hope takes hold, combusting in my abdomen, flaring up my throat and morphing into something brighter. The light inside me hasn't been completely extinguished. Where there is light there is hope. The question is, why didn't he kill me when he had the chance? Why the fuck am I still here?

'Move,' he says, his voice a grunt as he throws me onto the bed. 'Stay there and don't say or do anything.'

The knife is held between his knees, the blade pointing at my stomach as he crouches in front of me to tie my feet together. Now isn't the time. I'm tired, my arms aching. So I let him continue, watching as he goes through the motions, placing the gag around my mouth and *yanking it tighter, but already another idea has taken shape in my head. Either tonight or tomorrow, I will try again. He wants me alive, that much is clear. Why is a mystery to me, but the fact that I'm still here after trying to make a bid for freedom is enough to cement the idea in my brain that I can do it again. I can give it another go. I almost laugh. Almost, but not quite. It seems ridiculous that all this time I have complied with his wishes, been the perfect victim, meek and mild and fearing for my life thinking that at any moment, he could use the knife to silence me and keep me here forever, when in fact, he was never going to use it. It's a deterrent. An impotent one as I now know he isn't going to use it. I've been such an idiot, waiting for so long, being frightened and anxious, wondering every morning when I wake if today will be the day that I will die.*

'Stay here. And no noise.' He nods towards the photographs, as if the woman in them is actually here in the room with us.

More laughter bubbles up. I swallow it down, averting my gaze from him and from the photos. Later, when he feeds me, when I am able to speak, I will ask him about her identity, try to get him to open up. Who knows, we may even form a bond, the woman in the photographs uniting us, giving us something to talk about while I make plans on how to get out of this place. The fact he is alluding to the idea that she can actually hear us, is proof that his sanity is hanging by a thread. I need to make my move before that thread snaps and he becomes unreachable, any final strands of compassion and reasoning he once had, vanishing completely.

25

HELENA

Helena's jacket and trousers swamp her shrinking body, the fabric rumpled around her slim frame. She pulls at the stiffness of her collar and glances at Barbara, who is even thinner than she is. The weight has dropped off both of them in such a short space of time, the strain of the past few weeks taking its toll. Funny and horribly coincidental that their worries are linked and yet at the same time poles apart. Barbara has lost a daughter and Helena fears her own daughter may be the one who is responsible. She has prayed every day since spotting that jade ring that her fears are unfounded and without basis. Helena has prayed to whichever God may be listening to send her a sign to let her know that Rachel is telling the truth and that she did indeed simply find the ring on the floor. And yet something stirs within her every time she thinks about it, a worm of discomfort burrowing beneath her flesh and biting at nerve endings. A stirring that won't go away. Rachel hasn't ever shown any signs of violence in the past, but drugs do terrible things to a person's brain, skewing their thinking, making them do things they never thought possible before their addiction took hold. Also, the people Rachel calls friends, what if they coerced her into carrying out some unspeakable act of violence? There is no telling what people are capable of when they are desperate. The Rachel she gave birth to and reared wouldn't ever hurt anyone, but she isn't the same person any more. This is a different Rachel; a wretched, anguished version of the person she once was. And wretched, anguished people who are at their lowest ebb are unpredictable, volatile individuals.

A rustle of clothing, the shuffling of feet, the clearing of throats all signify the service is about to begin. Francesca's coffin is held aloft by a host of sombre-looking males who lower it onto a plinth in the centre of the aisle. Barbara's muffled shriek at the sight of her daughter's flower-adorned casket brings forth a torrent of tears from Helena. It feels like the beginning of the end, as if everything good in the world has shattered beyond repair. She can't imagine how Barbara and her family will ever move on from this, how any of them will ever find peace in their lives again. Perhaps they won't. A hole this big can never heal.

Barbara submitted a long-term sicknote last week and Helena has no idea when, or if, she will ever return to the library. Maybe after a few months she will crave some solace in the surroundings, a routine of sorts to provide stability and assist with her mental health. Knowing what to say or do to help has been almost impossible. Helena has rung a few times and spoken to Barbara and Jem, and she has visited twice. It's been difficult striking the right balance between being there for her friend and inadvertently overstepping that invisible boundary and being regarded as a nuisance. An unwanted presence in their lives.

A family liaison officer had just left when she last called

round to the house, Barbara's face puckered as she admitted that she was less than satisfied with how the investigation was being conducted and how it was progressing. Helena had tried to reassure her that it was early days, but reminded herself that if it was one of her children who had been murdered, she would want the perpetrator caught as soon as possible.

Murdered.

Visions of Francesca in her final moments enter Helena's head. Her screams. Her blind terror. She bats them away, refusing to allow herself to be drawn into a seedy, sombre trap of her own making. Such thoughts would only involve Rachel, and Helena has had enough of torturing herself. Francesca suffered and that suffering is now over, whereas Barbara's will go on and on and on. Which is why Helena needs to do the right thing and confront Rachel. The police have issued a press release stating they believe all the killings are linked. They bear all the markings of just one deranged psychopath. All were strangled and stabbed. All were found in town, which now has a heavy police presence. Vanessa's night shifts and her midnight callouts are now just something else to worry about. So much anxiety and terror in Helena's head; she fears just one more thing will be enough to tip her over the edge, sending her spiralling downwards into an endless void.

Francesca's eulogy is read out by a close friend, who manages to hold it together, her voice low and controlled, breaking only as she murmurs her thanks and leaves the pulpit. Helena watches the young woman take her seat, sliding onto the bench in a dignified manner. Her black trouser suit and dark sweptback hair serve as a reminder of how terrible a day this is. How young Francesca was. How abruptly and tragically she died.

The room swims. Helena bends over, tries to suck in as much oxygen as she can. Out of nowhere, she feels as if she can't breathe, the air in the church suddenly thin. She places a clammy palm against her forehead, desperate to stay upright, to avoid falling to the floor. She cannot faint here in this place. This situation isn't about her. Everything feels magnified, visions of Rachel and that knife looming large in her mind. Visions of Vanessa being stalked in the early hours of the morning as she heads into work. Today is about Francesca, and Barbara and her family. That's where Helena's focus should be, not on her own daughters, who are both still alive. Barbara's grief is going to be a harrowing journey without end. She is going to need all the help she can get from her friends who have to be strong for her. So Helena cannot be somebody who can barely walk in a straight line at the first hint of trauma. She has to be there for Barbara, a sturdy person who can be relied upon. Sometimes the oldest clichés are the truest ones.

The service is emotional, everyone acutely aware that it shouldn't be happening at all. They leave the church, a sea of dark clothing moving as one large silent mass. Helena watches as Barbara, Jem and Rhoda climb into the funeral car and leave. Others remain behind, milling about, whispering words of condolence, expressing their shock and anger at what has happened. Words escape Helena. What is there to say at a time like this? Everyone knows how deplorable this situation is and they all know that they are as sorry as each other, so perhaps saying nothing at all is as powerful as saying something pointless. Useless small talk; she simply cannot bring herself to do it and feels unable to stay, to mingle and smile when inside she feels like she too is slowly dying, so instead, she makes her way to her vehicle and drives home in a fog of fear and uncertainty, her mind raking over all the possibilities surrounding Francesca's murder.

By the time she pulls up on her driveway, a headache has

begun to pummel at her temples. Last night, sleep evaded her, the thought of today's event cluttering up her mind. Rays of sunshine beat down on her neck as she climbs out of the car. She stops and looks up, a hand shielding her eyes from its glare. It's wrong. Today should be a squall; a hurricane battering at the windows. Rain and hailstones and all manner of apocalyptic weather forcing everyone to take shelter. How can the day be so warm when Francesca has just been lowered into the ground?

The pain in her head increases. Dreaming of a nap on the couch before collecting the children from school, Helena unlocks the door and steps inside, her senses immediately attuned to the fact that something is wrong. The door to the living room is ajar. She is certain she closed it before leaving for the funeral. The welcome mat is askew, a scattering of dried mud ingrained into the fibres.

Fear stipples her skin, the hairs on the back of her neck standing to attention. She thinks of Vanessa, wondering why she would visit during the day when she is supposed to be at work. And then her thoughts turn to Rachel, and whether she still has a key to Helena's house. What if it fell into the hands of one the people she spends time with at the hostel? They could be here right now, or they could have rummaged around for cash and anything worth stealing so they can sell it for their next fix. She isn't sure which would be worse – being confronted with a stony-faced Vanessa or one of Rachel's accomplices.

As gingerly as she can, her hands and fingers trembling like leaves in the wind, Helena pushes open the door. A throb pounds behind her eyes, her limbs suddenly stiff with trepidation. She lets out a dry shriek when she sees him sitting there, hands clasped squarely on his knees, his shoulders hunched. His bottom jaw quakes when he tries to speak.

But before he has a chance, Helena's own voice drowns out his words, hysteria taking hold.

'Innes? How the hell? I mean...'

The question she wants to ask dries up in her mouth, her question trailing off, vanishing into the ether.

'I know,' he says softly. 'I'm really sorry, Helena. I know I shouldn't have taken her key for your house but I was desperate. Vanessa left me with no choice. I had to speak to somebody about getting access to my children.'

The vertiginous sensation she has been fighting all day suddenly defeats her. Helena slumps down onto the nearest chair and takes a juddering breath. The room whirls around her, a blur of pastel colours making her dizzy.

'But you left? You just took off without a word and nobody has seen or heard from you for years.'

His smile appears genuine, no derision or hatred. No tapered eyes or dark glances from beneath his brow. Innes shakes his head, a sudden flow of tears rolling unchecked down his face. 'That's a complete lie. I don't know what Vanessa told you, but I didn't leave voluntarily. She did things. Bad things. I had no choice but to go.'

It's been a long day and it's not even dinnertime. Helena wishes for it to be over, for this fatigue that is bearing down on her to vanish and for Innes to leave so she can be alone with her low mood and her exhaustion. He is about to unveil something she would rather stayed hidden. His words are about to further upset the already delicate equilibrium of her fragile existence; she can sense it. And she can't let that happen. As distressed as he is, her own troubles take precedence. She is running on empty, her reserves of sympathy for absent family members non-existent. And yet, as much as she wants to ask him to leave, somewhere deep down, his words ring true. Vanessa's temper. Again. Maybe, just maybe, her daughter lied to her. It's a distinct possibility but is something she doesn't want to consider. Not today. Not any day, but she knows that at some point, she will have to listen to him and attempt to unravel the truth, to unpick this damn piece of knotted fabric until the real picture is exposed. She needs to hear the unvarnished truth no matter how sour and distressing it may be.

'Innes, I have no idea what happened between you and my daughter, but today has been a tough one.' She doesn't want to raise her voice or beg him, but her energy is waning, as is her patience. 'Now if you wouldn't mind giving me back my key, maybe we can speak about this another time?' The map of creases on her palm as she waits for him to pass it over tell the tale of a woman who has lived a full, often desperate life. She stares at her hand, at her waxy skin. The size and shape of her fingers resemble those of her mother. There is no escape from Sylvie. Her DNA is Helena's DNA. No matter how loyal or kind or helpful Helena is towards her two daughters, Sylvie is embedded in every part of her. And them. What if one of her daughters is more like her own mother than she cares to admit? Not now. She can't torture herself any further. We are, thinks Helena, responsible for our own actions. The choices we make in life aren't pre-ordained by our family connections. There are plenty of people from damaged families who emerge as happy, healthy adults. Blaming shared DNA is just an excuse to avoid taking responsibility for bad behaviour.

'She won't let me see my children. I sent you a message a few weeks back. I'd called round to the house in the vain hope of seeing them and was given my marching orders along with a whole load of verbal abuse.' He shakes his head and rubs at his face, weariness oozing out of him. 'The kids were inside so I wasn't about to get into an altercation with her on the doorstep. Which is why I sent you the message. Not the best idea, I grant you, but my temper got the better of me. I was frustrated and upset and all out of ideas, so I told her I was going to call you.'

His words hit Helena like a speeding train. That text: *Your daughter is a fucking lunatic!* The one she presumed was from one of Rachel's counterparts. It was Innes. The father of her grand-children. The man who walked out on his family and cut all contact. Or at least that is what she has been told. What if he is telling the truth and it's her daughter who is the liar? Helena thinks back to the message and the call afterwards from Vanessa about something completely unrelated, asking about the chil-dren's school consultation; a ruse to see whether Helena had spoken to Innes. To determine whether Vanessa had been caught out in her lie.

No.

Vanessa is her daughter and she has to remain loyal to her. Once the loyalty has gone, then what is left?

'Innes, you chose to go. Vanessa told me this and as she is my daughter I'm more inclined to believe her over you.'

His voice breaks when he speaks, his timbre like the splin-tering of dry wood. 'Helena, please believe me when I say I had no choice. If I hadn't walked out when I did, the damage would have been irreversible.'

'To who?' She flings her arms up in the air, eyes wide, incredulity tattooed into her expression.

A voice at the back of her mind pushes itself forward, eager to be noticed.

Mummy is always angry.

Mummy smacks us.

Ignoring the voice is easier than addressing it. One disaster at a time. And yet she must face this. She has ignored it for too long now. The worry caused by her reticence to confront the issue is eating away at her, its corrosive path turning her insides to dust.

'To me.' In his lap, his fingers are interlaced, knuckles white as chalk. 'This,' he says, rolling up his sleeve, 'is what your daughter did to me.'

A silvery scar runs the length of his left forearm, its trajectory jagged, the skin around it pink and puckered. Flames lick through Helena's veins. She pulls at her collar, attempting to release the sudden burst of heat that is billowing beneath her clothing. An image of Vanessa attacking Innes balloons in her mind. Is there no end to any of this? Helena has never raised a hand to anybody in her life, so how did she end up rearing two females who clearly have a predisposition to such brutality?

She takes a rattling breath and speaks.

'I'm sorry, Innes. I really am, but I only have your word for it. I'm sure if Vanessa were here she would have a different story to tell.' A memory pierces her thoughts, unbidden. 'That was you in the back garden a few weeks back, wasn't it? Creeping around one morning, scaring the children. Scaring me.'

'They're my fucking kids!' He stands, fists flexed at his sides, towering over her. A vein bulges at his temple. A tic pulses at his jaw. 'She changed the locks to the house but I can still get into the back garden. I kept my key for the padlock on the back gate, and I'll do it again if I have to.' He spits out the final few words, his teeth clamped together.

Helena feels her bravery curl up and wither like ash, her initial flourish of courage suddenly no more than a smouldering ember. He is over six feet tall, his eyes now wild with unexpended fury and frustration. He wants to see his children, she understands that, but she barely knows this man. Her relationship with Vanessa was sporadic when she and Innes were together. Helena was kept at arm's length. Maybe this was the reason. Maybe his temper had her daughter running scared, possibly even fearing for her life. Vanessa too has a temper, always has, but she isn't and hasn't ever been violent.

Except to her own children.

Her fingers flutter to her throat to stem the tic that is thudding at the base of her neck. He's lying. He has to be. Perhaps they are both lying. An ill-matched couple who brought out the worst in each other.

With a hammering heart, Helena picks up her phone, brandishing it in the air while punching in the number of the emergency services. 'Give me that key, leave my house and don't think of returning until you have calmed down.' She shows him the number on the screen, the digits lit up for him to see.

Helena holds out her hand, doing what she can to keep it steady. The last thing she wants is for him to see how frightened she is. How vulnerable she feels. Her veneer is brittle, a flimsy shield, but he doesn't know that. This is her home, her sanctuary, and he has just stepped over an invisible boundary.

Innes is an immovable object, his growing anger and looming frame filling the room until Helena finally presses the button to connect the call, at which point he briefly closes his eyes and quietly drops the key into her hand.

Air shifts next to her as he exits the room, his movements light and silent, his expression stricken. Guilt is a rock-sized lump in her chest. She had to do this, to pick a side and not be swayed by a near stranger. Although Innes has suddenly softened, doing as instructed and leaving without a fight, she doesn't know him. Not as well as she knows her own daughter. Besides, this is the same man who sent her an abusive text. The same man who crept around her grandchildren's garden, scaring them. Scaring *her*.

A click of the front door. A rumble in Helena's chest as she exhales, a rush of sour air expelling itself from her lungs. He's gone. She is safe. She disconnects the call and turns off her phone.

With liquid limbs and semi-dextrous fingers, she locks the front door, then on impulse strides to the window and yanks the blinds closed. Another layer of safety. Another barrier between her and the outside world. A world that feels cruel and uncaring. A world that seems determined to grind her down.

Her phone hits the chair with a muffled thud as she throws it across the room, Helena letting out an exasperated howl. His words continue to ring in her ears. Words about Vanessa; about her behaviour. Her temper. Her lies. All the things Helena has chosen to ignore. There are clues there; clues as to why Vanessa and Rachel don't get along. Rachel is needy and Vanessa is intolerant. They are polar opposites, the only thing connecting them being the notion of the possible violence they mete out to others.

Finally the tears come, silent and unending. The creak of the chair as she slumps into it is the only sound to be heard. She is tired. She is pissed off. Helena is everything she never wanted to be. This isn't how she planned her life. She hoped for sunshine and flowers and contentment and has been handed dread and unease and a whole load of never-ending worry. As a child, she was told to never utter the phrase 'it isn't fair'. And yet as she sits, tears streaming, that is definitely how it feels; that what is happening isn't fair, that life isn't fair. She has always tried to do the right thing and yet it has been thrown back in her face. Two errant, damaged daughters. Two children who seem hell-bent on ruining their own lives and the lives of those around them.

Rest won't come until she gets to the bottom of this story. Until she gets Rachel back home where she belongs and Vanessa unveils what really went on between her and Innes. Something happened to send her youngest daughter off the rails, and Helena now knows that Innes left because of Vanessa's violent streak. It's apparent that somebody somewhere is lying, and Helena won't stop digging until she unearths the truth.

26

ALEX

Eight Years Prior

Alex rubbed at his eyes, the sting of the disinfectant irritating them. His skin burned, his lungs felt as if they had been scraped clean with a sharp knife. It was good. He felt good. Shoulders back, chest thrust forward, he inhaled, a deep swooping breath to appreciate the powerful stench of the bleach. The glassiness of the floor, the gleam of the kitchen surfaces, they all gave him a feeling of satisfaction that swelled in his abdomen. It had taken years of solid graft to get to this point; years and years of saving up his hard-earned wages and making improvements in the house wherever and whenever he could to ensure his home was no longer the sickening detritus-filled hovel it once was. And now, he could finally say that it was exactly the way he hoped it would always be. Clean. Presentable. Clinical even. No mould splatters up the walls. No ragged rugs or threadbare curtains. No stinking bedsheets. Every day, his cleaning regime would banish all filth, and the house would sparkle like new. Apart from one room, that is. Not everything within those four walls was as he wanted it to be. One room remained dirty. Her room. Despite his size and superior strength, she still managed to exert some level of control. But not for long. Her wizened body didn't have many years left in it. The damage was too great; her veins and organs had been subjected to so many decades of substance abuse, it was a miracle she was here at all. Still, at least he was now able to run the house as he liked, bringing some order back into his life.

The world outside his home was a little less easier to control, with people cluttering up his existence. Making him do things he knew he shouldn't be doing. It was difficult to stop. Not that he wanted to. Everything was too far down the line to go back. Besides, he was doing the world a small favour, ridding it of the weak and the arrogant, dispensing of folk of the lowest order.

He cast his mind back to when he was a child. That day down by the stream. The childlike screams. The gurgling. And then the silence. That still, protracted silence broken only by the shriek of one of the sisters. He had been too young to appreciate what had happened, to truly *enjoy* it, but now, years later, he is able to mull it over, to look back and think about how it felt. The pleasure he gained from that incident before the adults swooped in and took over, blaming the previous heavy rains and slippery stones. How little they knew. How stupid and ignorant they were.

And then there was that woman at the showroom where he used to work. She was his failure. Easier to think of it that way. He could barely remember her name. The way she walked, the overconfident way she had of commandeering every room she entered; those memories had stuck with him though, expanding in his mind for months afterwards until he was forced to do something about it to alleviate the pressure. His next one was much easier. A homeless woman, her clothes falling off her, her hair matted with dirt. She had reminded him of his mother, her shrunken form and gaunt features, the whine she let out as he crept up from behind and grabbed her. The deep, guttural lowing that leaked out of her parted lips as she took her final breath. It was easy, her tiny body no match for his size and superior strength.

That was over six months ago and since that time, the urge to do it again had left him. The problem was, she wasn't missed, her death making the news for only a few days. He had brooded over it, the lack of attention, how the public valued one life over another. Homeless people weren't worthy of headline-grabbing stories. Their lives and miserable endings melted away in a matter of days like snow in the first days of spring. So he had already decided that next time, he would change his routine. Do something bigger. Something better. More noticeable. If there was a next time, that is. For now he was content to toil in the house and do what he could to tend to his ailing mother. He didn't search for victims for the sake of it. He did it to relieve an urge, like scratching an itch.

The hot stirring between his legs brought on by those memories soon turned flaccid as a voice from upstairs filtered into the living room, the sound of his mother's nasally whine enough to drown out all thoughts. Their living arrangement had worked well over the past few years. It freed him up, allowing him to live his life without judgement or rancour. His most recent job also gave his income a much-needed boost. His commission-only position at the car showroom was a meagre wage and as a result he had lived a meagre existence. Only when he moved on to his new post at a larger garage with a regular salary was he able to expand his lifestyle and make his dreams a reality. It enabled him to move away from the boy he used to be, the socially awkward misfit that was Alex Broadwood, to the man he now was. With a vehicle as part of his package, he felt like a new person, his regular larger income permitting him to plough money into the house and make much needed-improvements throughout.

'Alex. Please help me.'

With pincer-like precision, he pulled off his rubber gloves and placed them in the bin before taking the stairs two at a time. That was another thing that he had gained control of – his levels of fitness and his body shape. Lithe and supple, he had shed his post-pubescence puppy fat and boasted a body that earned him glances from passing females. He knew that he had been blessed with good looks too, and yet none of that gave him complete satisfaction. There was a hole in his life. A craving for something else.

'What is it now, Mother?'

'I'm hungry.' There was a pleading quality to her tone, like a child desperate for love. Anything that would bring attention her way.

'Okay, let's untie you and sit you up. I'll get you a sandwich and a glass of milk.'

Every time her lifted her, he was struck by how tiny and vulnerable she was, her body mass decreasing with each passing day. At some point in the not-too-distant future, she would fade away completely. And who would miss her? With no friends, no work colleagues and a constant stream of transient neighbours who had come and gone over the years, there was nobody who called to check on her well-being. They had both lived their lives beneath the radar, telling nobody of their circumstances, managing to slip out of the clutches of social services. His mother's benefits were paid directly into her bank account, of which he had taken charge. Her previous drug debts were all cleared. They owed nothing to nobody, existing in a vacuum. Colleagues knew little of his homelife. He left work at the door each night. And that was how he liked it.

There had been a few women over the years. Not long-term partners; just the occasional one-night stand in local hotels. That was his preference; he needed space between any hint of romance and his homelife. His house was his sanctuary, somewhere he could hide and evade scrutiny. A place where he could cogitate and plan and scheme. Be himself without the roving gaze of a stranger assessing his every move.

The white walls of the room were in stark contrast to his mother's thin frame and dark baggy clothes as he propped her up in the armchair in the corner of the bedroom.

'Wait here while I go and get your food. And remember, no moving about when I'm not in the room.' He gave her the look he had perfected over the years, a dark-eyed stare that made her curl up with fear.

'I promise, Alex. I'll wait here until you get back. Such a good boy, you are.' Her voice trailed after him, a feeble rasp. 'Always such a good boy for your mother.'

* * *

It was like dealing with an infant, thought Alex as he prepared her lunch in the kitchen, with her childish demands and inability to fend for herself. It was while he was pouring her milk that he heard it – the scraping sound above him. Then a dull thud.

The creak and groan of old wood echoed, Alex thundering up the stairs to the source of the noise. His eye pulsed, a tic taking hold when he thought of her. Clumsy fingers pressed at his face, massaging his cheekbone and jaw to still the twitch.

He could see her in his mind's eye, her thin arms and bony

fingers pushing at latches, opening windows. Calling out to passers-by. Shouting untruths about their living conditions. Telling an empty street that she was being kept prisoner in her own home. She was wrong. Misguided. A liar. They were happy here. *He* was happy here.

'Mum? Mother?'

The doorway shrank around him, the ceilings lowering and the floor becoming sponge-like as he stood, staring down at the body of his mother, who was sprawled out on the bedside rug.

The grating sound that escaped from somewhere in the depths of her throat mottled his flesh; a death rattle echoed around them. He scooped her up and laid her on the bed. She was silent. Maybe the gasps had come from him. He couldn't be sure. Panic was blurring his logic. The blinds were still shut, small strips of daylight visible through the gaps. She hadn't made it to the window. He was safe. For now. For once in her life she had done the right thing, sticking to the rules.

As gently as he could, Alex covered her up, the duvet a mountainous wedge of fabric atop her small still body. He would let her sleep, bring up her snack later once she had regained her strength. It was just a fall. She had staggered and tripped. Maybe this would teach her to remain motionless in his absence. She had been warned and had ignored his instructions and was now paying a hefty price for breaking the rules.

The carpet was soft under his feet as he padded out of the room, quietly closing the door behind him, unaware it was the last time he would see his mother alive.

27

PRESENT DAY

It must be the weekend. A Saturday perhaps. It's light outside, shafts of yellow creeping around the edge of the blinds, and he is still somewhere in the house, the sound of his footsteps echoing. Taps being turned on. A kettle boiling. All normal sounds that bely the activities that take place inside this horribly abnormal house. Outside, traffic passes, intermittent engine noises, the rush of vehicles as they drive past, unaware of the atrocities taking place within.

Last night, I lay awake, chastising myself for my ineptitude, my lack of strength and inability to escape. After the incident with the towel rail, I knew I needed to find another way, change tack and use a different method to overpower him. That's when it came to me, the idea ripping me from sleep – his life. And my knowledge of it. I can use the element of surprise, try to talk my way out of here. Use my mouth to knock him off-kilter. The weeks and months I have spent here have given me time to think, to go over in my head how and why he chose me. It wasn't a coincidence. He didn't just happen to be driving past late at night and see me walking alone.

He had been watching me.

Stalking me.

I swallow and take a shuddering breath. All this time I have been fearing for my life, terrified he would slit my throat if I made one wrong move. Yesterday proved that he isn't the unbeatable man I thought him to be. I have found the chink in his armour. He needs me. He isn't going to kill me. I may not have his strength or a weapon, but what I do have is my brain and my mouth. And enough information about him to get inside his head and rile him. My memory of Alex Broadwood is of a man who was deeply uncomfortable in his own skin. A few of the girls at work thought him suave and handsome if a little socially awkward. I saw beyond his looks to the person beneath, and although it's easy to say now I have proof of his deeds, I never liked what I saw. It isn't hindsight speaking; it's the uncanny ability I have of being able to make snap judgements of people. And I judged Alex Broadwood as a predator. Which is why I often went out of my way to avoid being in his company, leaving a room whenever he entered, refusing to engage in conversation with him. Avoiding him on the walk to the staff car park in the surrounding darkness. I could see the monster behind the mask of conviviality. Others didn't, a few of the female members of staff doing their damnedest to hook up with him. He shunned their advances. Apart from one. I saw that coming as well but after leaving the place for a more secure position at the hospital, I have no idea if they are still an item.

'Time to get up.' His outline fills the doorframe, his shadow stretching along the floor, snake-like.

I haul myself upright before he tries to manhandle me. The thought of his fingers pawing at me makes me want to vomit.

He kneels before me and unties my feet. Kicking out at him is a pleasurable, satisfying thought, but a futile exercise. With my hands tied, fighting him off would be impossible.

'Get up. Come on, get showered, and no stupid stuff.'

I do as he asks, feeling brave, brazen even. We walk to the bathroom where he unties my hands and removes the gag. I stare at him as

I sit on the toilet and relieve myself, all the while trying to catch his eye to show him that I'm no longer afraid of him, but as usual, he half turns away, as if he is allowing me a modicum of respect. He isn't. I don't want respect. I want to go home. I will flee this place naked if I have to. I have suffered enough indignities in this house, been stripped of my worth and humiliated so often that running nude through the streets no longer holds any fear for me. It's better than spending the rest of my life in this house with him and those fucking pathetic photos plastered all around the room.

'Who is she, Alex?' I say as a stream of urine hits the porcelain. 'Who is that woman in the photographs? Is she dead?' I spit out the final word for emphasis, as if it is a toxic substance, lining my tongue and throat with venom.

No reply.

'Did you kill her?' I think of the bracelet, the blood-spattered bracelet he threw at my feet a few days back. He may not be violent with me but he is capable of it, that much I do know. A person who kidnaps people and has a weapon is capable of almost anything.

Still nothing. No response, but I can see that I have hit a nerve. His head is lowered, his spine curved, serpent-like. He rotates his shoulders and cracks his knuckles before resuming his usual position and standing at full height.

'Are you going to kill me too, Alex?' I am aware that I am pushing him hard now, seeing how far I can go before he cracks, but it's better than doing nothing. I need action. This inertia is rotting me from the inside out.

'Take off your clothes and get showered.'

I stand up, pull up my underwear and trousers, flush the chain, and wait. I wait for him to do something, say something.

'Why am I here? If I escape, you do realise there's no way out of this mess, don't you? I know who you are. I'll be able to lead the police straight to your door.'

I expect him to run at me, to hit and claw at me. To do something. But still he stands. Silent. Unmoving.

I shift away from shock tactics and try for friendliness, hoping it will disarm him. He is a cool one, rarely engaging in friendly dialogue. Always distant and aloof. Detached from reality.

'Do you still work at the same place, Alex? I remember when you and I were colleagues. Do you remember? Is that why you followed me? Was it because I ignored you when we worked together? Is this my punishment?' I tilt my head and manage a smile. Bravery is a growing thing inside of me, taking root and pushing me on. 'Or is it because I look like the woman in the photos? Is that it?'

'Get in the shower. Now!'

He clutches the knife and makes thrusting manoeuvres with it, slicing through the air like a child with a toy weapon.

Friendliness. That's the way to catch him off-guard; make him uncomfortable. Make him squirm. Not insults or a barrage of questions. Trying to connect as one human to another. That's what unnerves him. It's an alien concept for him, human attachments. Being friendly, affable. Normal.

Satisfied that I have finally found the courage to fight back, I strip off and step under the water, convinced that my route out of here is still within touching distance. I didn't fail when I ripped that rail off the wall and attacked him. I simply used the wrong type of weapon.

28

HELENA

She may as well get all of the dirty jobs over and done with in one hit, is her thinking as Helena steps out of her car and makes her way to her mother's house. With a sense of dread, she opens the front door and picks her way over the array of discarded tin cans and empty food packets that litter the hallway. The stink of cigarette smoke greets her when she strides into the living room, its acrid dry stench hitting the back of her throat like a punch to her gullet.

'You're back, are you?' Sylvie takes a long drag of her cigarette, the end of it crisp with layers of burnt tobacco. Helena watches, horribly mesmerised as the length of ash bends to one side, eventually dropping to the floor. Sylvie smears it with her foot, grinding a mass of grey powdery residue into already blackened tiles.

Helena disguises the revulsion that she feels rising up her chest. She learned a long time ago to keep her own counsel when faced with her mother's disgusting habits. Sylvie does it for a reaction, a way of provoking an argument. Helena has neither the time nor the energy for any of her little games.

'I'm back,' Helena replies, suppressing the urge to bundle up armfuls of rubbish and dispose of it outside.

She doesn't know how her mother lives like this, how she makes it through each day in this house, surrounded by a mountain of garbage and filth.

'I'm fine as I am,' Sylvie barks, her voice husky, laced with annoyance at Helena's unplanned visit. 'So don't go moving things and tidying up. It's my house and this is exactly as I like it. I know where everything is.'

Even after so many years of living apart, she can still read Helena like a book. She and her mother are so very different, their thinking and habits and lifestyles on separate continents, and yet Sylvie still has the ability to climb inside her head and pick apart her every thought. Helena doesn't believe that her mother does enjoy living as she does, but is too stubborn to change tack. Always mulish, age has only heightened her wilful ways, refusing every scrap of help that is offered to her. To back down now and live as others do would mean admitting she has been wrong for all these years. And Sylvie is never wrong.

'So what gives?' Dark lashes conceal a probing gaze that sweeps over Helena, burning deep into her soul.

She is exposed, every inch of her life on display, every family secret she has regarding her daughters and their lives suddenly revealed; her own mother, the last person she would ever confide in, is suddenly privy to her innermost fears. Helena wishes she was half the liar her mother is. She wishes she were better at masking her emotions instead of wearing all her worries and anxieties on her face.

'Nothing gives, Mum. I've just come to see how you're getting on.'

'Liar.' Sylvie makes a point of looking Helena up and down, nodding and frowning as her dark eyes roam over Helena's face and clothing, analysing every inch of her flesh. 'You haven't been sleeping and the weight has dropped off you. Take a look in the mirror at the bags under your eyes. You're a complete mess.'

'Thanks, Mum. Always good to know I can rely on you for moral support and compliments.' The crack in her voice causes her to stop.

She swallows, takes a few seconds to rebalance herself, to not allow her mother to have the upper hand. Sylvie hasn't earned that right, the accolade of being a fabulous mother something she definitely doesn't deserve.

'So what's up?' Another cigarette dangles from her mouth. She lights it and takes a drag while the previous one still smoulders in an ashtray next to where she sits. A dry cough emerges from somewhere deep in her chest as she laughs heartily. 'You can trust me; it's the people I tell that you can't trust.'

Enough. She has been here for seconds but already has had her fill of her mother's acerbic comments and lack of compassion. Helena turns and makes her way to the door, relieved to leave all of this behind her – the filth and the smoke and the constant stream of sarcasm. She shouldn't have come. She should have stayed at home and conserved her energy instead. There are more important things she needs to focus on, things more worthy of her precious time.

'Oh, sit down and don't be so bloody touchy. It was a joke for God's sake. You need to lighten up, girl. Here,' Sylvie says, removing a pile of clothes draped haphazardly over a chair and patting it with her long, painted nails. 'Sit down and talk.'

Smoke floats around the room, dust motes swirling amidst a cloud of grey fog. Helena doesn't turn to face her mother. She isn't in the mood for any of her mental gymnastics. She is too tired, too pissed off, too everything to endure a verbal beating from the woman who has the audacity to call herself a parent.

Sylvie forfeited the right to bark out orders to her daughter a long time ago. Helena has managed on her own for many years now and will continue to do so. This visit was a mistake. She should have waited until things have turned a corner, until her life felt a little less bleak. Every worry she has is engraved on her face, her anxieties about her two daughters evident in every crease and furrow. So she carries on walking, ignoring her mother's pleas for her to stay until one line catches her attention, forcing her to stop, her legs weak, her insides sloshing and roiling at the icy statement that punctures the silence.

'If you stay, I'll tell you about your father. It's about time you knew anyway.'

Her father. For so long now, Sylvie has batted away Helena's questions, refusing to speak of it. With no name on her birth certificate, his identity has remained a secret.

Until now.

The urge to drop to the floor and weep is strong. She ignores it, suppressing the irrepressible need she feels to scream and shout at her mother that that ship sailed many decades ago. But something stops her, the gnawing need to know that has eaten at her for most of her life overtaking every other urge and reflex.

'You've got five minutes, no longer. I've just about had enough of your mind games. Having you as a mother is like a form of torture.'

Helena watches, stupefied and aghast as her mum smiles; a lopsided crooked grin that reveals lipstick-stained teeth. Sylvie has taken that attack as a compliment. Her mother revels in hurting others, making their lives as difficult as possible. She lives for these moments, knocking those around her off-kilter in order to redress the skewed balance of her own life. Helena can see it in her eyes, how lowering the self-esteem of others, especially her only child, her only fucking *daughter,* elevates her, makes her see that her own life isn't so damaged and broken after all.

'Sit down and pin your ears back. Mind you, you might not like what I'm about to tell you. So don't go off on one, shouting and huffing if what I'm about to tell you doesn't meet your expectations.'

Helena slumps into the chair. It creaks and groans, the noise of old springs and the shift of damp wood ringing around them. Like many things in this house, it is just something else that is slowly shrivelling away before perishing and turning to dust.

She watches her mother, how she seems to have regained some normality in her usually bent stance. Her spine is suddenly poker straight, her posture rigid as if she is preparing for something monumental. Readying herself for a show; one where she takes the starring role. Sylvie takes a long drag of her cigarette, as if she is preparing herself for the moment. She makes a show of blowing out a stream of grey smoke before speaking.

'Your dad was a wrong 'un, but my God was he handsome. A right looker, he was. We met one night at a pub in town. He was propping up the bar when I walked in with my friend, Sally. I ordered a gin and he offered to pay. I wasn't about to turn down a bargain like that, was I? We clicked straight away but I knew him for what he was. I knew his type, had come across them before. He had that wicked twinkle in his eye, the look that told me he wasn't the type to hang around for long after an encounter, if you know what I mean.' Sylvie shakes her head and laughs, a thundering guffaw that vibrates in the tobacco-laden air. Helena takes a long trembling breath, trying to reserve judgement until she hears the whole story. Trying to surround herself with a protective shield, not let her mother's twisted words penetrate and wound. 'So anyway, at the end of the night,

I went off with him. Sally had hooked up with another guy so we went our separate ways.' A silence ensues, Helena waiting, every nerve ending sizzling with anticipation. She wants, and yet doesn't want, to hear the next part. It will be seedy and sordid and make for grim listening. This is her mother narrating the tale. Grim and seedy is who she is.

'We went back to my room, a small bedsit on the edge of town. He stayed the night and I never saw him again. Six weeks later I found out I was pregnant with you.' Her eyes land on Helena before continuing. 'I'll be honest with you, I did consider getting rid of you. I had a job in the local bookies, very little money and no prospects and was living in a squalid little place, but in the end, I decided against it.' She studies her long fingernails, turning them over and over, eyes narrowed in scrutiny. 'And now, here you are,' she says chirpily, 'an upstanding member of society. Not like either of your parents, eh?'

'I wouldn't know,' Helena replies, suddenly weary. She isn't upset or disgusted by her mother's revelation. This is exactly what she expected – this level of hurt and rejection. This level of depravity. Once again, her own mother has left her high and dry, given her only half the story whilst expecting Helena to be weepy with gratitude. 'You haven't told me anything about him apart from the fact he was a one-night stand you never saw again.'

'Ah,' Sylvie says, breathless with a surge of undisguised excitement that lights up her features, 'but I haven't told you the final part. When I said I never saw him again, what I meant was I never saw him in person. I did, however, see his mugshot in the local newspaper. He was arrested and sent to prison for murder when you were about two months old. Killed his best friend after a drunken squabble.'

A cold blade slices through Helena's sternum; a fist reaches in through the bleeding gap and squeezing at her heart.

Murder.

Her unknown, faceless, nameless father was a murderer. She shakes away her worries about Rachel and that damn stupid jade ring. And that knife. She is making a grave error linking her own daughter to a series of local killings. Isn't she?

'So what happened to him after he went to jail?' She isn't interested. She doesn't care. Why would she waste precious minutes and hours thinking of him? He means nothing to her. Not a damn thing. And yet she has to know, if only to convince herself that neither she nor her daughters are like him in any way, shape or form.

'I don't know for certain. I'd heard he died in there but got no proof to back up that story.'

'What was his name?'

Sylvie's grin stills Helena's blood. 'That's the stupid thing, I can't actually remember. I think it was either Alf or Albert. Pretty sure it began with an A. Maybe Arthur? Or Angus?'

It's as she stands up to leave that it dawns on her – Helena has spent her whole life curbing an inner rage brought on by the person who gave birth to her. Somewhere deep in her mother's soul is a demon, full of ill will, always ready to mock and make trouble for the innocent and the unwary. Helena came here with good intentions, hoping to build bridges with the woman who clearly never ever wanted her, and yet again, she has been let down. Treated like somebody who is unworthy of her love and attention; kicked aside like a discarded piece of trash or an unwanted family pet.

Perhaps it's true and her youngest daughter has indeed inherited her grandfather's miscreant ways. Can nurture really ever conquer nature, nudging aside genes that are deeply embedded and woven into our psyche? She has tried to love her children, give them everything that was missing in her own upbringing, and yet at this juncture, she is left wondering whether one of her daughters is a murderer and if so, in light of this latest piece of information about her own father, is she herself to blame for not loving her daughter enough, not giving her sufficient attention, or, as many psychologists believe, is the need to hurt and maim chiselled deep into Rachel's bones, something she was born with? Something that Helena could not stop because despite trying to guide and steer her girls along the right path, some things are just meant to be.

29

HELENA

Sleep evades her, the conversation with her mother going round and round in her head, a ghoulish ride of horror and hysteria she is unable to escape. Were it not for the fact she is the only family her mother has, Helena would take the decision to never see her again. Except she isn't sure she could live with the shame of her own flesh and blood being discovered dead by a neighbour, her mother's stick-thin limbs and skeletal body slowly rotting away amidst a sea of mouldy pizza boxes and cigarette ash. Helena has a strong sense of duty. Where she got it from is anybody's guess, but loyalty runs through her like a rod of iron. So she isn't about to abandon the woman who gave birth to her, but she takes the decision to lessen her visits if only to protect her own mental health. It's not the first time she has had this notion, only to bend and soften as the weeks and months passed, before gradually returning to the fold as if insults and a thousand derogatory remarks hadn't been fired her way. But not this time. She has enough going on in her life. Enough drama to make sure she spends every minute of every day worrying about her family and their many lies and secrets. And then there is

Barbara and her daughter. Tragedy on the periphery of her own troubles. Innes, Rachel and now even Vanessa, her stalwart daughter, all conspiring to dent her sanity.

Tomorrow, she will visit Rachel again. She will go into town and confront her, and if Rachel refuses to cooperate, Helena will threaten her with going to the police. It's the only weapon she has left in her armoury – threatening her youngest daughter with possible incarceration in order to force her into telling the truth.

Your father was arrested and sent to prison for murder when you were about two months old. Killed his best friend after a drunken squabble.

The vice around Helena's head tightens another notch. Her skull is slowly being crushed by the weight of her family's sins, her brain turning to mulch.

Beneath her head, the pillow softens. Her eyelids flutter. The pills she took earlier are now taking effect. It was the only way, the only thing she had at hand to fight off the incessant gnawing and pecking of the demons that kept her awake. She feels herself falling, falling, falling, the long drop to the bottom sweeping up to meet her, its hard surface still an easier and more comfortable environment than the safety of her own home.

One a.m. Gritty eyed and feverish, Helena sits up. Stares at the clock. Reaches for the phone.

'Hello?'

'God, Mum, I am *so* sorry. Medical emergency at the home. I've really got to go.'

Fatigue scratches at Helena's eyes, pounding and banging at the base of her head. She mentally counts the seconds, trying to find her voice. Trying to pull herself out of the deepest of sleeps. A blackness without end.

'Again?' It's out before she can stop it, her exhausted brain sans its usual filter.

A short silence, then Vanessa's reply; gentle. Low and soft. None of her usual bravado and brusqueness.

'I know. I know it's a lot. I promise I'll try to rearrange the rota so this stops happening as often. It's just with the manager being ill and—'

'I'm getting up now. Be there in ten minutes.'

She is too tired to engage in the whys and wherefores. That's a conversation for another day. A time when her brain is in gear and not clogged up with sleep. A time when she is feeling more pliable, her batteries fully charged.

The routine of pulling on clothes and grabbing at bags is something she can do with aplomb. If only the rest of her life was as smooth and effortless.

Her vehicle glides through the streets, curving around corners and slaloming past parked cars, reaching Vanessa's house in less than five minutes. It's quiet out, the neighbourhood still and silent.

With her usual predictive finesse, Vanessa rushes past Helena, the *too busy to chat* vibe even more obvious than it has ever been. Her eyes are lowered, keys clutched between her fingers.

Helena has visions of grabbing her daughter's arm, hauling her back inside to speak, to insist that Vanessa make other arrangements. To ask about Innes and why he left. To ask if she was violent towards her ex-partner. But she doesn't do any of those things. The timing is wrong. It feels like the timing is always wrong, other family dramas getting in the way of the important stuff. The conversation with her mother and the revelation about Helena's father took everything out of her. She left her mother's flat feeling deflated and depressed. As soon as there is space and time in Helena's brain for dialogue and dissection, something else slides in and settles itself into place. More trauma. Yet more heartache.

She will catch her in the morning, or perhaps when she returns in a few hours. If she does return, that is. Not only are these nocturnal occurrences becoming more and more frequent, they are also more prolonged. A part of her wonders if it's deliberate, a ploy of Vanessa's to avoid the obvious conversation with her mother. Helena will only allow this to continue for so long. Soon, she will pare back her assistance. See how her daughter copes without her. See who she dares to wake in the middle of the night for these emergency callouts. Because aside from Innes, she has nobody. Helena is her first and only port of call.

A splutter of the engine, a quick glare of headlights, and Vanessa is gone, the red glow of her rear lights disappearing around the corner before Helena even gets inside the house.

The familiar quiet hum of the house that she has become accustomed to surrounds her as she steps inside and locks the door. Every home has its own unique sounds and smells, and the scents and noises of this house are now like a second skin to her, her nightly visits so frequent, she can predict each creak and groan; the tick tick of the radiators as they cool, then the muffled whoosh of the boiler the following morning as the sun rises and the sleeping house slowly comes to life. Except tonight, something is different. Above her, the sound of footsteps. The strangled sound of a child's cry. Then the unwelcome groans of a sickly child as they lean over the toilet bowl and heave.

She takes the stairs two at a time, the stench of vomit hitting her as she enters the bathroom. Strands of Mabel's hair hang over her face. Her small limbs are trembling and tears are coursing down her face.

'Come here, sweetheart.' Helena places a cool palm over her granddaughter's hot forehead, pulling back her hair and making soothing comforting sounds to placate and ease her distress.

She fills a glass of water and offers Mabel a sip. The sound of the child's glugging, convulsing stomach reverberates off the tiled walls. Within seconds, her head is over the toilet bowl again, the splash of vomit and accompanying stench causing Helena to gag.

Ten minutes of almost continual vomiting sees Mabel pale and drained, her eyes heavy with exhaustion.

'Let's get you back to bed. Come on, my darling. Grandma will tuck you in.'

Mabel's hand is cool, her fingers dry and crepe-like. Helena wants to scoop her up, hold her close and wish away the illness as they shuffle along the landing together. Even in the dim light, Helena can see how Mabel's legs are weakened by the sickness, her flesh now the colour of freshly fallen snow.

Placing a dish by her bed, Helena sits, checking her granddaughter's temperature, wincing as Mabel's face grows hotter, sweat arcing her hairline while she shivers uncontrollably beneath the thick duvet. Even administering medicine does little to break the fever. After an hour, Mabel's eyes close, sleep allowing her a reprieve from the constant shivering, but only ten minutes later she wakes, her face burning, eyes wide.

'He's coming. We have to hide. You need to get under the bed. They're going to bomb the house.'

Mabel's delirious screams and rantings ring around the room, making the hair on Helena's neck stand on end. She leans forward, catches the child's eyes, but is met with a blank stare, as if they are strangers. Another touch of burning flesh is enough to alert her to what she must do next. Her granddaughter is ill. She needs her mother. Helena needs advice.

Her palm is hot, the phone slipping about in her hand as she punches in the number of Vanessa's office. This is a new undertaking. She will be busy, annoyed at being disturbed. Helena knows that doing this could cause problems for her daughter but has no choice. Mabel and Noah come first. Vanessa would do well to remember that. Work is something people do to earn money. It isn't the be all and end all. Family is more important.

A voice at the other end cuts into her thoughts with cold clinical precision.

'Oak Meadow Care Home, can I help you?'

Mabel's breathing is shallow, her eyes glassy and wide. Fear crawls beneath Helena's skin, snagging at her veins and organs as she watches her granddaughter. Trepidation is making her hot and disorientated.

'So sorry to disturb you at such an ungodly hour. This is Vanessa Portman's mother. She needs to come home. Her daughter is ill.'

'Vanessa?'

'Yes. This is Helena, her mother. I'm looking after her children because Vanessa got called out to an emergency at the home. Can you please let her know that Mabel is ill and she needs to see a doctor as soon as possible.'

A silence, then the sound of rustling and somebody breathing heavily into the handset, their words pulling away another piece of the scaffolding that holds Helena's crumbling world together.

'Vanessa isn't here I'm afraid. I'm really sorry, I'm not sure if there has been a misunderstanding between you and Vanessa but she hasn't been called out. We haven't had an emergency tonight. Have you tried calling her mobile phone as...'

The voice fades, Helena lifting the phone away from her ear as if it is white hot before disconnecting the call and dropping it onto the floor. This is wrong. Uncharacteristic. Confusion is a whirling vortex in her head. Vanessa has lied. Her daughter has dragged her out in the middle of the night, had her drive over here to look after the children, but for what? She isn't at work. There hasn't been an emergency. So where the hell is she? Where in God's name is her daughter?

Scooping up the phone once more, Helena calls Vanessa's mobile phone. As expected, it goes straight to voicemail.

Beside her, Mabel's breathing is now a rasp, the heat from her body enough to dampen the bedsheets and pillow, leaving a halo of perspiration around her head. A multitude of tangled thoughts fill Helena's brain. Her granddaughter is ill, and Vanessa is missing. Where the fuck is she? There is no emergency at the home. Maybe there haven't ever been any emergencies, each callout a fabrication, Helena's midnight dashes across town something that could have been avoided.

Tiredness and stress collide, a pain shooting up the back of her head and lodging behind her eyes. She has to gather her thoughts, do something positive. Be proactive. Right now, Mabel is her priority. She needs to be seen by somebody who can prescribe antibiotics, something to stop the vomiting and bring down her temperature. Once she has been seen, then Helena can turn her attention to Vanessa and her nocturnal disappearing act. Once Mabel is better, she will pin down her eldest daughter and ask her where the fuck she was when her own daughter was gravely ill, discover what is so urgent that she needs to head off into the darkness of the night, leaving her children and mother behind.

Helena calls 111, her breathing a rapid staccato rhythm, her voice cracking as she speaks to the operator and barks out Mabel's name, address and symptoms.

30

ALEX

Two Years Prior

They were all liars. Each of them scheming and plotting and fabricating evidence to try and oust him. And it had worked. He collected his box of belongings and walked to his car, relieved to be out of the place. The showroom was empty, none of his colleagues around to observe his demise. None of them present to offer their sympathies or apologise for being part of the witch hunt that sought to frame him. It had been banter, nothing more than harmless office banter. And she had taken it to management, put in a formal complaint against him. Told them he had sexually harassed her, following her home from work, demanding she get in his car. It was nonsense. He had asked if she needed a lift and she refused, telling other staff members that he continually stalked and abused her, swearing and throwing insults when she didn't take him up on his offer. And as if that wasn't bad enough, a stack of other women stepped up claiming he had abused them as well, making lurid suggestions, using inappropriate language in the workplace. Subjecting them to harassment. This was why he hated women. All their lies and rebuttals. Their unpredictable behaviour and volatile responses. He could do without it. He could do without them.

'You know, Alex, you're fortunate to get off without this going to court.' His boss's words rattled around his head as Alex leaned in and placed his meagre possessions on the back seat of his vehicle. 'You've walked away without a criminal record. Count yourself lucky.'

Rob had already declined Alex's request for references for future jobs, and he was supposed to consider himself fortunate? Rob, the general manager, was as big a liar as those women and a miserable nasty old bastard to boot.

This wasn't the end. He would get a job regardless of the lack of support. He had plenty of experience, had taken many sales courses over the years to improve and hone his skills. He refused to let this minor incident ruin his future. God knows he had weathered worse.

The engine let out a muffled roar, his foot pressed hard to the pedal as he backed out of his parking space. He glanced up, his chest and stomach suddenly knotted at the sight before him; they were all there, the rest of the office staff and sales team. Each of them standing at the large window, watching him leave. Their eyes danced about, each of them pretending to look elsewhere as he caught their judgemental gaze. Fuck them all. He hoped they all burned in hell. One by one they filtered away, too embarrassed, too full of their own self-importance to stay and actually watch him exit their lives for the final time. Except for one – Maxine. The bitch who started all this. The one who put in a formal complaint against him and started this fucking great ball rolling, asking others about his demeanour; had he said anything inappropriate to them? What did they think of his language, his unprofessional conduct? Were they prepared to back up her accusations, make sure something was done about his behaviour in the workplace?

Did his presence unnerve them?

Did they think he was capable of harming them when they were alone with him?

The questions were endless. The lies infinite.

He lifted his foot off the accelerator and slowed down, making a point of holding her gaze. She was a brave one, he would give her that much. Refusing to look away. Making sure her features didn't crumple, her stern glare and rigid stance never faltering as he sat with his engine running, heart thrashing around his chest like a captive bird making a desperate bid to escape. In the end, Alex was the one who broke the spell, looking away and shaking his head. He hoped she would see it – the pity he felt for her. The hatred and anger that welled up in his gut at the sight of her pale face and pinched features. Women like Maxine didn't deserve to exist. Some people were able to walk away from situations like the one in which he found himself, wishing the perpetrators no ill will. But not Alex. He wished the staff of that car showroom everything they would not wish upon themselves. He longed for misery and suffering and despair to litter their sorry little lives. He longed for them, Maxine especially, to suffer a litany of illnesses from which they would never recover, for bankruptcy and the death of a loved one to befall them.

Finding new employment would be his first task when he got home. Without a reference from his previous employer, it would prove difficult. But not impossible. Not all businesses relied on the word of a manager who may or may not hold a grievance against certain employees. He had skills. Somebody would be glad to take him on. And he would make it worth their while. He was a grafter. Reliable and loyal. At least he now owned his own vehicle. No more relying on the showroom for the use of a company car. Saving to buy his own had worked out well. He didn't need them. He didn't need anybody.

The evidence is overwhelming, Alex. You can either contest it and go through the courts or walk away with a month's salary and nothing on your record. Your behaviour counts as gross misconduct and overrides the need for a series of warnings. I know what I would do if I were you...

The look on Rob's face, every word he said, would forever be embedded into Alex's brain. Some things could never be erased.

Autopilot got him home, the journey a blur of thoughts of the countless ways in which he could have defended himself. Too late. It was all in the past. Time to plan ahead, get himself a new job with better prospects, a higher salary. He wanted to be the better man, always striving for improvement, but darkness was edging its way in, nudging aside all reason. His fingers twitched, his limbs suddenly fuelled by a surge of electricity that was firing up his senses. Certain yearnings overwhelmed him, searing themselves into his brain. They were difficult to ignore, those deep, hot yearnings. He had tried in the past, sometimes managing to work his way through the darkness, stumbling out the other side into the light, his mind and body infused with positivity. But those times were rare. It was becoming increasingly difficult to ignore the anger and rage that whispered in his ear, reiterating how stupid and thoughtless and fucking pathetic people were. Losing his job brought those urges closer, the voices growing louder, their whispers now a thunderous riot in his head.

Stepping into an empty house, his thoughts turned to his mother. Her final day. How she looked when he found her all those years ago. She was in the same position in the bed as when he had left her after her fall, legs poker straight, head turned to one side, the duvet atop her shrivelled tiny body. He hadn't realised she wasn't breathing, taking her stillness as a sign she was sleeping.

He had stood by the bed, waiting for it. Her voice, that irritating screech. When it didn't come, he had leaned closer and touched her face, her cold flesh causing him to jump away. He wasn't frightened of dead bodies. Far from it. They fascinated him. It was just unexpected. A shock to his senses. He soon became acclimatised to the change. That was when he took the photographs. He couldn't help it. She looked so peaceful. Not dead, just resting. The best she had looked in a long time, her body clear of the toxins she had pumped into it for so many years. It was as if death had sent a replacement. A decent mother. A calm tranquil version of the person she never was. The person he had wanted her to be. He had pulled back the duvet, opened her eyes, repositioned her body and began to snap.

Outside, the daylight was fading, the sky illuminated, dragging him back to the present. Streaks of burnt orange slashed through the clouds, stretched out like smears of blood. Soon it would be time. He would shower, change his clothes and go into town for a few hours. Battling his anger, that incessant clawing sensation, was too exhausting. Easier to go with it, to allow himself to be manipulated by those inner voices.

Alex continued to stare out of the window. Possible bad weather loomed, a downpour even. That always made it easier, everyone too focused on getting home, their eyes lowered to the ground and diverted away from him as they ran for cover from the rain.

Visions throbbed in his brain as he placed his balaclava in the well of his car and took his usual route into town. It would be dark by the time he got there, a wash of grey disguising his movements. He knew where the cameras were, which places to frequent to avoid being seen. The prospect of a possible kill lifted him, the tight ribbon of rage and resentment that had wrapped itself around his head loosening and falling away, fluttering to his feet like confetti.

Pulse thrumming, he turned on the radio, pressed his foot to the floor and drove off into the night.

31

HELENA

Three calls, two texts and still no reply. Fury drums at Helena's skull, climbing up her throat and banging at her temples with such power she feels as if the floor is about to fall away beneath her. The effort of trying to keep herself steady and upright has weakened her, her limbs suddenly flaccid and lifeless.

She is tired. Exhausted even. With the heel of her hand, Helena rubs at her eyes, trying to adjust her vision to the shifting hours, the change in luminosity that the new dawn is bringing. Shafts of light curl their way into the room, illuminating dark corners and banishing shadows. Helena arrived at Vanessa's hours ago. Hours; the fresh, clear sky outside, the dawning of a new day a harsh reminder of how long Vanessa has been gone. All night and still no word. Not a damn thing.

Helena stands, pulls the blinds to one side, her eyes searching the street for any signs of her daughter. In the distance a door slams, an engine revs. Tyres screech. The village is waking up, neighbours and people outside preparing for the day ahead.

Above her a creak. She moves away from the window, listens.

Ears attuned to every little noise. It's Mabel turning over in bed. The doctor left just over an hour ago. A dose of antibiotics helped bring down her raging temperature, allowing her some much-needed rest. The patter of Noah's feet as the doctor arrived was just another thing to deal with, the poor kid's distress evident when he spotted his sister and smelt the vomit on the bedside rug that Helena had scrubbed at without any real success. And now they are both asleep, the house still drowsy while she stands by the window and waits for Vanessa's return.

Helena has always thought that resentment is one of the most corrosive of emotions, eating away at our insides like acid, and she has been proven correct. Her stomach is folded into a tight knot, bile sloshing and gurgling. A band of bitterness, dark and festering like an untreated wound, shoots through her veins. Physical ailments brought on by her daughter's lies and thought-less ways. Her selfishness and stupidity. A thousand arguments have run through her head while she has waited for Vanessa's return. A thousand disagreements and fights while she paced the floor, listening out for the sound of her car, in between taking the stairs like a gazelle to tend to Mabel's cries. So many questions at the ready, loaded like bullets ready to fire at her daughter to try to work out why she has done such a thing. Why she has chosen to lie and ignore calls, vanishing into thin air while her child lies helpless and ill in bed. It's unforgiveable. Callous and horribly thoughtless, and Helena has every inten-tion of telling her so. She will hold nothing back. The dam will open and a volley of insults will come hurtling out. Her impo-tence and fear of confrontation has allowed Vanessa's selfishness to grow and multiply. Helena is responsible for allowing this to happen. She should have stopped it a long time ago, been the tough love mother and refused to babysit at the drop of a hat in the early hours of the morning.

For the hundredth time, Helena checks her phone, its silence already an indicator that Vanessa hasn't made contact. Unable to show restraint and simply because there is little else to do while she waits, she checks the main news sites, her insides twisting at the sight of the latest headlines.

Names. Photographs of dead people flashing on her screen. The smiling faces of murdered women.

The police have released details of all the victims, including Barbara's daughter. Helena can't breathe, a jagged chunk of air sticking in her gullet. Seeing their faces, their names stamped below, somehow makes it real. This is an announcement to the rest of the world that it is actually happening. That a serial killer is prowling their streets.

Tears mist her vision when she reads each name, stares at their images, their beautiful youthful faces. Sees their tender ages. Just babies. Snatched away from their families. Each of them somebody's daughter. Each one, somebody's beautiful child.

The jade ring. It flashes in her mind, a beautiful precious thing turned ugly. She thinks of Rachel. Her evasive manner. Her proximity to where the bodies were found. And that knife.

The sound of a car engine pulling up outside quashes all thoughts of her youngest daughter. Her eldest offspring is finally home. Her spoilt, thoughtless, eldest child whose propensity for selfishness knows no bounds. She blames herself. She has done this; in a bid to protect them, she has reared two selfish individuals. Helena pushes her phone back into her pocket, nerves jangling, skin flashing hot and cold. She will save the blame for later, for when she is alone and can think clearly.

Her stomach clenches. All evening, she has prayed for Vanessa to show her face, anger knotting and unknotting in her gut, and now she is here after vanishing into the ether, Helena has suddenly turned to jelly, every part of her terrified and unprepared. Hour after hour, she sat, fine-tuning her means of attack, carefully crafting each question, each phrase and sentence, and now that her errant daughter has finally returned home, she is unable to think clearly, her previous thoughts emptying out of her head and disappearing like water swirling down a drain.

She hears the dull scrape of Vanessa's key in the door, listens to her sighs as she wipes her feet on the doormat and bends down to remove her shoes. The rustle of her coat and the sound of her stockinged feet over the carpet; all regular sounds and movements that Helena would normally barely register, but today they are amplified. She wants to scream at Vanessa that the children are sleeping, that her near-silent sounds are too loud. Instead she stands, the trembling of her limbs and the weakness in her legs rendering her useless. By the time Vanessa enters the living room, Helena has slumped onto the sofa, a tumult of emotions draining her of energy. It's been a torturous few hours. She has mopped Mabel's brow, cleaned and scrubbed, and worried and paced, staring out of windows while biting at the skin inside her mouth, wondering where her daughter is. Why she lied. What she is up to in the dead of night.

'Sorry, Mum. I tried to get away earlier but it was tricky.' Vanessa manages a limp lopsided smile.

Helena is tempted to let her ramble, to listen to her fabrications. Let her daughter weave an even bigger mesh of lies, her deceptions so intricate and taut that she risks becoming tangled in them, snarled and unable to ever escape. Like a fly trapped in a spider's web.

But she can't. She is too angry, too anxious. Too everything to keep it all in. So it spills out of her like hot tar, spreading and scorching everything within reach.

'You haven't been at work, Vanessa. I rang the care home and they told me that you weren't there, that there hadn't been any callout. So where have you been? And why didn't you answer my calls or texts? Why has your phone been turned off?'

An uncharacteristic hoarseness has taken hold in her voice, gravel cutting into her throat. She wants to scream. She wants to shout and cry. She hasn't the strength for either. She is hollow. Spent and withered like a flower hidden in the shade.

The movement of Vanessa's jaw, the way her eyes bulge. The fact she is lost for words, standing mute in the middle of the room, tells Helena everything she needs to know. That her daughter is a liar. What else has she lied about? Thoughts of Innes pierce her brain. Helena opted to side with her daughter. It's clear now that she made a mistake. She should have listened to him, *believed* him, instead of ejecting him from her house.

'Mabel has had a raging temperature. She has spent the night vomiting. The doctor has been here. Where the bloody hell were you, Vanessa? Where the fuck have you been?'

Her voice is a shriek. She has neither the inclination nor the energy to disguise her fury, to play-act and tiptoe around her daughter. For years and years she has crept around Vanessa's moods, dancing to her tune to avoid arguments. But not any more. Time to change. Time to start telling the truth.

There is a small part of Helena that is enjoying seeing the look of horror on her daughter's face. But only a small part. Because at the heart of this situation is a whole load of dishonesty and underhandedness.

A groan of fabric as Vanessa slumps onto the chair. The sound of her laboured breathing. Then the croak of her excuse, every syllable like a punch to Helena's gut as she waits, listening. Hoping Vanessa's reasons stand up to close scrutiny. Hoping they are truthful.

'I'm so sorry. Mum, I am so, so sorry. I never meant for any of this to happen. I was going to tell you at some point, when things became a little more...'

Helena waits, the silence stretching out between them. She sits, listening, waiting. Waiting for the moment when Vanessa comes apart and reveals her hand.

'The thing is,' she continues, staring at her fingernails, 'there's this man I've been seeing.' Her eyes meet Helena's, her dark lashes fluttering wildly, a habit she has carried with her since childhood. 'And it's really complicated.'

'So why ignore my texts? Your daughter has been ill and you're sitting there giving me pathetic excuses. Your child is a greater priority than your love life!'

'I didn't have my phone turned on. I'm really sorry. How is Mabel?'

The laugh erupts out of Helena's throat. 'Now you ask? Now you're bothered about your daughter?'

Eyes bore into Helena's, drilling a hole in her skull. Vanessa's tone is suddenly cool and detached. 'Like I said, I'm really sorry. I didn't do this deliberately, Mum. I'm here now and I presume the kids are asleep?'

After Gavin's premature death when Helena lay awake night after night, unable to shut off to the horrors of her new life as a widow and single parent, she didn't feel this desperate, this fatigued and uneasy. Vanessa should be taking the stairs two at a time to see her daughter. She should be tearful and anxious. And she isn't. Her calm, composed manner unnerves Helena. Makes her wonder what is going on inside her head.

'Why did you have to meet this man in the early hours of the morning? Why not book a seedy little hotel room in your lunch-break like other people who conduct "complicated relationships"?' Helena hooks her fingers into the air, her voice brittle with anger.

At least Vanessa has the decency to look embarrassed. Colour creeps into her cheeks, spots of crimson peppering her face and neck. Finally, her daughter's flimsy façade begins to crumble. But not for long. In just a few seconds, Vanessa's usual bravado has been restored, her spine straight, chin held high.

Who is this uber-professional, hard-faced woman before her? This person she gave birth to and reared. Gave all her time and love to. She no longer knows her eldest child, this person sitting opposite her who is so removed from Helena's own ethics she may as well be a stranger.

'He works shifts. It's the only time he can get away. I didn't want to you to find out this way. I did plan on telling you at some point but—'

'But your daughter fell ill. I needed to contact you and you weren't where you said you were.'

The rod of iron in Vanessa's spine softens, her stance pliable again, the skin on her face suddenly pale and waxy, all the earlier colour draining away. Helena has shamed her, hung her filthy laundry out to dry. There must be something positive to come out of this – the fact that Vanessa has the propensity to feel degraded and humiliated. That's a start. If Helena can keep picking and digging, stripping at those protective layers, then the mask might just fall away, revealing the loving daughter and caring mother that lurks beneath. She is in there somewhere, she has to be. Anything else doesn't bear thinking about.

'I need to go home now, Vanessa. The children are both asleep upstairs. Mabel's medicine is in the bathroom. She needs another dose in two hours' time.'

Helena skirts past her daughter, their bodies almost touching. It's been a long time since they hugged. It's been a long time since they even sat together and simply talked.

She expects or at least hopes that Vanessa will call her back, hold her hand. Apologise profusely. Tell her how sorry she is and that from now on, her children will come first. But she doesn't. Helena wants to mention the visit from Innes, ask about his scar, about the fact he cannot have access to his own children. But nothing is forthcoming, the words drying up in her mouth. And so, with nothing to keep her there, Helena leaves the house, gets in her car, and makes the lonely drive home.

32

ALEX

Ten Months Prior

The last eighteen months had taken it out of him, the worry of his situation chiselled deep into the creases on his face, the furrow that appeared between his brow becoming more cavernous with each consecutive job application he slaved over, sitting up in the early hours, refusing to rest until each one was completed. He craved routine, waking every morning with a deep yearning for order and control. Being unemployed wasn't who he was, the situation an alien sensation that robbed him of sleep and took his mind down even darker routes that he had neither the energy nor the inclination to explore. But it was finally over. His stretch of having to take part-time jobs just to make ends meet now a thing of the past. No more weeding driveways or cleaning gutters for cash in hand. Trailing the streets, knocking on doors to offer his services as a handyman had been a low point in his life, something that was beneath him. This new post wasn't exactly highbrow, but after a year and a half of being denied benefits, because, as he was regularly informed by a series of smug-faced, pen-pushing, snotty-nosed little bastards, he had *chosen* to leave his position at the car showroom, it was a step up in the world. Fucking Maxine and her pathetic lies. And stupid spineless Rob for believing her.

Oak Meadow Care Home was a sprawling place on the outskirts of town, the type of building that was named after the very thing the builders felled and destroyed in order to create it. And it was managed by somebody whose name he instantly recognised. She barely gave him a second glance as he sat opposite her in the interview, willing for the penny to drop. Waiting to see that flicker of recognition in her expression. Even as a kid she had always thought herself superior. A cut above the rest. Granted, she had done well for herself, bagging a decent managerial post, but Alex knew Vanessa Portman for what she really was – a local woman desperate to shake off the shackles of her working-class childhood. He knew then that he would have to be careful. Even before he was given the position, when his financial future still hung by a thread, he had made up his mind. She would be his. He would make it his goal, something to aim for. Vanessa Portman was in his sights. And the most exciting thing about it was, she had no idea.

Afterwards, when his heart was still thrumming, her face burned into his brain, she had spoken to him, offering him the position, informing him of a few things, letting him know that he hadn't slipped beneath her radar, that she did indeed recognise him from all those years back.

'Best if we keep our association between you and me, Alex. You were the most suitable candidate,' she had coolly informed him, her eyes appraising him as he had sat, excitement pulsing beneath his shirt. 'But we don't want anybody thinking you were given any favours because of our previous connection, do we?'

She had winked at him, her pale blue eyes sparkling, setting off
a fire in his belly.

Only a week later, as he stood, staring at his reflection in the
bedroom mirror, his muscled torso a surprise even to himself,
Vanessa still figured in his thoughts. The day after being offered
the job, he had taken himself back to the care home, standing
behind the shrubbery at the far end of the badly lit car park,
watching as she slid into her vehicle and drove away. There was
no doubt in his mind; Vanessa was the one he wanted. She was
the glittering prize.

* * *

Groomed and satisfied, Alex dressed, putting every effort into
his appearance before venturing outside. He glanced around.
This street, this area, the entire town had seen better days. And
yet he still thought of it as home, the place where he grew up,
every cracked paving stone, every pothole, every boarded-up
window as familiar to him as his own features. He would never
understand why some people didn't give a shit about the place
where they lived. Part of him wanted to sell up, move elsewhere,
but he was anchored to that house. So many reasons to leave but
one solid reason to stay.

The past came to him in short bursts as he locked up and set
off, images of the times he spent walking the streets under the
cover of darkness. Searching, scouring for those encounters that
made him feel whole again. He enjoyed that segment of his life.
He missed the thrill of it, the need to do it once more a hot stirring in his groin. But not right now. Other things were calling,
like getting back into a routine, setting off for work each
morning and bringing some structure back into his life. A
haphazard approach wasn't his style. It would knock him off-

kilter, make him less focused. Susceptible to making mistakes. And he didn't want mistakes. He wanted satisfaction. Perfection. And that could only be achieved by having a meticulous approach. His adolescent foray into the murky world of robberies was a thing of the past. Something that made his toes curl with shame. He'd been a rough-edged teenager getting his kicks back then, trying to escape the confines of his mother's clutches. Thinking about it felt like a confession to a stranger, admitting that he was once a hooligan of the lowest order. What he was doing now was different. His methods clean and decisive.

The walk to the bus stop riled him; he had had to sell his car because some woman had let her mouth run loose and cost him his job. She was responsible for his life being put on hold, his plans and dreams curtailed. Still, things were finally looking up. His new position would bring in some much-needed cash. The benefits that were still being paid to his mother helped but they weren't enough for one person to live on. Food had to be bought, bills paid. Once he got some savings behind him, he would buy another vehicle. Taking the bus and travelling with the dregs of society was beneath him. There were lots of things that were beneath him, but for now he had to tolerate them, push them out of his mind. It was all just a means to an end.

This was his first day at the care home. Alex stepped on the bus and found a seat at the back, a sea of heads providing cover for him as he stared out of the window, telling himself that this was the fresh start he needed. A start that would help clear the cobwebs that lingered in his brain; a sticky mesh of memories he would sooner forget. They clogged up the pathways and neurons, made him slow and sluggish. But not for much longer. A new role, new people. And looking at the duties and responsibilities, he was practically his own boss. Answerable only to Vanessa. That excited and intrigued him. Nobody directly above or below him. Things broke and he fixed them. An ideal position that paid more than his last shitty job.

The traffic moved at a snail's pace, the bus chugging along, stopping every few minutes to pick up and drop off passengers. A line of grey-faced commuters slid on and off, eyes lowered to the ground, each of them forgettable. Alex drummed his fingers on his knees, impatience at their lackadaisical attitudes and listlessness gnawing at him. Soon this commute would be a dim and distant memory. He had a lot to look forward to, plenty of positives coming his way. And as far as he could tell, nothing could go wrong.

33

PRESENT DAY

Since my attempts to fight back, something has intensified within me. Small shoots of hope, fed and nourished by my growing bravery and the realisation that I am not going to die. I used to lie awake every night, terrified to sleep in case he crept into the room and killed me. Visions of me gasping for breath while he straddled my chest, his fingers pressing on my throat, filled my mind. I would wake, bathed in sweat, convinced he was standing outside the door, knife in hand, the gleam of it so real in my mind I could almost taste the tang of the metal, feel its icy-cold heft as he pulled back my head and sliced my throat open in one swift movement.

But none of those visions came to fruition. Many months on and I am still here. Rather than erode my confidence, being imprisoned in this room has allowed me to cultivate a level of quiet wisdom, the sort of wisdom I didn't possess when I was out in the world, working, travelling. Living my life. The trauma of being held captive has given me perspective; sharpened my senses and fuelled my bravery. Before being held here I was quiet and reserved. Quiet, reserved Maisie is dead to me, a part of my soul that has vanished, never to return. At this juncture, I will fight anybody to the death to get out of here.

Stockholm syndrome, another thing that has entered my thoughts before now. I cannot ever imagine being reliant on Alex Broadwood for anything. I would rather form an attachment to the devil himself than spend another second in this house with this repulsive man.

I stare at the photos on the wall, wondering where he buried her body. She is older than me, the picture faded and dated. Perhaps he has a type; small build, medium-length hair.

I have seen films and read books about people like Alex Broadwood; people who function at some acceptable level, holding down jobs, escaping the scrutiny of others by keeping their heads down and going about their day, their solitary lives their defining feature.

My memory of him when we worked at the same place is blurred at the edges, but I do remember him as a monosyllabic individual; dark eyes and impossibly good-looking. His handsome face wasn't enough to draw me in. I saw the sleeping serpent coiled within his veins.

My time working at the care home was a brief interlude, something I did between proper jobs. I paid scant attention to the staff, my focus homed in on the residents and their needs. Maybe that's why he chose me. Perhaps I didn't pay him enough attention, an imagined slight at my behaviour enough to warrant this sort of punishment. Or maybe I'm digging too deep here and I should pour all my energy into getting out of this house. Sometimes there aren't any reasons. Sometimes people do things; dreadful, unspeakable things that have no rational explanation.

Like keeping me prisoner in a room that is a shrine to somebody who may or may not be dead. Somebody who looks just like me.

Downstairs, I can hear him as he moves about. It's light outside. He will be leaving shortly for work. But before that, he will come up, feed me and take me to the bathroom. I will talk while I eat. I will talk while I pee, and I will talk while I shower, the words spewing out of me in the hope that a word or a carefully chosen phrase will hit the spot and weaken him. For every ounce of strength he loses, I will gain some. I will ask about the photographs; who is she? What is her name? Is she dead? But more importantly, will I be next?

Anything at all to knock him off balance, strip him of his usual reserve. I have been robbed of my dignity. It's about time the roles are reversed. If I can't match him in physical strength, then I will match him another way, by using my brain and my razor-sharp tongue. And then when I have chipped away at his veneer, his bravado eroded, displaying his soft underbelly, I will strike. For so long now I have been quiet and compliant. It's time for the new, robust, powerful version of me to emerge and hit him where it really hurts.

34

HELENA

The house shrinks around her, the walls pressing her into a tiny compressed husk of a person. The lies. All those dreadful unnecessary lies. It doesn't make any sense. Why all the turmoil just to see a new partner? Whatever happened to candlelit dinners and romantic weekends away? Have things really moved on so rapidly that Helena no longer recognises what constitutes the signs of a new relationship? No, there is more to this than Vanessa is letting on. Something shadowy and sinister.

Her thoughts turn to Innes, his words ringing in her head. Turning her insides to water. What if he isn't the liar? What if her hardworking, professionally minded daughter is the one with all the issues? The one who caused all the problems in their relationship, ending it abruptly and forcing him to leave his home and his children. Refusing him contact with his own flesh and blood. For a while now, Helena has suspected this is the case but she has been too busy, too frightened and too damn cowardly to admit it, even to herself. What mother wants to see the flaws in their own children? Far easier to go with the flow, pretend the obvious isn't happening. It has taken an ill child for Helena to see it even though the signs have been there for much longer.

Ice needles her flesh. Her fingers are poised over her phone, her stomach plummeting as she thinks back to his message. She blocked his number. There is no way of getting in touch with him to check the veracity of his story. She doesn't believe her own daughter and is now stuck in the middle of their relationship breakdown with nowhere to turn. No allies or anybody she can call on for support. There was a time when she would have called Barbara, cried on her shoulder while her friend listened, interjecting with sage advice on what to say and do, but Barbara has her own ordeal to face.

Through the swirl of fog in her head, Helena searches online on how to unblock a number, not even certain if it's possible to do so. A small flame ignites inside her chest as she reads a set of instructions, relieved at how simple it all appears to be.

Within seconds, she has found her call settings and now has a way to contact Innes to find out the truth about her eldest daughter, to ask if he knows why she is behaving so irrationally. Why she has chosen to tell so many lies.

The silence in the house is broken by the sharp trill of her phone, its vibrations sending tremors up her hands and arms, like ants scurrying across her skin. Vanessa's name flashes up on the screen. Swallowing hard while trying to still her pounding heart, Helena answers, her voice disembodied, heightening her feelings of solitude. Her fear that something deeply unpleasant is happening. Something she can neither predict nor control. She has been blind. Blind and too forgiving, her efforts focused on Rachel when all the time the target was right in front of her.

'Yes?'

'Mum. I just wanted to apologise again. Mabel is a lot better. She is sitting up in bed eating a slice of toast and I've kept Noah off today. He's sitting watching *Paw Patrol* and thinks all his Christmases have come at once for having a day off school.'

Myriad scathing insults bulge within Helena's brain. She is close to saying something that once said cannot be unsaid, but instead gives a simple *okay* in return. Sometimes the smallest of responses says more than a thousand words ever could.

She waits, the silence between them loaded with so many hidden meanings, the heft and magnitude of it an unbearable weight that presses Helena deep into the ground. As a mother, her policy has always been to remain neutral, keep her thoughts hidden for fear of upsetting her children and them taking umbrage. But what if she has been wrong for all these years? What if her ineptitude and weakness as a parent has caused this?

Cushions groan when she slumps down onto the sofa. Dust particles swim and drift around her. How long has it been since she gave her home a thorough clean – days, weeks or even months? Her mind is always engaged elsewhere – her job, her children and grandchildren. The problems her family create. A stream of them that she battles without question, desperate for a peaceful solution so life can continue on its way. But this feels different. She can't explain it, but knows that something is terribly awry and this time, she isn't sure she wants to face it.

'The thing is,' Vanessa, says, an edge to her voice that makes Helena think that her daughter has for once picked up on her mother's annoyance. Vanessa is so used to floating in and out of Helena's life, she rarely takes the time to study the lasting damage caused by her actions and it has always been this way. The daughter she loves and would die for has always been thoughtless and selfish. 'It's not just his shifts, this guy I'm seeing. He's a colleague. And the rules of the home strictly forbid any romantic connections.'

And there it is. A simple sentence tagged on to the end of her explanation that is anything but simple.

Everything Helena has planned to say leaves her in a cold rush. For the first time as a parent, she is all out of ideas. No motherly advice. No soothing words or attempts to calm troubled waters. All this time, all those frantic visits in the dead of night to look after her grandchildren, and all so their mother, *her daughter,* can sleep with a colleague. How many rules is her daughter willing to break to get what she wants? If caught, Vanessa runs the risk of losing her job and subsequently her house. Mind blank, Helena does something she would never have thought possible. She disconnects the call and lays her phone on the sofa next to her, staring at it as if it is a weapon of mass destruction. All those years of protecting her children, trying to ward off the blows of a cold, callous world, and this is the result. Her daughters have now become the cold, callous people she tried to protect them from.

She sits back, thinking she has caused this – this catastrophic breakdown of relations between her and her two children. Her need to protect and provide has turned them into demanding, hopeless creatures, unable to navigate their way through life in a becoming manner.

One hand pressed to her forehead to alleviate the ache that is setting there, she makes the call to Innes, hoping he doesn't cut her off or ignore his phone when he sees her name on the screen. He picks up after just two rings, an eagerness in his voice that almost breaks her.

'Helena? Everything okay?'

She tries to keep a matronly manner to her tone, a crispness to her voice that will help control the direction of their conversation, but fails, a crack in her throat like shattering glass slicing through her words.

'I need to see you, to speak with you. If you can call round?' Anxiety threatens to pull her under.

'I'm at work at the minute. I finish at 6 p.m. if that works for you?' They agree and Helena ends the call, ashamed that she doesn't even know what Innes does for a living, has possibly never known. He was practically a stranger to her. And here she is, attempting to reel him back into her life as a possible ally.

Until this moment, she thought herself in tune with the lives of her daughters. How silly and naïve she has been. They are strangers, a wall dividing them. A huge fucking wall that is too high and too wide to ever scale. She has been thinking that Rachel's problems can be solved with an application of love and deep persuasion, but it's now clear that it isn't going to happen. She needs more than any mother can ever give. She needs professional help. And as for Vanessa, she is too old to lecture. Helena should have done that long ago. The time for badgering her about how to live her life has long since passed. Vanessa is an adult who makes her own choices, even if they are questionable, bordering on seedy.

The day looms ahead of her, all colour leached out of it since her daughter's revelation. Her terrible unthinkable lies. Helena's conversation with Innes cannot come soon enough. She will take note of everything he says, store it in her head and try to match it to the person who is her daughter. In the meantime she will clean this house. She will dust and wash and scrub and scour in a bid to clear the grime from her brain.

As if in a daze, Helena tidies the living room, throwing open windows and allowing the icy chill to bite at her exposed arms, before cleaning the kitchen and then heading upstairs. She refuses to stop. There is no time to sit down, no need for taking a break, her appetite non-existent. She will keep going until every speck of dust, every smear and fleck of grime has been banished.

In the bedroom, Helena stands in front of the wardrobe. For so long, she has made a promise to herself to sort it out, to get rid of the unnecessary clutter and start afresh. Something crawls along her skin, her scalp tingling as she steps forward and flings open the door. This used to be Vanessa's room. It's her daughter's old wardrobe, some of her teenage belongings still taking up space at the back. Vanessa's young life packed into neat storage boxes.

Sitting cross-legged, Helena reaches in and slides out the small stack, anxiety sitting at the pit of her stomach, heavy as a rock. The first box is an array of birthday cards. She leafs through them, smiling despite herself. Pictures of flowers and balloons and teddy bears and cakes painted in pastel colours, forcing a lump into her throat. She swallows it down, refusing to shed any tears for the child that her daughter once was and the deceitful woman she has become.

The next box is a small bundle of photographs – Vanessa and her childhood friend, Crystal. Time stops, the air in the room thinning as Helena takes a deep breath and places a splayed hand across her forehead.

Crystal.

Sweet, charming, sensitive little Crystal. The photograph trembles in Helena's hand, her fingers holding it so tightly, a small crease appears on the lower half of the picture. As if burnt, she drops it before picking it back up and trying to smooth out the edges, clearing away an imaginary layer of dust with trembling fingers. Strange how she thought of Crystal not so long ago, how an image of her sweet face crept into Helena's mind, as if she is trying to tell her something. Some important piece of information that Helena has missed.

Visions of that summer, that day by the stream, catapult into her brain. Unlike last time, she allows them in. For too long she has denied access to those memories, thinking if she ignored them, they would fade. They haven't. They are still there. Incidents like that don't ever leave. How long ago was it that it happened? Twenty-five years? Guilt scratches at her flesh. The date should be emblazoned in her mind, etched into her thoughts with a permanent marker. At one time it was, but she has buried it deep, unwilling, or unable to continually rake over that day. Trauma never leaves no matter how hard we try to ignore it. It sits dormant, ready to strike unbidden. Like now.

Vanessa was ten years old, Crystal a year younger. It was a hot day, summer at its height. The children had gone down to the woods to play, Rachel tagging along with Vanessa, complaining vociferously about having to babysit her younger sister. And that boy as well. The one whose name she cannot remember. He was there too. It was one of the rare occasions when Helena was relieved of parental duties, choosing to spend the time sitting in the garden, reading a book and drinking lemonade. Like a scene from a movie, the sweet sound of birdsong echoed around her, the distant laughter of children at the end of the road gliding over her skin like warm honey. It was a glorious day. Everything was perfect.

Until it wasn't.

Ripped from her soft gentle daydream by the scream of a child – her child – Helena had raced to the back door, catching Rachel as she tumbled into her arms, her howls buried into Helena's midriff. She expected the usual tales of sibling rivalry, of arguments and spiteful behaviour. What she didn't expect was what came next, the words that tumbled out of her youngest daughter's mouth.

'She's dead. We can't wake her up. She isn't breathing. Vanessa said to come and get you because Crystal fell in the water at the edge of the woods and we've shouted and shouted but nothing is happening and even though Vanessa has shaken her and called her name, we just can't wake her up.'

35

ALEX

Now

He sits in his car outside the care home, watching. Waiting. Last night was good. But it wasn't perfect. She was quiet, more reserved than usual. As if she was having second thoughts. Then today, complete radio silence. No word from her at all. He will only sit here for so long, hoping to find out what the problem is when she arrives and then he will head inside, take up his usual position in his small cubbyhole-sized office and get on with his day. It's an insult, expecting someone to work in there, to provide a service for a care home of this scale when his surroundings are barely bigger than a box bedroom. He will speak to her about it at some point, start making demands. He is valued for his skills. He works hard. It's about time he was shown some respect. Both in and out of the workplace.

Things with Vanessa didn't initially work out as planned. Forging a connection with her took time. For the first few days in his new position, he stood at the end of the road after leaving work, watching as she drove past, her spine rigid, expression imperious. She was oblivious to the figure crouched behind the shrubbery. It took time to build a link and for that link to expand to a proper relationship. She was an enigma. An elusive butterfly he wanted to catch. He spent day after day trying to work out what his next move would be. He expected the usual rush of resentment and anger whenever he brushed past her in the corridor. But then something happened. Something unexpected. Her presence in his everyday life resulted in a variety of new and unusual thoughts that roamed around his brain. Her efficiency, her expertise and need for order were even greater than his own. She was unique. An adult version of the child she used to be. And he liked it. Rather than being repulsed by somebody who was often direct and aloof, it aroused him. Made him want to spend more time in her company. So he asked if she wanted to go for a coffee one afternoon, take an hour away from the office and stroll into town. And she agreed. He had already braced himself, ready for the rebuff, for her to sneer and curl up her lip in disdain. Instead, she had smiled and raised a perfectly arched eyebrow, claiming they had to leave the care home separately to avoid any suspicion.

They met in a small coffee shop, sitting at a table in a dark corner, reminiscing about the past. Speaking briefly of that day. The one down by the stream. And rather than drive an uncomfortable wedge between them, it brought them closer together.

Things have moved on since that first coffee. They are now an item, albeit a secret one, their clandestine meetings taking place under the cover of darkness.

He thinks about her recent request to visit his house, to discover where he lives. She is clearly unaware that he still inhabits the same house in the same street. A grown man still living in his childhood home. It was on his letter of application, but Vanessa has clearly not taken notice of such a minor detail. Either that or she is toying with him. He pushes that thought away. She has moved on from her past while he is still anchored to his. A small amount of humiliation sits within his gut. He should have moved house years ago but can't. It's impossible. He is stuck there, his mother once again running his life. Dictating to him from beyond the grave. And now Vanessa is asking to take things a step further, to visit his home. His safe place. His sanctuary. It's something he will give thought to today while he sits in his tiny room, checking his stock and waiting for that ancient boiler on the top floor to stop working again.

Ten minutes pass and still no sign of her. Probably a good thing. It's still meant to be a secret, their relationship; speaking furtively in the car park would probably rile her anyway. Give her a good reason to pick an argument. There is a slight imbalance of power between them. She's his boss, and seems to revel in the idea of barking orders his way in the presence of other members of staff. He will speak to her about that as well. He's her employee. He isn't her personal slave.

The idea of inviting her back to his continues to dangle in his mind as he waits for her to arrive. It's about time they took their relationship to the next level, spent more time alone instead of driving around in his car, trying to decide on the perfect location to suit their needs. Still, at least one positive is that this job pays him enough to run a car. The time he spent using public transport tore at his guts. With a new motor, he can be his own man, not reliant on anybody or anything.

Except Vanessa.

He continues to sit, eyes darting to the main gates, hoping to spot her white Mazda. It's ridiculous, having to conduct private conversations in a car park like fucking schoolchildren. There has to be a better way.

It's the rigid approach that the care home owners have about fraternising with other members of staff that has stifled their relationship. Vanessa could lose her job if they are discovered. Worse still, he could lose his. That would end him. Tip him over that cliff edge and have him tumbling into a bottomless well of misery. Once was enough.

He glances at the clock on the dashboard and sighs. She isn't coming. Or she's late. And Vanessa is never absent and never late. He thinks of car accidents on the journey into work, illnesses, all manner of reasons why she is suddenly unavailable. Why she has gone to ground.

Another quick swipe on his phone tells him she hasn't returned his calls or replied to his texts. Panic is a tight knot in his chest, a deadly unfurling creature about to strike. Something has happened. Something that is out of his control. Has she been stopped for speeding on the A19? Is she currently sitting in the back of a police car? He swallows, runs his fingers through his crop of dark hair. Will it turn into something bigger, and more importantly, will she lead them to him? To his house?

He shakes his head, aware he is blowing her absence out of all proportion. He's letting panic get to him, his deepest darkest fears manipulating his thoughts and sending him into a tailspin. He is above those sorts of reactions, isn't he? Anxiety-fuelled responses are for the small people, the weak and the lazy who don't have enough intelligence or foresight to think logically.

One day. That's all he has to get through until he can contact her, find out what the problem is. Find out if *he* is the problem. This is the thing with relationships – it's the not knowing, the sudden switch in emotions and temperament. He isn't used to it. He needs control and order. Anything else makes him view the world through the lens of suspicion. And anger. God, the anger that he is trying to keep a lid on, it burns within his veins, scorching the marrow of his bones.

Enough.

The sound of his footsteps as he strides across the car park to the building is a lonely echo, booming in his head and reminding him of how far he has come. And how far he would fall should anything untoward occur.

With a streak of confidence that ebbs away like the retreating tide the closer he gets to the care home, Alex pushes open the door and walks inside, determined to speak to her. Find out where she is. Why she has been ignoring his calls and messages. All of a sudden, her efficiency and reserved demeanour is losing its appeal, morphing instead into a cool detachment that he doesn't care for. By the time he reaches his office, his temper is unravelling, heat rising from beneath his collar. He trusted her. He thought they had a future. And now this.

An hour later, a sharp rap at his door prickles his flesh. The stretch of his leg from his seat is just long enough to kick it open into Miranda, the receptionist, who is standing outside, glasses perched on the end of her nose.

'Vanessa has sent a message saying she won't be in today. Illness apparently, but she asked if you can do your usual round of checking the rooms on floor six. Make sure the radiators are all working properly.'

The slam as he pulls the door closed again is enough to send Miranda scuttling away. He yanks at his collar, the heat of his growing fury making him sticky and uncomfortable. Who the fuck does she thinks she is, sending orders his way when she can't even be bothered answering his messages or turning up? She may be the acting manager of the place, but he and Vanessa are equals in every other respect. That was the allure, part of the attraction, but this new set-up, the power suddenly being snatched away from him, is his breaking point.

He suddenly realises as he sits alone, trying to keep his temper in check, that he doesn't even know Vanessa's address. They are an item, a proper couple in every respect, and he doesn't even know where she fucking well lives. He needs to find out. He needs to call round and see the startled expression on her face when she opens the door to find him standing there. Not so powerful then. Except of course he can't. Unless he can get inside her office and access her files, that is. All the human resources files are on her computer. The addresses of each member of staff. Including his. And hers. He also knows her password, once standing close to her chair while she typed it in.

Praying her office isn't occupied or locked, he stands, an idea of how to talk his way into getting in there already formulated in his mind. That's the beauty of his job – he can fabricate a broken radiator or a window that won't open properly. Even changing the batteries in the smoke alarm in the corner of her office. Any of those excuses will allow him access. Replacing door hinges would work, allowing him to close himself inside under the pretence of unscrewing the door from the frame.

He bends and picks up his toolbox. She should have known who and what she was dealing with when they hooked up together. He remembers the initial spark between them, that sizzle of anticipation at the interview as she leaned across the desk and asked him when he could start if he were to be offered the position. And all those evenings they spent together, the memory of those nights that still set a fire raging in his belly. Did none of it mean anything to her? He had to speak to her, get her back in his life. They couldn't be apart. It was unthinkable. It is the first and only time in his life he has felt a connection to somebody. They are fused together; minds and hearts. He has put everything he has into this relationship, handed over parts of himself that have never been exposed to anybody else.

The heft of the toolbox pulls at his shoulder, his fingers curled around it until his knuckles turn white. Tension tears at his spine, pulsing in his jaw. The corridor that leads to her office is empty, most of the staff tending to the residents; getting them out of bed, dressing and feeding them. His timing is perfect.

The memory of him pulling the door of his cubbyhole closed with force pierces his thoughts. You never knew where you stood with Miranda the receptionist. Some days she is friendly and approachable, the next, stiff as parchment, her eyes roving over him as if he were a creature that had crawled out from under a rock. He hopes she hasn't reported him, made a call to the board of directors or some other shit organisation who run the home and hold the purse strings and all the power. If Vanessa had been here, the complaint would stop with her. She would make all the right noises, assuring Miranda that she will speak with him whilst doing nothing. But she isn't here and that bitch Miranda has free rein. She is probably on the phone right now, whining and moaning and making her voice heard. All the more reason to get inside Vanessa's office and access her computer while the place is empty.

The smell of cooked breakfasts wafts his way, punctuated with the occasional stench of vomit or some other bodily fluid shed by one of the residents during the night. It's always the same in this place. Everyone else seems inured to it, their senses dulled by time and familiarity. Alex isn't sure he will ever reach that moment. Every sound, every smell feels like a physical assault on his body, the occasional howl of a disgruntled resident like nails being dragged down a chalkboard.

By the time he reaches Vanessa's office, Alex is convinced she is actively avoiding him. Probing into her personnel records is recompense for abandoning him. This is a small punishment. He is capable of so much more. He also knows that her request to visit his home is her way of humiliating him. Of course she has seen his address. She knows exactly where he lives. It's listed in the same files he is about to access to find hers. Wanting to visit him at home is just her way of exerting control. Letting him know that while she has moved up in the world, he is still stuck in the same childish groove, his inability to move on to bigger and better things proof that she is superior while he is still stuck on the bottom rung of life.

A vibration of anger and excitement runs through his body, small tremors that send his pulse racing. His movements stealthy and silent, he slides inside the office and closes the door with a muffled click. In the name of authenticity and honesty, Alex opens his toolbox and spreads an array of screwdrivers across the floor. Then he pads over to the computer and types in her password.

Crystal123*

She has made it so easy for him. Within a second or two he is logged in and has access to everything he needs. Everything, that is, except time.

Outside, footsteps disturb his plan. A breath is suspended in his chest; the sound of his own heartbeat roars in his ears. He waits, counting the seconds, before letting out a trembling sigh as the shuffle of footsteps recedes and fades away.

Alex isn't IT savvy. He knows enough to get by, but is faced with dozens of folders, their titles esoteric and meaningless. All he needs is a small detail, something that will lead him to Vanessa. He scans list after list of documents and folders, and official-looking papers and files. A small, inconsequential-looking folder simply named *Staff*, catches his eye.

Glancing over his shoulder, Alex spots the angle of the

blinds. Too exposed. Vanessa's office is on ground level close to the main entrance. A careless move to not shut them. Not like him to be so sloppy in his methods. Not like him at all. This is what she has done to him; made him edgy. Made him lose focus. He pulls the cord and is plunged into near darkness, then clicks on the file and scrolls through the long list of names and addresses until he finds exactly what he is looking for.

36

HELENA

The hours drag, the wait for Innes calling round to speak with her seemingly endless. Crystal's face stares up at her; a grainy photograph of a child long since dead lies idly on her lap. In Helena's hand is a collection of papers, yellowing at the edges, the ageing, musty smell catching at the back of her nose and throat. Memories she has suppressed for so long snag at her brain, rough-edged pieces of a jigsaw waiting to be slotted into place. Old school reports. She found them in a shoebox at the back of the shelf, neatly folded and stacked in a small pile. Reading them again after all these years was like having cold water poured over her. With each word, Helena felt her muscles tighten, the tendons in her neck stretched and taut. Something else she had forgotten. Or ignored, painting over the real meaning with pastel colours to stop the truth from leaching out. Another thing she deliberately pushed to the back of her mind, as if none of it ever took place. Like Crystal's death. Fragments of the past, the pieces of her daughter's childhood coming back to haunt her.

She stares down at the handwritten reports.

Although very bright, Vanessa appears withdrawn and rather sullen.

Helena had reasoned that she was still grieving, Gavin's death leaving them in turmoil.

An incident with another child involving an injury...

A tumble in the playground that had got out of hand. That was what she had told herself at the time.

Sometimes Vanessa can act in an intimidating manner towards other pupils.

She was simply a bright child, emotionally ahead of the other children, that's all it was.

We feel that Vanessa might benefit from some assistance from an external body. We have completed an assessment and would like to set up a meeting with you at your earliest convenience.

Helena had rung the school, told them she was a single parent who worked full-time and that they would simply have to do what they had to do to make sure Vanessa behaved and didn't upset the other children. She recalls with toe-curling clarity that conversation, her dismissal of their words, telling them they were wrong, that they were simply unable to manage a particularly bright child who needed extra stimulation. She felt sure that was all it was. She had another child to care for, a demanding job. She didn't have time for nitpicking when it came to her child's behaviour. Vanessa's work was always excellent, coming top of the class in all areas. She told them they had no reason to complain and single-out her daughter, claiming she had emotional needs and behavioural issues. But what if Helena was wrong? What if all the signs were there and she chose to ignore them, putting everything down to the death of Vanessa's father?

A cold wave of fear washes over her. There are so many unanswered questions. So many areas of her daughter's life that are a mystery to her. Areas she should know. She should have asked more, tried harder. Got to the bottom of things. That is her job as a mother. To care. To protect. To know.

A knock at the door drags her back to the present. Not a loud insistent rap; a gentle tap as if the caller is too embarrassed to announce their arrival.

Helena stands and heads to the hallway, pulling open the door and shivering at the blast of chilly air that brushes over her face and bare arms. He is here. The wait is finally over and Vanessa's ex-partner is here.

'Innes. Please come in.'

He is being intentionally unobtrusive, his footfall light, his movements slow and considered. After their last encounter, Innes is doing what he can to put her at ease. It won't help. Unless he is about to inform her that his previous statement about her daughter was a lie, unless he can magically erase the worries that are gnawing at her brain; worries that she as a mother missed the vital signs that her daughter is a pathological liar and possible narcissist, then nothing he says or does, no matter how discreet and modest, will help to smooth out the wrinkles of discomfort that sit deep in her flesh like barbed wire.

'Thank you. Sorry I'm a bit late. Traffic was a nightmare.'

Is he late? Time seems to have passed her by, her mind

fogged up with long-forgotten memories that have hindered her ability to think clearly.

'Tea?' Her voice sounds ethereal, the question falling out of her mouth, manners and years of conditioning taking over.

'I'm good, thanks. But I do want to thank you for inviting me back. Last time we spoke I was rude and—'

Helena holds up a hand to silence him.

'No need to apologise. We were – *are* – under a great deal of strain.'

Behind her, the antique clock she bought for no other reason than it caught her eye and she needed a nice-looking timepiece in the house ticks away, its relentless pulsing drawing attention to the strained atmosphere. It's as if every item in the house, and even the house itself, knows what is about to be said. Every inanimate object bracing itself for the unveiling of horrible truths that for too long Helena has ignored.

'Please, Innes, tell me about your time with Vanessa and the problems you had with her. Don't feel you have to soften your words for my benefit. I'm at a point in my life where I need to know who my daughter really is.' She swallows and lets out a trembling sigh. 'What she is and what she is capable of.'

He nods, his elbows resting on his knees. His navy trousers expose an inch of ankle as he taps out a nervous rhythm with his feet.

'It began after Noah was born, although if I'm honest, it started long before that. It just got worse after his birth.'

Helena raises an eyebrow, nodding at him to continue.

'Vanessa would fly into rages at the slightest thing. She once threw my phone at the wall because somebody rang while she was watching TV. She said it disturbed her and she panicked.' He stops, takes a rattling breath, rubs at his eyes with the heel of his hand before continuing. 'I loved her. I wanted to make it work, I really did, but her rages got worse. There was this one time when I said I was going out with a few of the boys, just to the local pub for a couple of beers. She went mental, screaming that I was having an affair, that she was going to follow me and if she saw me look at another woman, then she would produce a knife and kill me.' Another brief silence. Helena says nothing, allowing him to gather his thoughts. She swallows to try to still the tic that is pulsing in her neck. 'And then one time, she did actually take a knife to me.' He glances up, meeting Helena's gaze. 'Hence the scar on my arm.'

'Did—' A lump forms in her throat, blocking her words, forcing her to stop as she fights back tears. She lowers her head and bites at her lower lip, the rush of pain a welcome reprieve. 'Sorry, Innes. I just need a few seconds.' A rattling breath, then, 'I'm so sorry she did those things to you. Did the children ever see any of this? Did they witness her abuse?'

A second or two of throat-clearing before he shakes his head. 'No, they heard the shouting but a lot of what took place was while they were in bed.'

Guilt for feeling relieved washes over her. She feels sympathy for this man, but had to be certain her grandchildren hadn't witnessed the violence. What Vanessa did to Innes is unforgivable but if the children had observed it, then there would be no telling what could happen. The cycle of harmful, destructive behaviour could perpetuate, their fragile minds warped and reprogrammed, thinking it was normal to behave in such a way. It would go on and on and on. There would be no end to this awful, dreadful cycle.

'The night I left, she was going crazy, threatening to stab me while I slept. A colleague had messaged to say she was sorry for a misunderstanding that had taken place at work earlier that day, and Vanessa had seen it and assumed it was from another woman, shrieking at me about a lover's tiff and how she wished she had never met me. She came in from the kitchen with a long knife, and I knew then that I had to leave.'

'Why did you not go through the courts to get access to the children?' It isn't that Helena doesn't believe him. He has the pained look of a deeply damaged man. Broken, even. But if Vanessa had been challenged a little, met with resistance from a legal team, then perhaps she would have backed down.

'That was my last resort. I was sure doing that would exacerbate things. I wanted to keep her calm, try to get on her good side. She always said that if I didn't back off, she would take the kids and leave with no forwarding address.' His voice cracks. Innes runs his fingers through his hair and rubs at his eyes.

'That would never happen. Vanessa has a job, a house. The children are both settled in school. Where on earth would she go?'

More head shaking. 'I... It's difficult to see or think clearly when you're in the middle of a situation like this one. I've spent months and months and months trying to see the kids but to no avail. After my last attempt to get in the house, I went to speak to somebody at the Citizens Advice Bureau and they recommended seeing a solicitor.'

'Which is exactly what you should do.' Helena is overcome by an urge to place an arm around his shoulder, to let her know that she feels his pain. That despite Vanessa being her daughter, she is on his side.

'Solicitors cost money. I'm still paying the mortgage and giving extra cash for child support.'

A pain shoots up the back of her head, wrapping itself around her skull like a vice. Is this why he made contact a few weeks back? Is it money he's after? She shuts out that thought. She was the one who contacted him, arranging this meeting.

Helena has some savings, a small pension and the salary from her job, but knows that legal costs would eat through what she has in a matter of months.

'There has to be a way, Innes. You have a right to see your children. They are your flesh and blood.'

The sudden narrowing of his eyes coupled with the quizzical expression on his face send a rush of fear through her; a snake slithering beneath her flesh, fangs bared, ready to spit out its deadly poison.

'You don't know, do you? Vanessa has never said anything, has she? Not that it makes a difference to my feelings for him. I'm still his dad. I'm the one who brought him up, rocked him to sleep at night, cuddling him when he woke in the early hours after a bad dream.'

She doesn't want to hear the next part. Helena wants to cover her ears and pretend none of this is happening. Innes's voice cuts through her thoughts, his voice vibrating around her.

'Noah isn't my biological child. Vanessa had an affair. It didn't last long – just long enough for her to fall pregnant.'

'But how—'

'How do I know Noah isn't mine? Because I had spent the last few months sleeping in the spare room. We were having yet more problems and I thought it best to give her space, allow her some time to clear her head, hoping distance would make her heart grow fonder and all that. Clearly, it didn't work.'

The thump in Helena's chest is so powerful, she fears she is going to slide off the sofa onto the floor. So many secrets and lies. So many things she doesn't know about her own child. One more revelation just might be the undoing of her.

'I am going to speak with her. This needs sorting.' She doesn't tell him about Vanessa's current relationship, the callouts in the dead of night. The clandestine meetups. The gnarled web of deceit she has spun.

If Innes can sort out his issues, then she will focus on hers, get Vanessa to open up and tell her the truth about her life. It's time for Vanessa to come clean, to be honest and open so they can start afresh.

'I'm going to call round and speak with her tomorrow. I'll call you and keep you updated. I will tell her that I know everything, that you have a right to see your children.' She stops and takes a juddering breath, sucking in so deeply she feels lightheaded.

'He may not be my biological child, Helena, but he is my son. I still want to see him. I still love him as if he's my own.'

She nods, her thoughts spiralling, a negative thread tugging at her that reminds her how difficult access might be if the subject of Noah's real father is ever brought up should the courts have to intervene. But that doesn't mean they shouldn't try. Because something has got to give before the whole sordid pack of cards comes tumbling down around them, crushing them all beneath the weight of her daughter's sins.

37

ALEX

Now

He snaps a photo of the computer screen just in time. With seconds to spare, he slips his phone back in his pocket, shuffles over to the door, and drops to his knees. Alex is unscrewing one of the hinges just as Miranda walks in. His eyes travel over her face, searching for any sign that she knows what he has been doing, and is met with a blank stare, her voice brimming with its usual competence. Everything seems normal. No frosty reception. No clipped tone or sibilant demands.

'Did you manage to see to those radiators?'

'Off to do them as soon as I've sorted this door. Hinge was hanging off. I could see it from the other side so thought I'd fix it while I was passing.'

She doesn't question it, matters related to general maintenance a mystery to her. Miranda is always more concerned with paperwork and residents and their needs, and making sure all the documentation is up to date.

For the briefest of moments, their eyes meet, her gaze penetrative and dark. Christ, she is hard work. Alex wonders if she lives alone with a dozen cats roaming about the place. Then he remembers and realises his error. She isn't onto him. She is waiting.

'I need to apologise for earlier – the slamming of the door, that is. Been a hectic few days. Didn't get much sleep last night.'

She hitches an eyebrow up, her face cold and impassive.

'It's my mother, you see. She's disabled and I'm her main carer.'

It hits the spot, her face slackening, a look of tenderness creasing her eyes. 'Oh, Alex. I had no idea. I'm so sorry to hear that.'

'It's okay. I'm used to it.' He gathers up his tools and slides them back into the box, closing it with a snap. 'I'll go and sort those radiators now.'

'You know, if ever you need any respite or any assistance, I know of an organisation that could—'

'It's fine.' He stops, aware his voice is sharper than he would like. Sometimes it's difficult keeping it all tucked away. 'Sorry, Miranda. I'm fine. Honestly, we're all good, Mum and I. Yesterday was a bad day but today is better. But thanks for the offer. I'll certainly bear it in mind.'

She does the head-tipping thing that people do when they hear a tale of woe. Even if that tale of woe is a complete fabrication. She doesn't need to know that. Nobody does.

The rattle of his toolbox cuts through the silence that follows. As soon as he leaves, she will be out there, telling the rest of the staff about his torturous homelife, how he is a marvel for looking after his poor mother, and that everyone should treat him with a little more respect given what he has been through and what he has to endure every night when he gets home.

He suppresses a smile, wanting to laugh at the absurdity of it all. Some people are so easy. So fucking easy. Like tricking a small child. Or a particularly dense person. And Miranda is so incredibly dense. As thick as treacle with a face that could curdle milk.

She leaves the room, giving him a simpering grin. He has visions of ramming his fist into her face and pressing his fingers around her throat, watching her eyes bulge and listening as she gasps for breath. Except she isn't his type. No make-up. No skin-tight clothes or midriff on display. Miranda is middle-aged and dresses in tweed skirts.

A tune of old, one of his favourites from back in the day, implants itself in his head. The sound of his whistling fills the corridor as he makes his way to floor six to check those radiators that he already knows are working just fine, with Vanessa's address tucked safely in his pocket. He wonders if Miranda realises how lucky she is. How her drab appearance and sour expression has lent itself to her remaining safe. And staying alive.

The rest of the day passes without incident, one hour blending into the next, until he is finally able to head home. A change of clothes, a few jobs to do around the house, and he will be ready to make his unannounced visit, the vision of Vanessa's face blooming in his mind. Her shocked expression, her garbled explanation. The way she will suddenly realise that she has mistreated him. And then her apology, her profuse, grovelling apology that he will savour and cast to memory, storing in a special place at the back of his mind, bringing it out when life grinds him down and he needs a flicker of light in the oppressive darkness.

His pulse is racing as he pulls up outside his house, the idea of seeing Vanessa enough to arouse him. It isn't her face or the thought of her naked body that pushes his buttons – it's her

possible meekness and humility for doing him wrong. Her fear-
fulness; the way she will look at him as he forces his way past
her into her home, his fists and mind angled towards violence.
He never wanted it to come to this but she has stepped over a
line. He refuses to be the browbeaten one in this relationship.
Soon she'll come to see that he isn't the underdog, somebody
she can bark orders at whenever she wants.

But first, he has things to do. He needs to see to *her*. She is
fast becoming a nuisance. An annoyance he cannot dismiss.
Letting her go isn't an option even if the sound of her voice is
enough to make him want to punch the nearest wall.

Inside is cool and tranquil, the silence wrapping itself
around him like a welcoming embrace. He showers, eats a sandwich and then enters the room, a rush of adrenaline spiking his
energy levels as he sees her sitting there, staring at the photos of
his mother.

'Here,' he murmurs, leaning down and placing a sandwich
and a drink next to her feet.

He readjusts her attire, allowing her to eat, then watches as
she slowly chews and takes small sips of the juice.

'Who is she?' She tears her eyes away from the pictures that
cover every wall and stares at him.

'Why do you need to know?' Alex is feeling generous. He has
had a good day, discovering Vanessa's home address. He will
allow her this indiscretion. This uncalled-for personal question.

The shake of her head and curl of her lip forces a rock-sized
lump into his chest. Is she laughing at him? Mocking him even?

'You're a fucking lunatic, you do know that, don't you? Where
is she? Did you kill her?'

The pulse in his neck makes him dizzy. He suddenly realises
he has forgotten the knife. In his haste to see Vanessa, he has
left that jagged bladed weapon in the kitchen. It doesn't matter.

She is too slight to do anything. She tried before and failed. One punch and she would slump to the floor like a ton of bricks. And he would punch her too if she tried anything untoward. He doesn't want to kill her. She is too like his mother. A reminder that he finally managed to control his life by controlling her. But neither does he want her mouth running loose. Sarcastic bitches rile him, make him want to do things to shut them up.

'I fucking hate you.' Spittle flies out of her mouth as she fires insults his way.

'Get up. Go and get showered. And hurry up.'

She doesn't move, her legs jutting out in front of her, her eyes locked onto his.

'Fuck off.'

A flutter of annoyance dances around the edges of his brain, a frisson of annoyance he ignores.

'You're making me late. Get up and get in the shower.'

'No.'

The annoyance slowly augments into a wave of agitation. He is busy, has things to do. Places to go. Problems to sort. She is slowing him down.

'Is she buried in your back garden?'

The question catches him off guard, like a punch to his solar plexus.

'Shut up. Stop talking and get up on your feet.'

No movement. No fear. No trace of the terror that once resided in her eyes. Instead, she sits motionless, watching him. Waiting for a reaction. Laughter bubbles up his throat. He knows what this is. It's all she's got. Denial and disobedience, her only form of power. He will grant her that. Everyone has to have something.

'Right,' he says, bending down to pick up her plate and

empty tumbler, 'bathroom next. Even if you refuse to take a shower your bladder must be bursting so—'

The pain is blinding, his feet struggling to gain purchase as he stumbles back. A sudden smack. He felt it between his eyes. A line of pain, like an explosion inside his skull. She has head-butted him, taking him by surprise. By the time he is able to stand upright, she is on her feet and marching towards the door.

'You bitch! You fucking crazy bitch!'

Panic and searing pain paralyses him, rooting him to the spot. The knife. He needs to get to that knife before she does.

As if pushed on by an invisible hand, he finally moves, galloping down the stairs after her, the thud of his feet like the roar of thunder. She is at the bottom, pulling at the door handle, trying to get out. The sharpness and volume of his laughter is as big a surprise to him as it is to her. Hair fanning out around her like a halo, she spins around, mouth agape.

'Did you really think I'm stupid enough to leave the key dangling from the lock? What the hell do you take me for, eh?'

Alex lifts it out of his pocket, his finger looped through the fob. He swings it back and forth, smiling. Teasing her. Enjoying the moment. He has taken back the power with both hands and is once again in control. No bids for freedom from her. Not on his watch.

Like a tiny insect, she spins around and darts past him, slipping out of reach. Alex lets out a growl. She's heading for the kitchen, trying to get to the back door. He can't let that happen. He needs the knife. There isn't a single part of him that wants to use it against her, but he cannot let her leave this house and will do whatever it takes to stop her.

'Open that fucking door!' She is standing pointing at it, eyes wild with fury. In her hand, grasped between her fingers, is a long metal skewer. Just as dangerous as any knife.

He sighs, his breath hot and sour. This has gone on for long enough. He is tiring of this particular game.

'Okay, okay!' Hands held up in surrender, he lifts a key out of his pocket and steps towards her.

He makes a show of stabbing it into the lock, waiting for her to edge closer, ready to flee once the door is swung open. Around him, the air vibrates, her barely perceptible movements making the hairs on the back of his neck stand on end. So very slowly, he turns the key, the heat of her body so close he can almost taste the tang of her body odour, is able to smell the pungent aroma of her stale, unwashed hair. One day without a shower and already she smells like death. Like the rotting corpse of his beloved mother who is safely nestled beneath the floorboards of the living room. He wrapped her in plastic to stop any smells escaping but for months afterwards, he was convinced he could detect the whiff of her decomposing body filtering up through the rug.

Alex counts to ten; waiting, listening, his senses attuned to every breath that exits her lungs. Then with as much force as he can muster, he brings back his arm, his elbow smashing into her face with such force, she is propelled into the nearest wall. He hears her cry, feels the soft splatter of flesh and cartilage, then turns and smiles at the bloodied heap lying on the floor at his feet. Beside her lies the skewer. A scrape of metal as he kicks it away out of reach.

It was easy. His work here is done. Carrying her back upstairs is an effortless task, her body as light as air.

'I really should increase your food portions,' he says as he lays her on the bed, tying up her hands and feet and smoothing down her hair. 'You're as light as a feather.'

A soft moan escapes from her, her head rocking from side to side when he leans closer, their faces almost touching.

'Shhh now.' His fingers untangle the blood-spattered strands of her hair, stroking and smoothing and coming to rest against her collarbone. 'I need you to get better. You remind me of her so much. That's why I can't let you leave. You being here helps keep her memory alive. You help to keep the balance just right.'

The duvet is soft and warm as he tucks it under her chin, turns out the light and leaves the room.

38

HELENA

A new day, a different outlook. That is what Helena tells herself as she rises out of bed after a restless night. Body aching, she showers and gets dressed. In her head is a list; tasks she has lined up that need to be completed. Ringing in work and speaking to Cassandra, claiming she is sick, is her first priority. Ordinarily, it isn't something she would ever contemplate doing, especially with Barbara's absence, but these are not ordinary times. Sometimes, decisions have to be made, families cared for. Lies and secrets unpicked.

She makes the call, apologising profusely, her cheeks burning at the white lies and embellishments she tells her manager, who in turn is wholly sympathetic when none is due, then she pulls on her jacket, wraps a scarf around her neck and leaves the house.

Speaking to Rachel is next on her agenda. After Innes left last night, she studied the photograph of Crystal, a few memories niggling. Memories that had been pushed aside, Gavin's death squashing so many incidents, pressing them into a dark corner of her brain that she didn't have the energy to tackle them. Until now, that is. Now she has a burning desire to unearth every truth, to pick at old scabs until they bleed.

The drive there gives her time to think, to sort through and ponder over the things that have led to this juncture. Did she do something terrible to warrant having two selfish children? Both grown women with countless problems in their lives. Is any of it Helena's fault? She tries to think back, wondering if she at any point neglected their needs, dismissed them because she had her own emotional issues to deal with. And then she thinks of her own upbringing, how her own mother played a background role in Helena's life. And yet she turned out okay. Didn't she? A good enough mother. A phrase that can mean one of two things – either she was good enough in all areas, raising two healthy, happy individuals who are equipped to deal with whatever life throws their way, or she was just good enough, providing them with scant attention and love, just enough for them to survive. Which was she?

Tears prick at her eyes. She swings the car into a parking space and takes a deep breath, swallowing down her misgivings and swiping at her face with balled fists. Enough of this self-pity. Wallowing in misery won't solve her immediate problems. Neither will ruminating over a past she cannot change. Her own upbringing was character building. Not something she would wish on anybody, least of all her own children, but it did equip her with resilience and an inner strength that many people lack. Maybe, she thinks as she slides out of the car and heads into town, she should have given her daughters more independence, spoilt them less. Loved them more. Wrapping them in cotton wool has weakened them, made them impervious to the feelings of others.

She stops, takes another convulsive breath, sucking greedily at the air. Her chest aches. Her head aches. She is tired of this constant cycle of torture, blaming herself for the faults of her children. There are people out there who have greater issues. She thinks of Barbara. And then she thinks of Rachel and that ring and suppresses a sob. It never ends. Jesus Christ, it never bloody well ends.

The phrase 'this too shall pass' rattles around her head while she strides towards the place where she is meeting Rachel, who thinks she is about to be given an invitation for Mabel's birthday party when the real reason she is here is to be questioned about Crystal. And that day. The day that poor child tragically lost her life in the stream. There is something about that incident that never seemed to fit. That feeling coupled with the recently unearthed school reports have kept her awake most of the night. Helena wants to hear Rachel's version of events. But then, can she really take the word of somebody who is wearing the ring of a murdered woman whose killer has yet to be found? The answer to that is that she has no choice.

Through a gap in the foliage, she can see Rachel sitting on a bench, shoulders hunched. Her hair has been brushed and she is wearing the clothes that she wore for the meeting with Mabel and Noah. An effort has been made. It's a good sign. A small one but enough to give Helena impetus to pick up her pace and greet her daughter with a nod of her head and a hug.

'You look well!'

A shrug, then a tentative smile, Rachel's mouth hitching up at the corners as if she has forgotten how to be happy. How to be comfortable in her own skin.

'Thanks.' Rachel glances around, her eyes darting everywhere before coming back to rest on Helena. 'Cold, innit?'

'Here,' Helena says, unwrapping her scarf and handing it to Rachel, 'I'm warm from the walk.' She smiles and cocks her head to one side. 'Besides, it's my age. I'm always warm. You keep it. I've got plenty more at home.'

She waits, expecting a refusal, and feels her chest expand with a small amount of relief as Rachel nods and wraps it around her neck, pulling it tight and stroking it as if it were made of silk. Another small step. Helena daren't hope. She simply will not allow herself to get ahead of things.

'So you said you had an invitation for me?' Rachel's voice is quiet, her usual gruff demeanour and sullen countenance, absent.

Here in the park, away from the traffic and the general hubbub of the town centre, every sound feels amplified: the rustle of Helena's clothing as she digs into her pocket, the scrape of paper as she pulls out the photograph, the pounding in her head. She is about to ask the unaskable here, and her blood bubbles like hot tar at the thought of it.

'We haven't got them written out just yet. It's in a couple of weeks. I just wanted to give you plenty of advance warning. It's going to be at the soft play area in the Parkway Centre. I'll pick you up and take you there.' Helena has fabricated it all. Vanessa hasn't booked a party. But she will. Helena will make sure of it. 'Rachel, can you tell me what you remember about that day? The day Crystal died?' She thrusts the photograph towards her, placing it on Rachel's knee.

It's immediate – the change in her daughter's demeanour, the way her eyes cloud over, her teeth biting into her bottom lip with a savageness that chills Helena's flesh.

'What? I mean, why? Why ask now? It was so long ago. I'm not sure I can fully recall it. A lot has happened since then.'

'Maybe just tell me what you can remember?' A sudden breeze curls its way down Helena's spine. She shivers and pulls up her collar, her neck suddenly cold and stippled with goosebumps.

'Why are you asking me? What's done is done. It was years ago. All in the past.'

Helena shrugs. Tries a smile. 'I found this photo yesterday and it took me back. Talking about it doesn't harm anyone, does it? The poor girl shouldn't be forgotten. We should remember her, speak openly about her, don't you think?' Helena leans forward, trying to catch Rachel's eye. She needs that connection. She needs her daughter to see the compassion and longing in her gaze. Most of all, she needs her daughter's help.

Above them, a bird takes flight, soaring upwards, its sleek wings fanned out, its small body swooping and swirling until it picks up speed and disappears into the distance, its small body swallowed up by a vast blue sky.

'If I tell you, it stays between us, okay?'

It's a deep thrum, the pulse that starts up in Helena's neck. She swallows and nods her head, doing her best to appear calm and unruffled when all the while her insides are squirming. She was right. Her suspicions about that day are about to be confirmed. She couldn't see it back then, blinded by maternal instincts. Blinded by fear and grief. Besides, why would she suspect anything untoward had taken place? They were children. But even at the time, she was struck by Vanessa's calm reaction afterwards, her lack of tears and terror compared to Rachel, who was beside herself with grief. It's becoming clearer now, the passing of time allowing her enough hindsight to see the truth she has never ever wanted to see.

'I won't tell another living soul, I promise. I just need to know.'

Rachel spins her body around, eyes scanning the area before leaning forward and speaking.

39

PRESENT DAY

I'm going to die here. Everything feels hopeless, freedom slipping further and further away from me. I've had my chances to try to escape this place and each time I have failed. Images of my family and friends fill my mind. I would do anything, give anything to see them again.

The relief I felt when I realised he wasn't going to kill me has been replaced by despair. I would rather die than spend the remainder of my days cooped up here, held as a prisoner in this place, slumped on the floor in this hideous shrine. Maybe once I die, he will bring in another and then another until we are all piled up, one on top of another. A house full of buried bodies lying side by side.

I haven't the strength to fight any more. I thought I could do it but my positive attitude has been smashed into a thousand pieces. Everything feels bleak. I would rather he killed me than leave me here for the rest of my days. Either that or I could kill myself. Refusing food and drink would be enough. One week without fluid and I will be dead. No more of this room. No more of having to stare at those photos, and more importantly, no more of Alex Broadwood.

'How's your face? Swelling's gone down now I see.'

He is standing in the doorway surveying me, his eyes travelling over my face and body. My immediate instinct is to curl up away from him but the rope around my ankles and hands is so tight, and I am so damn tired, I haven't the energy to move. So I do the only thing I can do to shut him out. I close my eyes, imagine I am at home or at work. Anywhere but here. He doesn't seem to notice, speaking in a calm, soft voice, as if he didn't try to break my nose. As if this entire set-up is normal.

'You must be hungry and thirsty. I'll bring your food and then you can go to the bathroom. Do what you need to do.'

My eyes remain closed. I can sense him standing there. Watching me. Waiting. Then footsteps receding, the sound of him moving about downstairs. Humming. He is fucking well humming. I can't hold back the tears. I made a promise to myself shortly after being brought here to not waste any energy by crying, but a deep depression is pushing me lower and lower. So low I can almost feel the soil and dust and clay as it fills my mouth and throat, clogging up my lungs and stopping me from breathing. I weep for my predicament, for my previous life and for the future I no longer have.

'Here. You need to eat and drink something.'

My eyes snap open. He is back again, his shadow filling the doorframe. A plate of food and a tumbler of juice is placed next to me.

'You need to promise me that when I take off your gag and untie your hands, you won't try anything.'

I am rigid. No nodding or shaking of my head; nothing at all. In his hands is the knife. I feel so low that if he stabbed right now, death would feel like a release, an infinitely preferable future than spending week after week, month after month, in this awful room. It's a dead house. I think of the cars that pass by every single day, the pedestrians and buses that rattle and chug past, filled with commuters and shoppers, and once more am astounded that they have no idea what lies behind these walls. What kind of macabre set-up he has got going on in here.

A whiff of disinfectant and aftershave fills my nostrils when he steps close to me, bending to untie the fabric that is wrapped around my face and to loosen the rope that is cutting into my wrists and ankles.

I turn away from the food, shuffling my backside around until I am facing the other wall and he is behind me, the sound of his low breathing irritating and terrifying me in equal measure.

A scrape of porcelain crashes in my ears, the plate of food appearing beside me as he pushes it forwards.

'No food,' I say quietly. 'No juice or water either. I'd rather die so you should just kill me right now or I'll kill myself. I will dehydrate and be dead within a week.'

Silence.

Then a shuffle of feet, his shadow appearing in my peripheral vision, looming over me like a spectre. A vision of imminent death.

'Stab me. Strangle me. Do whatever you need to do. I'm done here. I am fucking well done.' My voice rises to a shriek. I can't help it. The last vestiges of dignity that I have tried to cling on to for so long have vanished. There is no point to this farce. There is no point to anything.

I swallow, trying to stem the panic and anger that is rising in me. Maybe this is it. Maybe I will rile him enough to make him use that knife against me, driving it in my back and twisting and twisting until my lungs deflate and there isn't a single pocket of air left in my body.

But he doesn't do that. Something twists in my throat when I see him squat on his haunches, his face close to mine. So close I can smell toothpaste and coffee on his breath, feel the warmth of his body, small waves of it pulsing in my direction. Revulsion unfolds in my gut. A toxic cloud of dread and loathing.

When he does speak, his voice is no more than a whisper, not a hint of anger present. And yet his words still terrify me. Even when I am at my lowest ebb, about to give up on everything, he still has the power to frighten me.

'You know I chose you for a reason, don't you? You're here because I let you live. Not like the others.'

A chill skids across my flesh. I shiver, refusing to look his way. I won't give him the pleasure of seeing the fear in my eyes. Fear at the thought of what he did to those other women.

'I don't want any special treatment.'

A laugh and a shake of his head, as if I am a particularly stubborn child or a stray dog who is begging for scraps.

'I saw you with her a few days prior to taking you. The pair of you were heading into town.'

I say nothing. I refuse to ask who he is referring to, sitting with my head lowered, trying to avoid his gaze.

'I didn't know you knew her. I guess it's a small town. I knew when I saw you together that I had to punish her for what she did to me. So if it makes you feel any better, none of this is because of you. When I worked with you at the same place, I quite liked you. You're not like the others, with their push-up bras and short skirts and thick, brash make-up.'

Curiosity is burning a hole in my gut but still I refuse to engage with him. This is bullshit, a way of coercing me, getting me to do exactly as he wants. He thinks I'm weak and childish enough to fall for this nonsense. I'm not and I won't.

I lower my chin to my chest and shake my head, lightly at first, then so vigorously, it begins to hurt.

'Yes,' he says, his eyes assessing my every move, my every reaction. Every breath that exits my body is being surveyed by this monster. This hideous beast of a man. 'She must have told you about me, surely?'

I gulp back a guffaw. His ego is so out of control, he actually believes I spent time talking about him to other people. I barely remember him. He was a forgettable character, a dysfunctional strange little man on the periphery of my existence. He didn't figure in anything I did.

'No. I know nothing of you and your life.' The final word spits from my lips as if I am ridding myself of a deeply unpleasant residue that clings to the roof of my mouth. A particularly foul-tasting morsel of food that makes me want to vomit.

A prolonged silence while he watches me, his eyes drilling into my body, my face. My innermost thoughts.

'Maxine,' he says finally, her name ringing around the room, the sound of it bringing a round of fresh tears to my eyes. 'I saw you with Maxine, that bitch who got me fired. And of course with you looking so much like her.' He stares at the array of photos, then back at me, his eyes glassy with some hidden emotion that make me want to heave. 'That was when I knew I had to have you. I had to make you mine.'

40

ALEX

Now

She needs to know. Deserves to know. He has an overwhelming compulsion to inform her of why she is here. Why she is still alive. It's not a random occurrence, him taking her. Keeping her. None of them have been random. That's not how he operates. Alex likes order, craves it even. Order amidst the chaos of life. Yin and yang. He takes people, does things to them to keep the balance right. Maisie is here in his house because of Maxine. Simone was because of a rebuff from a pub one evening. Francesca was because her sister was an old classmate, one of the bitches that reported him to the teachers time and again for purported lurid behaviour. She was a lucky find. He saw her one evening in the pub and it went from there. And Arabella, well, she was a practice run. She helped him sharpen his skills in preparation for the others.

He is slowly reeling her in, her eyes widening at the mention of Maxine's name. There is fear there. She doesn't need to be frightened. That isn't his intention. He had to tell her about the resemblance. That's another reason for taking her. Keeping her as his own. He knew when he saw her with Maxine that it was a sign. The stars had aligned and everything was perfect, everything pointing towards what he had to do next. So he waited until she was alone one evening. He had studied her, checked her route. His initial plan was to follow her car from the hospital when she left work, so when she walked rather than drove, he took it as yet another indication that it was the right thing to do. He knew there and then that he had to have her.

'You look just like her when she was young and handsome and not pumped full of drugs and alcohol.' He nods towards the old photos of his mother, taken by his father before their lives turned to shit and his mother turned to drugs and alcohol. His eyes rove over the other pictures, the ones he took of her dead body. She looks peaceful. At rest. She doesn't look dead. Dead was when she was alive and drinking herself into a stupor. Dead was when she was still breathing and injecting drugs into her veins. Death isn't always the end. Some people stop living before they draw their final breath.

'Who is she?' she barks, her eyes briefly flicking away, perusing each snap before moving back to him. Her head is resting against the wall, as if sitting doing nothing is the most exhausting thing in the world. 'And what the fuck has being friends with Maxine got to do with me being kept here?'

Now he has her. Now she is interested and willing to engage in conversation. He knew he would get there eventually. He knew that if he persevered for long enough, she would come round to his way of thinking.

'She,' he says, his voice softening, an expression of fondness in his eyes that only took hold once she was dead, 'is my mother. A real likeness to you, don't you think? Of course, she is no longer with us but I like to keep her memory alive. Which is part of the reason why you're here.'

'Did you kill her?' Her voice is a near shriek. 'Did you fucking well kill your own mother?'

A swarm of angry hornets bite at his skin, sneaking beneath his flesh, attacking his muscles and soft tissue.

'Stop! Of course I didn't kill my own mother. What do you think I am – some sort of monster?'

Her head is shaking, her cheeks wet with tears. He is torn between wanting to dab them away and raising his hand and slapping her hard across the face. Instead, he does nothing, speaking freely about his motives, about who he is. Why he does what he does. It's to make the world a better place; cleaner, less cluttered with troublemakers and spiteful women. Women like Maxine. He couldn't get to her. Besides, that would have been too obvious a move. A police investigation into her background would have led them straight to him. But he could get to Maisie. And he did. With ease.

'Maxine got me fired from my job. Made false allegations about me. You need to choose better friends, Maisie. Friends who are truthful and don't go around trying to ruin other people's lives.'

'No!'

Her howl of denial catches him off guard, momentarily stopping his thoughts. But it is only a momentary thing, because now is his time to speak, to let her know that he is doing this for a reason, that she wasn't just some random female he took off the street. Her being here has meaning. It helps restore the balance in his life.

'She must have told you about that time?' He shifts his gaze up to the ceiling, as if deep in thought. 'Maybe she didn't. It probably meant nothing to her, saying what she said. Doing what she did. But it meant everything to me. That's the type of woman your friend is – thoughtless, callous and selfish.' He shifts about, still crouched on his haunches, his face now only inches from hers. 'So if you want to blame anyone for this, then turn your attentions to your friend, Maxine. She is the one who put you here. She is the reason I had to take you. I'm saving you from her. Saving you from the selfish, dreadful ways of the world. You're better off here with me.' He leans forward and plants a dry kiss on the top of her head, resting his chin on her hair as he speaks once again. 'I'll keep you safe from the rest of the world. You're going to be just fine here with me and my mum. I can sense it.'

He stands, knowing he is right. And although she might not agree with him at this moment in time, she will eventually come round to his way of thinking. He'll make sure of it.

* * *

Still no communication from Vanessa. No texts or calls. Not a damn thing. Upstairs is silent. She'll eat when she's hungry and she will drink when she's thirsty. He'll try her again in an hour, spoon feed her if he needs to; hold her nose and shove the food and drink down her throat. He'll do whatever it takes to keep her alive.

The resemblance was immediate to him, her facial features strikingly like those of his mother in her younger years. Before her substance abuse took hold, addling her brain and damaging her skin and outlook on life. She was once beautiful, his mother. A stunning young woman. Naturally pretty. Not like the women of today; all lashes and lip gloss. Maisie is the same, possessing an organic look that outstrips other females around her. Which is another reason to keep her apart from them. He doesn't want her tarnished by their superficial shallow ways. She is special. Different. A bit like him. They have more in common than she will ever know.

He checks his phone again. Still no contact from Vanessa. Not that it matters any more. He has already worked out what his next move will be. Making plans, sticking to them, making sure they are carried out properly always gives him a sense of satisfaction. Chaos and disorder make him restless and edgy.

Soon, he'll visit Vanessa, make an unannounced call at her house and see what she has to say for herself. See if she is thinking of backing out of this relationship. He won't let that happen. They are an item now. A proper couple. A relationship built on trust.

41

HELENA

Cold air rushes through Helena's body. Her feet are pressed to the floor as she sits, trying to remain steady, not float away or be blown sideways by the slightest of breezes. All her life, all the things she has ever done, all the things she has ever said or learned or taught others, has led to this point. That is, if what Rachel is telling her is true. Because both of her daughters' track records are hardly shining examples of how to conduct oneself in public, or even in private for that matter. And yet, there is something about Rachel's expression, something about her voice and body language that makes Helena want to believe her.

Not *want*.

She doesn't *want* to believe any of what she is hearing, but she feels duty bound to nod and give Rachel the space she needs to unload this terrible burden. A heavy burden she has carried for many decades now, its heft crushing and grinding her until she hardly knew which way was up. Driving her to do the most terrible things to her own body in a bid to blot out those memories.

'I didn't see it all. I was too frightened, but I heard the

splashes and the screams and I heard Crystal shouting and crying, begging them both to stop.'

Tears bubble behind Helena's eyelids. She blinks them back, fearing their power and the acidic burn of their salinity as they trail down her cheeks and drip off her chin. This is the worst thing she has ever heard. She is all out of answers. She has no idea what to do next. Walking into the police station and reporting a historic incident that involves her eldest daughter and a young boy killing another child is an unthinkable scenario. And then informing the officer that the story came from her younger daughter who is a homeless addict. Already she can see the look of disbelief on the faces of the officers; she would know by the roll of their eyes and suggestive glances that they think her unhinged.

She bites at the skin on the inside of her mouth. Why is parenting so fucking difficult? Why does the worry never end? Her children have caused her more heartache as adults than they ever did as infants.

A glint of colour catches Helena's vision. That ring. The moment to discuss it is here. If not now, then when?

'Please tell me the truth about that ring, Rachel. I need to know. And after you've told me, I'll let you know why I've asked.'

Rachel stares down at it, her eyes suddenly wide. Full of fear.

'I didn't steal it. I'm not a thief.'

'I know you're not a thief. I just need to know how you came by such an expensive-looking item.'

Silence. Only the sound of her own breathing roaring in her ears. Just when Helena has given up hope of ever knowing how it came into the possession of her homeless daughter, Rachel speaks, her words the final straw that breaks Helena, cracking her ribcage wide open and exposing her beating heart.

'I met up with Vanessa a month or so back. She gave me it,

said it was a gift for me, something to cheer me up, help me get back on my feet.'

Helena's brain freezes. If this is true, then her world is about to shatter into a million pieces.

'I thought you and Vanessa hadn't seen each other for a long time?'

She is searching for the truth, that elusive ethereal thing that dances about on the periphery of her life, like a butterfly that refuses to be caught and held fast.

'She saw me in the park one day and came over. Told me I should go to a hostel, that the town was no longer safe.'

Hope burns brightly in Helena's mind. Surely Vanessa wouldn't warn her own sister if she had anything to do with those atrocities? Maybe she is placing too much importance on this ring. Maybe rings like these are ten a penny, a piece of costume jewellery that is available in almost every shop in town.

Helena once again questions Rachel about that day down at the woods. She needs facts. Not pieces of flimsy evidence or distant memories that her youngest daughter has misinterpreted. All she wants is the truth.

'Rachel, are you absolutely certain that Vanessa and Alex deliberately hurt Crystal in the stream at the edge of the woods?'

Rachel's eyes are sharp as flint as she turns and stares deep into Helena's face. 'I know what I heard. Vanessa had already threatened Crystal saying she would hold her head underwater if she didn't do exactly as Vanessa asked.'

'And...?'

'And when I finally dared to turn around, Crystal had gone quiet and Vanessa was straddling her, her hands covering Crystal's face while Alex stood close by and watched. He was smiling. As soon as she saw me, Vanessa began to cry, saying Crystal had slipped and now she wouldn't wake up.'

Helena pulls out a wad of notes from her purse and stuffs it into Rachel's hand.

'I need to get home. Get yourself some food.'

She no longer cares if the money is spent on drink or drugs. Her immediate focus is on getting back to her car, driving to Vanessa's house and demanding that her daughter for once in her life, tell the truth. About that day by the stream. About her current relationship. About everything.

'Mum, are you okay?'

The softness in Rachel's voice brings forth a flood of tears. Helena is unused to such tenderness and so unaccustomed to somebody generally giving a shit about how she feels, that it overwhelms her.

'I'm okay. Had better days but I'll be fine. I always am. In the end.'

Arms envelop her before she can say anything else, the closeness and sensitivity of Rachel such an alien encounter that her silent tears escalate into a dramatic sobbing session so vivid and all-encompassing, she fears it will never end.

They part, her face wet and streaked, Rachel watching her as she pulls out a tissue and dabs at her eyes and blows her nose.

'You look tired, Mum. Really tired.'

Helena smiles, a laugh feeling like a step too far. Tired. Rachel has no idea. She is beyond tired. She would give anything to simply be experiencing a mild bout of tiredness. What she is feeling right now is like nothing she has ever felt before. It is something that is robbing her of every bit of light and warmth and comfort she had in her life. It is a dead end with no means of escape.

'I can't come home with you, Mum. Not just yet.'

Another half-smile and a nod. 'I know, love. I know.' She starts to walk away, the ground spongy beneath her feet.

'But I will soon. I promise. I'll really, really try.'

Helena stops, a rattling breath trapped in her chest. Everything hurts – her head, her stomach, her back. Even her teeth, an ache setting in at the back of her jaw. It's all the crying, all the tension. All the everything that she has just been told.

Nodding her head causes her pain, but she does it anyway, to let Rachel know she has heard her. It may be an empty promise but right now, it's all she's got to hold on to. An armful of empty, hollow promises.

Shoving her hands deep in her pockets to disguise the tremble, Helena dips her head and makes her way back to the car.

42

PRESENT DAY

Every time I think of the kiss that he planted on the top of my head, I have to swallow down bile. The fact he was even that close to me makes me want to vomit. Him seeing me naked, seeing me dry myself after a shower, him being present while I squat on the toilet; none of those things repulse me as much as that kiss. It was intimate, as if we are close. Lovers even. I would sooner gouge out my own eyes with a blunt instrument than be that close to him again. Unless I am driving a knife deep into his chest, that is. If that happened, I would lie next to him and watch him bleed out, taking pleasure in seeing him gasp his last breath. That type of closeness I could tolerate. I'd welcome it. And then I would grab the key for the door and run and keep on running, never looking back at the place that has been my prison for so long now.

But all of that is a dream, because all my attempts to get out of here have failed. I am useless. A hopeless case.

He is downstairs, pacing, muttering to himself. Something has got him riled up. Or somebody. His noises, the creaking of floorboards as he paces back and forth allows me to shuffle about, to attempt to loosen the rope on my wrists. I keep my movements light, doing what I can to avoid being heard.

I glance around, looking for sharp edges, somewhere I can rub against to fray the twine in the hope it will slacken and eventually snap, but there is nothing. Even the radiators are rounded. No pointed corners. Nothing jagged I can use to free myself.

Continuing to shuffle, I manage to haul myself up onto the bed and worm my way behind the closed curtains. Trying to open the wooden shutter blind proves way more challenging. I could continually bang my head against it to attract attention, but he would hear me. I would also cause myself an injury. If I do it once he leaves the house, I could use my feet and then maybe, just maybe, somebody will hear me and knock on the door to see if everything is okay.

The wait for him to go is torturous, every minute feeling like an hour. Downstairs he continues to walk about, muttering and swearing, the sound of his voice interspersed with the occasional clatter or crash. I presume he is throwing things or kicking furniture and wonder what is causing his foul mood. It's not me, that much I do know. I am being given a long leash. I'm not a free woman but at the same time, I'm not dead.

I sit on the bed and wait, trying to think of other things. Trying to remember if Maxine ever mentioned anything about him. I don't know why she would, why Alex Broadwood would ever crop up in any of our conversations. I cast my mind back, raking over old memories and dialogue. And then it comes to me, the memory rushing like a surge of cold air whistling through my brain. The guy where she worked. The one who stalked her, tried to corner her in the staffroom, making lurid comments about her clothing and hair and perfume. The same one who told her she was a bitch and a whore and that women like her didn't deserve to live after she turned down his offer of a date. He had been given his marching orders and Maxine's life went on as normal. I recall her being frightened for a few weeks afterwards in case he tried to follow her home from work, but as time passed and nothing happened, she forgot about him. And so did I. Until now.

Below, a sound cuts through my thoughts; an important sound. The scrape of a key in the door. A slam. And then the splutter of an engine as he drives away, leaving me alone in the house.

The relief I feel is so overwhelming, I feel tears bubble. A lump swells in my throat. I swallow it down, refusing to give in to self-pity. All my energy needs to be conserved for what I am about to do next.

I lie back on the bed, twist myself sideways and lift my feet so they are resting on the windowsill and pressed against the blinds. Then I use every bit of strength I have and begin to bang on the window, gently at first, then increasing the power until I am kicking wildly, using my bound feet as one powerful hit. Over and over I pummel at the glass and the wooden shutters until my hips and lower back ache and sweat coats almost every inch of my flesh.

Breath hot and sour, I wriggle beneath the curtains, hoping to see some damage and let out a roar of frustration when I see that nothing has changed. The heavy wooden shutters remain intact. Undeterred, I shuffle about and try again, hammering and kicking and pounding until I am so tired I can hardly breathe.

This time, I let the tears fall. Three attempts to escape and each time I have come undone. What the fuck is wrong with me? He never needed that knife to keep me in line. Getting out of this place is impossible. It's like a fucking fortress.

I take a sharp breath and give it one more go, determined to do something and not be a victim. I'm a fighter, always have been. I think of Maxine and how she would have coped if she were the one held prisoner in this place. She would have scratched and fought and kicked and bit, knife or no knife. And that's why he hates her. It has nothing to do with her reporting him for sexual harassment. It's the fact she refused to kowtow to his bullying, misogynistic ways.

With another roar and a monumental rise of anger, I slam my feet *against the blinds and feel something shift. A movement. A splintering sound. One of the wooden slats coming away under the pressure. Excitement simmers in my gut. I daren't let myself get too carried away. I've been here before, thinking my route out of here is within touching distance, and then had my hopes and dreams cruelly snatched away from me.*

I continue kicking until I am so tired I can barely move. Counting slowly in between gasps, I wait until I am able, and then sit up, the ache in my shoulders from my hands being tied so tightly now a throbbing, searing pain. Dipping my head behind the curtains, I can see that one of the wooden slats has become dislodged. It's not a lot, but it's something and something is better than nothing. Using my shoulder, I knock it out of its frame and it lands on the bed next to me. My fingers grapple for purchase, my body twisted as I grab it between my hands and clumsily slide it beneath the duvet. A makeshift weapon. I have my own makeshift weapon. I just hope that he doesn't glance up when he is outside and notice the gap.

I have another chance to fight back and get out of here. This will be my final opportunity. I need to use it wisely, not waste it by being weak and pathetic.

The sudden depletion of adrenaline leaves me exhausted. I lie back on the bed, my head resting on the pillow. A few seconds. I just need a few seconds to restore my energy levels before thinking up a new bullet-proof plan.

43

ALEX

Now

Still no communication from Vanessa. His growing anger is a bubbling mountain of magma that is eating at the lining of his stomach. He has waited and waited, allowing her time to sort out whatever is going on in her life, but he isn't prepared to put up with it any longer. He has paced the living room so many times, waiting for her to return his call, he feels certain he has left a furrow in the wooden flooring. He has a choice – stay and feed Maisie, or go and face Vanessa. Maisie is determined. A force of nature, her own anger and resentment difficult to contain; a common thread they share. Usually calm and unruffled, his temper has completely unravelled and he needs to do something about it.

Another glance at his phone. Nothing. Enough now. He has waited long enough. Being kept dangling like this is an insult to his intelligence. He thought they had something special. Clearly he was wrong.

Vanessa lives approximately twenty-five minutes away, in a

village on the far edge of town. It occurs to him as he starts the engine and heads out onto the main road that he knows very little about her current homelife. He knew her as a child, but people change. Hell, she could even be married, although he somehow doubts it. She is too strong a character for that set-up. The type of person who likes to take charge and make no compromises. That's what attracted him to her. Sharp-minded, fiercely independent and somebody who doesn't have a hidden agenda. Not like other women who tease and flirt and get their kicks by trapping and manipulating unwary admirers.

The voice of the radio presenter is enough to make him holler and hammer his fists on the steering wheel, their simpering reports on missing and dead females so conde-scending and dripping with faux sympathy he actually laughs out loud. How many of these people who purportedly show concern and pity for these women would stop and help them in the dead of night if they showed signs of distress? He is willing to bet that the answer to that question is zero. Everyone is too busy with their own miserable lives; too busy tapping away on their phones, posting on social media, displaying to the world how perfect their houses and children and bodies are, that they forget to stop and look around them. They have no right to act outraged when something untoward occurs. They are all selfish, looking only inwards when the world in which they live is slowly rotting away.

He turns off the radio, the immediate silence a soothing balm for his troubles and worries. He needs this moment to prepare for what comes next. In truth, he has no idea what he will be confronted with when he knocks on Vanessa's door. She may smile, step to one side and invite him in, or he may be greeted with a curl of her lip and a volley of abuse. He does know that he is not prepared to be strung along like an idiot.

The shame and disappointment of it is that he thought her different to the others. Sophisticated and intelligent. Turns out she is just like the rest of them – self-centred and thoughtless. Hostile and heartless.

By the time he swings the car into the end of her road, his heart is pounding, his anger an uncontrolled raging fire ready to swallow everything in its path. Engine idling, he stops and stares at the numbers on each door. Vanessa is twenty doors down. Inching along, he stops five houses away and waits, watching for any signs of movement within. And then he sees it – an older woman pulling up in her car and striding up the path. She opens the door and lets herself in, and for a few seconds Alex panics that he has got the wrong address. And then he spots Vanessa standing at the window. He is too far away to be seen, hidden by other vehicles, but lowers his head anyway and slides farther down in his seat, watching as she turns and moves away from the window. He presumes the other woman is a friend or maybe her mother? He casts his mind back to the times he spent at their home as a child, wishing he lived there. Wishing he could swap places and be their sibling. But his memory is a blank. All he remembers is a female figure, kindly and quiet. Warm and welcoming. Everything his own mother wasn't.

Minutes pass, Alex wondering how long he should wait, how long he should sit here in his car in the half-light like a needy child craving attention. It's demeaning and only serves to heighten his anger. What if this other woman lives there with her? What then? Does he knock? Barge in and demand to speak with Vanessa? Or does he do the gutless thing and go back home? He is no coward. He refuses to be browbeaten by a woman who is using her professional managerial status to keep him in line. If that's how she thinks this is going to go, then she is sadly mistaken.

A movement in his peripheral vision. The door opens and the older woman bustles out with two children in tow, each of them carrying a small backpack. They turn and wave and within seconds the door has been closed and the three of them are ensconced in the car. Alex waits, unsure what to think. Did Vanessa mention children? He doesn't think so; the personal lives of staff are rarely discussed at work, especially in his presence. He's a lowly maintenance man, unworthy of idle conversation. Unworthy of anything at all.

A fresh wave of anger washes over him, Alex pulls up his hood, tightens the cord around his face and steps out of the car, ready to do battle. By the time he reaches the front door, he is prepared.

Before he can raise his fist to knock, the door swings wide and a startled Vanessa is standing there, mouth open, eyes bulging. Her gaze darts from side to side as if looking for anyone who might be watching. Before he has a chance to say anything, she steps to one side and beckons him in.

44

HELENA

It feels as if a drill is boring a huge hole in her chest cavity, a line of pain shooting through her ribs directly into her heart. This is unchartered territory. She is about to speak to her eldest daughter about things she would have once thought were unthinkable. There is no easy way to navigate her way through this awful unruly mess. No guidance or handbooks. Nothing concrete she can cling on to for assistance This is a rutted path and one she must walk alone.

She collects the children from school and they drive to Vanessa's house with Noah and Mabel asking a barrage of questions about why they aren't going to Grandma's house first.

Frazzled and tired, Helena pulls up outside the house, managing to bundle the children out with bribes of ice cream and extra screen time.

'I want chocolate ice cream, please, Grandma.'

'And I want vanilla!'

She agrees to all of their requests and they traipse inside, the children kicking off shoes and throwing down coats while Helena slumps on the sofa, her head and body heavy as lead.

She just wants this to be over with. She wants Vanessa to be honest but what she wants more than anything else is some peace in her life. Tranquillity and happiness. And the truth. She desperately wants to hear the truth no matter how uncomfortable or unsavoury.

In the kitchen, Helena prepares dinner with some spare for Vanessa when she arrives home. Despite the nervous tension that is burning in her core, she cannot do nothing. Maternal instincts are her driving force, controlling everything she does. It's an intrinsic part of her make-up. It would take something catastrophic to switch it off.

Like one of your daughters being convicted of murder.

Shame creeps over her. A week ago, she suspected Rachel, and now she is about to question Vanessa about a childhood incident and how that jade ring came to be in her possession. All roads lead back to her daughters.

Thoughts of her absent criminal father and equally feckless mother puncture Helena's thoughts. Thoughts of how she would like to interrogate them, ask why they passed on faulty genes to her precious daughters when all she has ever done is love them unconditionally.

She dishes out chips and sandwiches, and fruit and ice cream, watching misty-eyed as Noah and Mabel eat. It's a tonic for the worst of ailments, seeing hungry children consume the food she has prepared. She welcomes the noise, each scrape and clatter a distraction from what is to come. A distraction from her dark thoughts and worries about what the future may hold.

The growl of an engine chills Helena's blood. She wants to have this conversation almost as much as she doesn't. The time isn't right. It will never be right and yet if not now, then when?

Vanessa bustles in all efficiency and power, her mouth set in a thin line, her self-aggrandising manner a clear indicator that she is prepared for this moment after reading Helena's message about her need for an urgent conversation.

The children are greeted with a forced grin and a hug and then chivvied upstairs by Helena, the promise of being able to eat their ice cream on Mummy's bed while watching the television up there enough to send them scuttling away.

'It's been a busy one, Mum, so I'm not sure what this is about?' Vanessa perches on the edge of the sofa, her reticence to engage in conversation as solid and heavy as the bricks and mortar that surround them.

Terror at being ejected from the house with the threat of never being allowed to see her grandchildren again lodges in Helena's chest, growing and branching out through her veins. And yet at the same time it is tempered with a smattering of something else; the knowledge that her daughter needs her. With few friends to call upon and a partner she has banned from her life, Vanessa is very much alone in her endeavours. And the sad thing is, Helena isn't even sure if her daughter recognises that fact. With her brusque, prickly demeanour that Helena for so long now has mistaken for efficiency and professionalism, Vanessa has isolated herself.

Rather than dipping her toe into the tepid, mildly toxic water to test its potency, Helena opts for diving straight in.

'You saw Rachel a few weeks back. Why didn't you say anything?'

As expected, Vanessa's spine softens for a second or two before straightening again. 'She's my sister. Why wouldn't I go and see her? What a strange question!'

'You haven't seen her for months and months, if not years, then a visit out of the blue to give her a gift?'

Colour dapples Vanessa's cheeks, cerise dots speckling her pale skin.

'Again, why not?'

Helena pulls out her phone and scrolls, searching for the screenshot of the victim, searching for evidence of the jade ring.

'This is why not.' The phone is thrust under Vanessa's nose with Helena watching, scrutinising every flicker, every pulse and eye twitch on her daughter's face.

More colour peppers Vanessa's cheeks, her voice a low growl when she finally replies. 'What am I supposed to be seeing here, Mum?'

Helena's patience is waning, her temper wafer-thin. She is not one of Vanessa's residents at the care home or a poorly paid member of staff and she will not stand for any more of her condescending ways and dismissive responses.

'The ring that you gave Rachel, it belonged to this lady. One of the women who was murdered in town. Where did you get it, Vanessa? Tell me where you got that bloody ring from.'

Vanessa's dry laugh and response prickles Helena's scalp. 'Mother, a ring like that can be purchased anywhere! I mean, what the hell are you implying? That I somehow stole a ring from a dead body?'

Helena has no idea what she is actually implying. Saying it out loud now sounds ridiculous. Outlandish. She continues anyway, everything too far gone to suddenly back out.

'Why, Vanessa? Why not take Rachel a sandwich or a scarf or even a new coat to help keep off the chill while she wanders the streets at night?'

Vanessa's head shaking, her tapered eyes and look of bewilderment on her face raises Helena's temperature. Her insides are burning, her flesh ice cold.

'I gave her the ring because it was a gift to me from somebody. I didn't like it so gave it to Rachel because I knew she could pawn it for some cash. You have no idea, have you, Mum? No idea how addicts and homeless people operate on a day-to-day basis.'

'Who gave you it?'

A deep sigh. Vanessa is working hard to undermine her own mother. This is her forte, her speciality.

'Who gave me it? My new partner gave me it if you must know. He bought it on a trip to the Lake District a few months back. I didn't like it so saw Rachel in town once and passed it on to her.'

It sounds feasible. Vanessa's expressionless face making Helena restless. Making her doubt herself.

'I saw Innes recently. His story is very different to yours. He said you were violent towards him.'

Vanessa jumps up out of her seat as if burnt.

'And you believe him? You actually believe a virtual stranger over your own daughter?'

Hearing it said out loud is a wake-up call to her senses. Cold water closing over her, filling her lungs. And yet something deep inside her gut is pushing her on, like a large stone rolling down a hill. Despite Vanessa's contrition and apparent horror, Helena cannot stop.

'He also said a few things about Noah.' Her words dry up. She sits, waiting for Vanessa to fill in the blanks.

Cushions groan in resistance as Vanessa slumps back down. 'Noah,' she murmurs, tears now coursing down her face.

'I need to know, Vanessa. In order for me to trust you after those fake callouts and your secret relationship, I have to know. I still love you. You're my daughter and no matter what, I will always love you, but please start telling me the truth about what the hell is going on in your life.'

More tears come. Helena resists the urge to wrap her arms around Vanessa, her maternal instinct tempered with caution.

'Innes told you, then?'

She nods, waiting for more. Waiting for her daughter to let her back into her life.

'It was a brief fling. Innes forgave me and agreed to treat Noah as if he were his own.'

'Which is admirable, don't you think?' Helena replies, trying to keep her tone soft and non-aggressive. 'Many men would have fled at that point.'

A protracted silence until Helena breaks it.

'And in the end, you told him to leave, anyway.'

Vanessa doesn't deny it, sitting quietly instead, her eyes fixed on a point in the corner of the room.

'Look,' she says suddenly, 'I know I've put you through a lot lately, but I promise that things are going to improve. I'm going to end this relationship with the guy at work, maybe even look for a different job. Things will get better. And if you must know, I haven't been in work today. I've taken a few days sick leave to think things through. I've been in town to meet up with an old acquaintance about a possible job interview.'

Before Vanessa can say anything else or smudge away her mother's rough edges with love and tender words and promises of better times ahead, Helena interjects, her need to know over-riding all other sentiments. 'I found an old photo of Crystal the other day. I was tidying up a cupboard and it was in a shoebox at the back.' Her eyes never leave Vanessa's face. She watches for signs of guilt or embarrassment but sees nothing, Vanessa's expression open and guileless. No recognition at the mention of Crystal's name, which she thinks, sadly, is far worse. 'Poor Crystal,' Helena says softly. 'All these years she has missed out on. All the chances and opportunities that we've all had and she hasn't experienced any of them.'

Helena wants to say more, to drive the truth out of her

daughter, but fears overstepping that invisible boundary. A loose, thin line that could cut all contact if broken.

'Not sure I remember much about that day,' Vanessa finally says, her features unmoving, eyes still fixed on something other than her mother. 'It was such a long time ago.' She bites a nail and sighs. 'Yeah, poor Crystal.'

'Tell you what,' Helena says, trying to ignore her daughter's contrived manner, the dull, deadened expression in her eyes, 'why don't I take the children out to the park for a while? Give you some time to yourself?'

Before Vanessa can reply, Helena stands, pulls on her jacket and calls up the stairs, both youngsters appearing with wide smiles at the mention of the park and roundabouts and taking a bag of bread to feed the birds.

Feet thundering, they run down, grab coats and small bags of breadcrumbs and head out into the street before Vanessa can refuse or protest.

45

ALEX

Now

'What the fuck are you doing here?' She is standing in the hallway next to him, eyes boring into his.

Rage balloons inside him, her tone, her glare, all causing him to stand that little bit straighter, to give him a few inches' advantage over her. To let her know his capabilities. What he could do to her if she doesn't start being honest with him.

'And why the fuck haven't you answered any of my calls or messages?' He tries to remain calm but his fury at being ignored like an admonished child is gathering pace. Forcing images into his brain. Dark images. Things he would have never considered possible in her presence. He thought she was different. Unique. More like him. Turns out she is just the same as the rest of them. Casting him aside like a speck of dust.

'Things have been... tricky.' She lowers her eyes, guides him into the living room where they sit in adjacent chairs.

He glances around the room. Children's toys litter the rug. An overturned box of kids' books sits in the corner of the room.

His flesh prickles. He never imagined children. He never imagined this level of clutter. This changes things. Makes them complicated. The room feels overly hot, the detritus hemming him in, making him uneasy. Restless.

'Why don't we go for a drive, talk things over?'

She sighs, her hands clasped over her knees. 'Maybe. I'll need to message somebody first if that's okay?'

He nods, desperate to leave the house, to leave the mess behind and wait outside where the air is clearer. Where he can breathe properly. Instead, he sits, watching. Waiting, while she taps out a message. She is likely asking her mother to keep the kids. He doesn't ask. He doesn't want to know. Vanessa's mother is a throwback to a life he would sooner forget. A life when he was a needy, unloved child. Discarded and despised by many.

'Right, let's go.' She stands at full height, her posture something he has always admired. Confidence without arrogance. Now it riles him, makes him want to slap her, to push her against the nearest wall and spit in her face.

He pulls his hood up and they leave the house and slide into his car, his anger dissipating. He has her now. They are finally alone. Turning to face her, he notices how perfect she is, her skin blemish-free. Her eyes ice blue, shot through with flecks of gold. A face like that deserves forgiveness.

'I've got an idea,' he whispers, turning on the engine and swerving out onto the road. 'We'll go somewhere different. Somewhere you've never been before. We can talk things through.'

He takes her lack of response as affirmation and makes a right turn at the junction, heading to the place he knows best. The place where all will be well again. The place where he grew up and still lives. It's about time Vanessa visited his home. Soon she will get to know his true intentions, see who he used to be, who he has become. Who he will always be. There are some things he needs to tell her. Things she doesn't yet know.

Excitement grips him as he presses his foot to the floor, the roar of the engine filling him with hope and making him feel alive.

46

HELENA

She no longer knows what to believe or think or say. She has done the worst thing imaginable and accused her daughter of killing another person. And now she cannot unsay it. She had to voice those thoughts. Keeping them in her head was like harbouring a deadly disease, its toxic clutches slowly eating away at her, killing her from the inside out.

The shriek of excited children bursts into her thoughts. The innocence of youngsters. She watches them throw breadcrumbs into the water, laughing and clapping as ducks fight for scraps of food. If only the rest of her life was as easy and simple as this moment, this snapshot that belies the horror that is her current existence.

She knows she has done a terrible thing, daring to wonder if either of her daughters was involved in the deaths of those women. All Helena has is belief in her own family. And cold hard logic. If her daughters choose to lie, there is nothing she can do about it. And yet Vanessa's reaction when she mentioned that ring snags in her brain – her horror. The tears. That gives Helena hope, makes her realise she may have blown everything out of proportion. Has blind fear skewed her judgement? Then she remembers Rachel's description of that day in the stream and a storm explodes in her mind, fat drops of rain splashing on mud leaving behind a murky, indelible stain.

'Can Noah go on the slide, Grandma? He's too little to climb the steps on his own.'

Helena rises, the sound of Mabel's voice and the warmth of the low winter sun on her neck rousing her out of her dark reverie. Vanessa mentioned looking for another job. A possible new start. A positive step forward. Sometimes leaving the past behind is a tonic for all ails.

'Be careful up there!' Helena's voice is carried off by the breeze.

Noah stands proudly at the top before crouching and sitting. 'Catch me, Grandma!'

She stands at the foot of the long slide, arms ready to sweep him up. His squeals prickle her flesh, her smile feeling like the only thing that is real and genuine.

They spend another fifteen minutes at the park, Vanessa messaging to say she is going to see a friend for a short while and will be back before the children go to bed. Perhaps she has gone to break it off with this man at work. Helena wonders if her daughter is being intimidated by this person; the nocturnal meet-ups, the secrecy of their relationship. A clean break is probably a good thing. Vanessa can start again, get a different job, make new friends. She can begin to live. Be the mother her children want her to be. The daughter Helena would like her to be. Anything is possible. With some therapy and a caring environment, the future may prove to be a happy one.

The house is still empty when they arrive back. Switching on lamps lightens dark corners, casting a soft hue over the mess of the living room. Helena begins the process of tidying up while the children eat their supper and watch television. She stares at the clock, wondering when Vanessa will arrive home.

An hour later, children bathed and in their pyjamas, they sit together on the sofa, leafing through books, Helena reading story after story until Noah's eyes droop and Mabel lets out a wide yawn.

'Right, you two, let's have you up to bed. Teeth cleaned and then we'll get you tucked in ready for Mummy coming home later.'

'Where is Mummy?' Noah asks, his small fists rubbing at tired eyes.

'She's just gone to see a friend. She won't be long.' Helena prays all is well, that her request to end the relationship has been met with agreement and conciliation. That is, if she with him. She could be anywhere. Still the secrecy continues.

The urge to send a message is strong, to make sure things are okay, but doesn't want to disturb her. Helena understands the need for privacy. For enough time and space to mend their broken lives. Instead, she helps to brush small teeth and reads enough bedtime storybooks to fill an entire library.

With the children asleep, she sits, pondering over the many possibilities as to what is going on. Where her eldest daughter is. Shadows creep into her thoughts. She attempts to banish them with a light-hearted romcom and fails. Nothing holds her attention. Only as night-time arrives, its darkness sweeping into the house, does she finally send a text asking when Vanessa will be home. Helena pulls back the blinds, glancing into the street. Her eyes searching. Scouring the roads for signs of Vanessa's approach. Her car is parked outside. Has she walked? Taken a taxi? Streetlights illuminate the road with a spread of amber, the path and rooftops bathed in an orange hue. People walk past. The occasional car. But no Vanessa.

The wait is an eternity, her eyes flicking to her phone every few minutes. Still nothing. She wonders how long she should leave it before she actually calls. Helena doesn't want to interrupt what may be a private, delicate moment, and yet time is moving on, the hours ticking past with still no word. How long is too long? An hour? Two hours? Time drags as she waits, checking her watch, staring at the clock, at her phone, hoping that things are being resolved peaceably. Because if they're not and this guy has a temper...

Helena rubs at her face, as if to smear away that thought. It will be fine. Everything is going to turn out just fine. Vanessa is a strong woman. She can handle herself. All Helena has to do is sit here and wait.

47

PRESENT DAY

A key in the lock. I lie still, my breathing ragged. Adrenaline pumps around my system, masking my aches and pains. Then something else. Something that sparks hope in my chest. I hear a female voice echoing from below. My heart beats so fast I feel certain it is going to force its way out of my chest. This is it. This is my key to getting out of here alive. Finally, fate has handed me a chance. I have no idea what this woman is doing here and neither do I care. All I know is, I am going to be helped. She is going to find me and together we will over-power him.

'Upstairs,' I hear him say. 'The surprise is upstairs waiting for you.'

I want to scream that it's a trap, that he is a fucking maniac. I want to shriek at her that she needs to run and to keep on running, to call the police and shout at the top of her voice until somebody arrives and frees us both.

The sound of two sets of footsteps on the stairs makes my skin prickle, my nerve endings blazing with fear and anticipation. I sit on the floor next to the bed, the wooden slat of the blind pushed under the duvet. It was the best I could manage with my hands tied and my feet bound together. It's not much but it's better than nothing. When she gets up here and sees this macabre scene, she can untie me and we can escape together, me and this mystery female who is walking into a horrible trap.

And then she is here and I see that it's her. I suck in my breath when I spot her features. That authoritative scowl. The way she has of commandeering the room. Vanessa, my old boss from the care home, steps into the room, her expression crestfallen as she sees me slumped on the floor. I attempt a smile but the gag is too tight. Despite trying to hold them back, the tears begin flow, relief opening the floodgates and a tsunami bursting through.

'Alex, what the fuck?' Her hands are raised in confusion, her voice a boom in the surrounding silence.

She looks from me to the many photographs spread over every wall, and then back to me again.

He steps closer to her and I worry that he is going to hit her, to do to her what he has done to me. That would end everything. Vanessa is my ticket out of here. She is my only hope.

Her voice goes up an octave when she speaks again, each word shrivelling my insides. 'You need to get rid of her! Why the fuck have you kept this one? Why is she so special? Get rid of her like you did the others!'

I'm dizzy, the room whirling around me. My world has cracked in half and I am being smothered by the aftermath, rocks and stones raining down on me, burying me alive. She knows. Vanessa knows. She is a part of this sick and twisted game. She fucking well knows.

'Sshh,' he says softly, stepping out of the shadows and kneeling next to me. 'I'm going to feed her and give her a drink. She's been cooped up in here all day.'

Before Vanessa can respond, he has untied the rope around my hands and feet. His fingers rest on my head, stroking my hair before taking off the fabric that is cutting into the soft flesh of my mouth. I don't have time to feel repulsed by his touch. That's a sentiment for another time. Right now, I have to take my chances wherever and whenever I can.

Feigning a stretch from being bound all day, I reach back, slide the wooden slat from under the duvet and swing it at his head. It meets his skull with a satisfying wet smack. In my peripheral vision, I can see him lying on the floor, blood seeping out of him. A nail from the wooden slat is embedded in his temple. Before Vanessa can do anything, I am up on my feet and running at her, my fingers splayed. I press my hands into her chest and push her backwards, roaring into her face, an expulsion of anger and euphoria at the thought of escaping ballooning in my chest.

Her eyes are wide with shock as I propel her backwards, pushing and pushing until we are at the top of the stairs. Her hand reaches out and grabs at the handrail, her body steady and firm, but adrenaline is pulsing through me and I am stronger than she is. I have more at stake here. She will lose her liberty when this is all over. If I don't succeed I will lose my life. If Alex recovers, he might not kill me but I can tell by the look of horror and hatred in her eyes that she definitely will.

I try to knock her hand away with my shoulder but she holds on, her body recovering from the shock of being caught off guard. I will do whatever it takes to win this battle. Anything at all. I scream once more and spit in her face, real malice behind it. In one swift reflex motion, she removes her fingers from the handrail to wipe at her cheek and that's when I use every bit of strength I have to push her hard, watching as she tumbles backwards down the stairs, landing at the bottom in a crumpled, disfigured heap.

The sound of me running down and leaping over her rattles in my head. I don't stop to check if she is alive. Time is my enemy. I need to find a key to either of the doors and get out of here. Neither locks have fobs dangling from them. Exactly as expected. He will have them in his pocket. I can't waste precious minutes going back up there and rummaging. Instead I open cupboards and cabinets, knocking things aside in a frantic search for a spare set.

Nothing.

The windows are double-glazed. Little chance of me being able to smash them. I try anyway, hurling a chair at the glass and seeing it rebound.

I grab the kettle – a large old metal thing – and pick it up ready to swing it until something stops me. A tugging sensation. Something, or somebody pulling it back. Body braced, ready for a fight, I turn around and see her standing there, eyes blazing, anger and determination etched into her expression.

Again, I run at her, the kettle pressed hard into her chest. She's strong, I'll give her that, but for every ounce of strength she has, I can match it with willpower and fortitude and an unparalleled urge to escape.

She is pushed up against the wall, hitting it with a crack, her backbone crushed against the tiles. I see her wince and squirm and press even harder, forcing myself against the metal between us, hoping to squeeze every last drop of air out of her lungs. I use my arms, my shoulders, my whole upper body to try to crush her.

'I'm here to help,' she gasps. 'I know what he's done and I've come to get you out of here.'

Doubt creeps its way in. Panic is evident in her eyes, the way she is looking at me. The pleading tone to her voice. Did I misinterpret her words earlier? I could have sworn I didn't, but what if she was trying trick him whilst attempting to help me?

Her breathing is shallow as I continue to push the heavy metal kettle against her chest. I take a chance and bit by bit remove the pressure, stepping back, watching her to see what she says and does next.

48

HELENA

How long, she wonders, before she makes that dreaded call to the police to report her eldest daughter missing? Two hours? Four or five? Or should she wait until morning, give Vanessa some time to sort out her troubled relationship? Helena knows nothing about this man. Who he is, where he lives. Not a damn thing. She does, however, know where he works. It's a start should she need to make that call and file a report. Every fibre of her being hopes that Vanessa will walk through that door any minute, but Helena being the cautious creature that she is needs a contingency plan. A childhood filled with uncertainty has resulted in her always being one step ahead as an adult. Always needing to know what comes next. Nasty surprises leave a sour taste in her mouth.

The television is one long stream of monotonous programmes, each blending into the next until in the end, she can no longer differentiate one from the other. Feet tucked beneath her body, Helena once again checks her phone, hoping for a reply or to see a missed call, and feels her stomach sink when she is faced with a blank screen. One hour; she will give it another hour and then she will phone the local police station, see if they have any guidance on what her next move should be. Her initial worries could be correct. For all she knows, this chap from work could be violent and controlling. If Vanessa went with him intending to end the relationship then who's to say he didn't do something awful to her? Something destructive. For all her daughter is strong and fiery, she couldn't possibly fight off a grown man. Biology dictates that she has lost before the fight has even begun. And then Innes punctures her thoughts. His injuries and that scar. She pushes that notion away. Innes is not your average tough guy. He is reserved. Malleable.

Helena swallows and leans her head back, staring at the ceiling light, the sharp glare of it burning into her retina. She wishes for Rachel to come home and for Vanessa to find herself a life partner, and for all of them to live happily with their children. Is that too much to ask for? To want what other families have?

All she needs is for her eldest daughter to walk through that door unharmed. And then she thinks about Crystal and Innes again, and runs her fingers through her hair, wondering when and how all of this is ever going to end.

* * *

It's dark, the room chilly when she wakes. A feeling of despondency circles her, anxiety lodging itself in the pit of her stomach. For all she knows, Vanessa may have snuck in during the early hours and left Helena sleeping on the sofa. She could be curled up in bed right now.

Even as she climbs the stairs, her footfall light to save waking the children, she knows that she is going to find an empty bedroom and Vanessa's bed unslept in. Call it sixth sense or mother's instinct, but as soon as she peers around the main bedroom, she knows that Vanessa hasn't come home.

She heads back downstairs, a sense of dread biting at her. Making that call to the police is the thing that will make this scenario real. Instead, she sends another message to Vanessa.

> Just another message to ask where you are and when you're coming home. Please call me asap xx

The screen feels cold against her fingertips as she types in Vanessa's name and presses the number to call her. And again, as expected, it goes to the answer machine. Frustration is a fiery bulbous thing in her gut. There are children asleep upstairs. In just a few hours they will wake and ask where their mother is. What is Helena supposed to say to them? That she doesn't know, or is she supposed to lie, just as Vanessa has been lying to her for all these months? The chain needs to be broken. Refusing to be honest will only make things worse. It's a dark latticework of deceit. The lies need to stop right now. There is another possibility; one she doesn't want to consider. Thinking of it makes her dizzy. Nauseated. A serial killer in town. Dead bodies, all of them female.

Please God, no.

Fingers trembling, Helena searches for the number of the local police station. She takes a sharp rattling breath, inhaling so deeply she feels sure there isn't any oxygen left in the room, and then makes the call.

49

PRESENT DAY

Her expression, her smile, the way she tilts her head at me; she is too difficult to decipher. I wish I could see inside her mind, read her thoughts. Pre-empt her next movements.

'Thank you,' she says, bending over to catch her breath. 'Maisie, isn't it?'

I nod, tears welling at the sound of her voice, the way she lifts her head and smiles at me. The kindness in her timbre. I got it wrong. I was clearly mistaken.

Except I wasn't. It takes me by surprise, the slap across my face, the way she grabs a knife from the block and thrusts it at me. Part of me knew that this was going to happen and I'm prepared for it, an inner strength taking over. I duck out of the way, for once my small frame an advantage. Vanessa is bigger than me. Clumsier.

As I move under her arm, I use my whole body to knock her sideways. She collides with the wall, the knife falling from her hand. It clatters to the floor, spinning wildly and landing at my feet.

A scarlet line trickles down her neck, a gash on her head bleeding profusely. Her hair is matted with dark blood. Whether it's from the fall down the stairs or the collision on the wall isn't certain, but I do know that it's slowing her down. She is suddenly cumbersome and woozy.

Even with her in this dazed state, I cannot escape until I find a key and I don't want to go back upstairs to search his pockets. I hope he is still unconscious; he would be down here if he was awake and able to move, but I'm not prepared to take that chance.

I can see her at the edge of my line of sight, stumbling. She could be doing it on purpose to try to fool me. Anything is possible. I turn and give her another shove, watching as she topples to the floor. My body pulses as I bring back my foot and kick her hard in the stomach. I have never kicked or hurt anybody in my life; it's an alien sensation, my foot meeting with the soft flesh of her abdomen. She lets out a wail and curls up into a foetal position, hands clutched over her midriff.

Behind her is a door. I step over her and open it, gasping when I see it – a cupboard that contains cleaning equipment and beyond that a large single-pane window. It's old, the wooden frame thick with many layers of paint that have begun to flake away. It's my only way out of this place. I am not letting this chance go.

On the floor is a plastic bucket and a mop. No heft or weight to the bucket but the mop has a long wooden shaft. I pick it up and ram it into the glass. The window shatters on impact. I almost cry out with relief. All this time I have been here; all this time I could have simply stepped inside this small space and escaped.

I pick out the tiny shards that jut out of the frame and am about to hoist myself up when I feel it – a hand grabbing my ankle. Fingers pressing into the bone and holding me fast. It's a reflex action to kick back. My foot meets with flesh. I turn to see Alex crawling towards me, blood pouring out of his head, his face streaked with it. Even though I hate him, even though I am fighting for my life, bringing back my foot and stamping on his skull with as much strength as I can muster feels horrific. I do it anyway. Kill or be killed.

Blood bubbles out of his mouth as I bring my foot down on his face over and over. His grasp on my ankle doesn't lessen. I do it again and again until I can barely find the energy to move. Sweat runs down my face and neck, gathering in my clavicle. I rub at my eyes and nose with my sleeve and take a shuddering breath.

His arm slumps by his side. I don't hang around to see if he is still breathing. Not enough time for pity or assistance or for guilt to get a stronghold over me. I use the underside of the bucket as a step and haul myself up through the window frame, my legs flailing for purchase as I clamber through the open space. I don't scream. Not yet. Not until I am out of this fucking awful house.

A noise from behind me. It can't be him. I kicked and kicked and stamped until he was unconscious.

'Stop! It's not what you think.'

Her voice is distorted, warped by pain and the swelling to her face. I don't stop. I have no intention of doing as she asks. She is a liar. This is a last plea to try to clear her name, for her to try to stop me from going to the police.

Before I can wriggle through the frame completely, she has grabbed a handful of my hair and is wrapping it around her fingers and pulling me back. It's now or never. With a final surge of strength, I place a hand on my scalp to lessen the pain and throw myself out into the cool clean air. A lack of natural light has weakened my hair, handfuls of it coming away in her fist. It doesn't matter. Nothing matters except getting as far away from this place as I can.

I drop down and am wedged between a brick wall and a rickety old fence that is about to collapse. With only a foot or so in which to manoeuvre, I slide between them, my feet twisting beneath me. I am exhausted, the adrenaline rush now dissipating. Just a few more steps to freedom.

A shaft of light at the end of the gap is enough to keep me going, my earlier flood of energy now in decline. I continue pushing myself sideways, eventually emerging into a shaft of daylight.

It's a strange sensation, being outside after this long. I bend over, my hands resting on my knees, my breath coming in short bursts. I almost laugh at the absurdity of it all, but can't quite summon up enough power or momentum. I'm an empty shell, nothing left.

To my right is a movement, a flicker of something dark. I turn to see her standing there, face set like stone. He may be dead but Vanessa is very much alive, doing what she can to stop me from leaving that house. Doing what she can to stop me from passing her name on to the police. The sound of her footsteps as she approaches echoes around us.

Before I can move, she is beside me, hissing in my ear. 'Don't fucking move.' The knife glints in her hand, concealed by her coat.

She slides it up her sleeve out of view. This isn't the end. I've come too far to lose now. This is just the beginning.

My options are limited, my energy waning, so I do the only thing I'm able to do – I open my mouth and I scream and scream until my throat is sore, until my voice is hoarse and I feel as if I am choking on thin air.

We are surrounded by row upon row of derelict houses, some thankfully still occupied. People emerge from inside, standing in doorways, watching me. Watching us.

'It's okay,' Vanessa shouts, keeping her gaze locked on mine, her head dipped away from the sea of eyes. 'She's my sister and she's not well. I'm going to take her home now.'

Low murmuring, a clicking of tongues. Audible sighs. A few of them disappear back inside. Panic claws at me. I can't be alone with Vanessa. I need somebody to do something, to say something. To fucking well stop her.

So again, I open my mouth and scream, 'Help me! Somebody, help me!'

Before I can continue, she steps closer to me, her hand wrapped around my forearm, and yanks me inside the house. Somehow, she did what I wasn't able to do, and she found the key. I manage a quick glance around the street before I'm pulled in and see that it's empty, everyone too immersed in their own lives to give a shit.

I should have run while I had the chance. I should have ignored the knife, dug deep into my reserves and summoned up enough strength to push past her and sprint across the road into one of the other houses, begging for them to help me. But I didn't, and now I'm back in this place with her. And a knife. Back to the beginning. Everything I have done, all that I have suffered, the risks I have taken; it's all been for nothing.

Frustration and anger fragment in my gut, sparks igniting, pushing me on. I'm tenacious and determined, always have been. But more than that, I want to live. I want to get back home to my family and friends. So I run at her, knife or no knife. I use the element of surprise, wrestling her to the floor. Her head hits the bottom stair, more blood spraying out and smearing over the wall. I punch at her face, using my nails to scratch, doing anything and everything I can to disarm and injure her, but she is strong, refusing to be beaten. I feel myself sailing backwards as she throws me off, my body as light as a feather.

My spine hits the corner of the wall with a crunch, momentarily winding me. The knife is laid on the floor between us. I leap for it but she is faster. She comes at me with it held firm. I kick and I punch, and I scream and I spit. Anything to get her away from me. Anything to make her stop.

My feet and hands meet flesh, but at the same time I feel a sharp pain, a slicing sensation around my midriff. I stare down and see a crimson wet ring around my stomach. So much blood. My vision begins to blur, a coldness wrapping itself around me. I can't see the knife. Vanessa is sitting on the stairs, her head in her hands. Blood is seeping through her splayed fingers.

I watch, mesmerised and exhausted, as she slumps backwards, eyes glassy, her gaze fixed on the ceiling. She might be dead. Too difficult to tell. I think I'm probably dying too. So cold, so tired. Every ounce of energy I have is leaching out of me. My legs weigh nothing. I drop to the floor, a numbness, a welcome lightness surrounding me. No more pain. No more tiredness or fear. Just silence and a few seconds to stop and catch my breath.

My eyes are heavy, as if being pulled downwards by a large anchor. Too fatigued to fight it, I allow myself to be carried into oblivion. Nothing but darkness.

Nothing at all.

50

VANESSA

Two Months Later

I glance around the tiny bare room, a space filled with things that aren't mine. I'm where I should always have been. Where I deserve to be. That much I do know. I'm not one of those people who denies their crimes, convincing themselves they are innocent. I'm too aware, too intelligent for that sort of shit.

A neighbour called the police. A decent-minded neighbour. I'm not a decent person but I'm also not an idiot. I know right from wrong, it's just that sometimes I choose to do the wrong thing. Bad things. Things that set me apart from others. Things that have resulted in the media and the public calling me a psychopath. A heartless bitch. A cold-blooded murderer.

I think of my mother, how she is coping throughout all of this. And my children. I may not have been the best parent or daughter but I still love them. They are a part of me and I am a part of them. Forever entwined no matter how repulsive and stupid my actions were. And they were. I got carried away in the slipstream of Alex's thoughts and anger, his stories of how he was wronged by his mother, firing up my senses. I admit that part of me was excited by it all. I didn't kill any of those women but I lured them in, made his appearance seem innocent. Females don't do that sort of thing. We are the sensitive sex, the caring, nurturing sex. I feigned friendliness, pretending we had broken down in the car while he did the rest. I'm such a coward, I can't even speak openly about what he did. What I allowed to happen. What I witnessed.

I'd like to be able to list the reasons why I let it happen, but I can't because there isn't one single solid explanation for any of it. Loneliness, anger, maybe even gullibility. I don't want to admit that he fooled me; I like to think of myself as more rational than that, but maybe he found my weak spot and I crumpled under pressure.

I was angry at the world in general; still am. My mother would say I was born angry. Or maybe she wouldn't. She has always worn rose-tinted spectacles when it comes to me and my sister, desperate to see the best in us to the point where she was blind to our faults. And we had faults. Still do. I'm living proof of that. Being incarcerated here is proof of my badness, my many flaws and shortcomings.

Still, being here has given me time to think, to rake back over my past, search for the cracks in my character, the fissures where the darkness crept in. Crystal was the first thing I thought of. I know my mother thinks that something sinister took place that day by the stream in the woods, but she is mistaken. Whatever Rachel told her is a pack of lies. Or at least I think it is. Every time I try to delve into the store of memories in my head, I come up with a blank. A big fat nothing. So maybe the papers are right, and maybe I am a psychopath. An unfeeling, hard-faced bitch. I like to think that Alex egged me on, dared me to do it. Perhaps he initiated it while I assisted. Perhaps we will never know the answer to what happened that day. Some things are best left alone.

I've admitted my guilt in the case of the recent deaths; I had no other option. When the police arrived and kicked in the door, they found me unconscious on the stairs with a large gash to my head and numerous broken ribs. They found Maisie with a deep stab wound to her abdomen. My fingerprints were on the knife. My injuries were superficial even though they hurt like hell. The neighbour saw me drag her back inside the house, fear forcing them indoors while they watched from behind half-closed blinds. And of course, they had a statement from the woman herself, telling them what I said when I saw her in the bedroom. After being rushed to surgery, she was able to recall every little detail, leaving nothing out. I guess I admire her for that; her tenacity and her will to live. She did it. Maisie finally got out of that house.

Some of the more cerebral newspapers have already begun assessing my relationship with Alex, blaming him for intimidating me. Forcing me to do those things. They're wrong. I am my own person. I have a brain, albeit a dysfunctional one bordering on depraved, but I am nobody's fool.

Alex isn't around to tell them anything about me. He isn't dead, but he might as well be. He has been in a coma for months now and isn't expected to come out of it. The doctors are talking about turning off the machine. The sooner the better as far as I can see. His mother's corpse was found under the floor of his living room. The autopsy showed no signs of trauma and they are saying she died from natural causes. I guess we will never know.

Rachel and Mum are playing happy families while I'm locked up in here, my sister suddenly the perfect daughter, the prodigal aunt and child. She is coming to visit me next month. I have said I don't want to see her but she is coming anyway with Mum as a back-up. Let's wait and see how that visit goes.

The worst part of all this is the fact that Innes has applied for custody of Mabel and Noah. He has finally got what he wanted. All it took was for me to drop all the balls I was juggling and while I bent down to pick them up, he stole my children.

My time in here will be a long stretch. So long that my children will be adults by the time I get out. If I ever do. The court of public opinion always judges women more harshly than men. I may not have killed those young females but I didn't stop it happening. To many, that is worse. I hope that one day soon, Mabel and Noah will be allowed to visit me. It's their faces I see at night when I close my eyes, the sounds of screaming and the banging from the women in the other cells rattling in my head as I shut my eyes and pretend I am elsewhere. Anywhere but here.

I have one wish; I don't dream of being freed from this place or for my sentence to be reduced; those type of wishes are stupid, predictable pie-in-the-sky desires. My one wish is that my children don't inherit any of my character traits. I pray the badness ends with me. My grandma isn't exactly a saint and was a terrible mother to my mother. Maybe that's where I got it from. Maybe badness and cruelty are genetic and inescapable. I hope not. I was loved unconditionally and grew up to do terrible things. So my question is this – if love can't break the cycle of hatred and violence, then what hope is there for any of us?

51

HELENA

She is nervous. Although their phone call was cordial, Helena still feels her legs weaken when she spots Maisie in the distance, striding towards her with all the confidence of somebody who has overcome adversity and trauma and exited the other side, relieved to be alive and ready to embrace freedom and happiness. Ready to embrace each day and all that comes with it.

Innes has taken the children to the park and then to the café for lunch afterwards. Helena wasn't sure who was the most excited as she waved them off, Innes's grin so wide she feared his face would split in half.

Maisie's pace slows down the closer she gets to Helena. Her gait is still slightly off balance after the attack, her injuries so severe she was in hospital for over a month and needed over fifty stitches. She is lucky to be alive. And all because of Vanessa.

A lump is wedged in Helena's throat. She swallows it down. She has shed enough tears to fill a dam and refuses to weep any more for a daughter who did the most atrocious things imaginable. After it all came out, Helena considered moving house, selling up and settling in another part of the country, taking the children with her, but then something happened; the village in which she lived and the people in it took her under their wing, protecting her from the many insults that were fired her way from those who didn't know her. She awoke one morning to find neighbours washing away the graffiti that had been daubed across the front of her house during the night. That was when she knew she had to stay. Those people were more than just neighbours; they were her friends. Her saviours. They have helped her through the most difficult and traumatic of times, never questioning or passing judgement. Always kind. Always there.

Speaking to Barbara has proven to be way more difficult, Barbara and her family refusing to communicate with Helena, and she doesn't blame them for that. With the guidance of a counsellor, Helena has written a letter to her friend which she has yet to send. She keeps it in a safe place and sometimes adds extra words or removes phrases as things become clearer in her head. Even if she never sends it, it is a cathartic process that has helped her to try to come to terms with what has taken place. With what her daughter did to their daughter. Helena shudders. Even saying it in her head makes her dizzy, her skin flashing hot and cold. There are mornings when she wakes, feeling as if the light will never come back into her life. And then the children wake and she forges ahead with her day, their presence and the accompanying busyness that comes with them stamping out all dark thoughts. Until the following evening. Because nights are the worst. Those long, lonely evenings when sleep refuses to come and misery and anxiety nestle beneath her skin like old bedfellows, taking root and branching out. A splash of light the following morning and she is able to see through the darkness and the fog that muddy her thinking. This thing is never going to go away – she knows that – but hopefully day by day, her outlook will improve, even if it's only by a small amount, too tiny to measure. At some point things will get better.

There are a few positives to come out of this dreadful, unspeakable mess, and that is the stranger who appeared on her doorstep one morning, his features and mannerisms as familiar to her as her own. As expected, Sylvie had lied about her father. He didn't die and neither did he go to prison for murdering another man. He moved to Sheffield shortly after meeting Sylvie and lived his life unaware he had a daughter who lived only two hours away. After the story hit the papers, he somehow managed to track down Sylvie and demanded to see Helena. He is a retired marketing manager and a decent man. His presence in her life is a blessing but it rules out the idea she had in her head that Vanessa has inherited his genes and predisposition for being a cold-blooded killer. Which begs the question – where did her daughter's dysfunctional, depraved ways come from? A woman from a loving, caring family turned accomplice to a savage murderer. Newspapers are likening her to Myra Hindley, suggesting she was so enamoured by Alex Broadwood, she would do anything for him. But Helena knows that isn't true. The death of Crystal sticks in her mind, despite Vanessa's protestations she had nothing to with it. Despite Vanessa's protestations that it was probably Alex who killed her. Rachel has given more details on that day, opening up to Helena since Vanessa's arrest. Rachel has no reason to lie, but Vanessa has every reason to deny. An admission would result in an increase in her sentence. Mabel and Noah will be adults by the time their mother is released from prison. They could have children of their own and would never see her again if Vanessa admits to the part she played in Crystal's death. There is some good news, nestled amongst the horror. Rachel is undergoing a rehab programme and currently living with Helena. It's not easy. They have good days and bad days but at the moment the good days outweigh the bad. And they can't ask for more than that.

Sylvie remains the same person she always was, claiming Vanessa was misled by Alex Broadwood. Helena knows better than to disagree, sitting instead, listening to her mother's diatribe about how the courts have got it all wrong and that Vanessa is simply misunderstood and should be released. An hour every week, that is what she is prepared to endure. Visiting a woman who defends Vanessa's actions, a woman who lied about Helena's father is a test of her patience and strength. A woman who cares more about herself than her own daughter or the people who were murdered in her hometown, dismissing the evidence that highlighted Vanessa's part in their deaths as fabricated nonsense. Sylvie cares only for those who mirror her own life – the harmful, dangerous people. The ones who walk their own path, unaware of the damage their actions inflict on others. She feels an affinity with them, afraid that doing anything positive would mean she would be held to account for her past misdemeanours. Her lies and lack of care and compassion. Helena knows that her mother won't change her ways. She is who she is and the way things are going, she'll possibly outlive all of them. She is untouched by all the emotions that Helena has been forced to experience, Stress plays no part in Sylvie's life. If the cigarettes and cheap wine don't see her off, she will still be around when Helena is an old woman, and that is a thought that makes her go cold.

'Helena?' Maisie is standing in front of her, her eyes sparkling like diamonds under the glare of the sun.

'Maisie, so lovely to finally meet you. Thank you for coming.'

They walk together, the warmth of the sun on their backs like a gentle caress as they stroll through the park ready to converse.

52

RACHEL

Who knows why people do what they do. We are an unfathomable species, human behaviours confounding the most intelligent and qualified of psychologists and mental-health specialists. So why did I lie to my mother about that day by the stream? Why did I tell her that Vanessa killed Crystal? Maybe it's because I have always resented my older sister. Perhaps it's because I too am also a pathological liar. Or maybe it's because I wanted to cover my own tracks and blame some-body else for a dare that went horribly wrong. A dare that resulted in our childhood friend losing her life.

It was my idea for us to clamber over the wet moss-covered stones in the water. My idea to shout at Crystal, to tell her she was a sissy for not wanting to do it. My idea to give her a little push to help her along. Vanessa was the one who jumped in to help her, but they ended up thrashing around in the water, their limbs and hair entangled. All Alex did was stand by and watch, a strange wry smile on his face like he was enjoying it.

We dragged Crystal out and laid her on the grass by the side of the trees, the dappled sunlight dancing on her face. Making us believe that she was still alive. It didn't take me long to realise she wasn't breathing. That's when the idea came to me. I couldn't take the blame for what had happened; I wasn't prepared to let Vanessa off and have my name muddied. I already hated her, my sister; the favourite child. The one who received all the attention after Dad's death while I was left alone to cope with my grief. So I ran home, screaming that Crystal wouldn't wake up, that Vanessa had been playing with her in the water when it happened. I can't recall my exact words but I did imply that Vanessa was somehow to blame. I should have known that nothing would happen, that once again the golden child would emerge from that situation blemish-free, her reputation untarnished.

I have hung on for the longest time for the subject to be brought up again. Good things come to those who wait. All my story did was hammer the final nail into Vanessa's coffin. Make sure our mother finally, after all these years, took notice of me and was on my side.

Did I end up an addict because of my homelife, because of the guilt that has stayed with me after that incident? Perhaps. My gradual slide into addiction is too complex a thing to study, too many details involved to pin it on one solid reason. All I do know is that I now have my mother's ear after being nudged aside for so many years. I'm living back with her until I get my own place. It's not easy. She is often overbearing, smothering me with love and maternal advice, but at least Vanessa is no longer around to steal all the attention. The best thing that ever happened was Alex Broadwood applying for a job at the care home. That's where it all began.

Just goes to prove that sometimes fortune really does play a huge part in how life pans out. And right now, Lady Luck is definitely shining down on me.

* * *

MORE FROM J. A. BAKER

Another book from J. A. Baker, *The Good Daughter*, is available to order now here:
    https://mybook.to/GoodBackAd

ACKNOWLEDGEMENTS

My goodness, this was a difficult one to write. Without the help of my editors, Emily Ruston and Jennifer Davies, this book would a mish-mash of badly drawn characters with plot holes big enough to drive a truck through, so first and foremost, my thanks go to Emily and Jennifer for your sage words and guidance.

The team at Boldwood Books work incredibly hard so I would like to extend my thanks to them for all the marketing and wonderful cover designs for my books. Thank you also to Rachel Sargeant, my eagle-eyed proofreader who sees the many things that my tired eyes miss!

Writing is a lonely old business and work colleagues are in short supply. However a few names need mentioning, so huge thanks to Valerie Keogh, Anita Waller, Diana Wilkinson, Clare Swatman and Jessica Redland for their unending assistance and kind words during the low points. The authors at Boldwood are a deeply supportive lot, so thank you to everyone for always being there.

I would like to thank my wonderful ARC readers for their unwavering support and always getting those reviews out there in such a timely fashion. You guys are ace! I won't mention names for fear of leaving anybody out, but you all know who you are.

Thank you to Book Mark for always promoting and championing us less well-known authors. We need people like you to make sure our books get noticed, so thanks to Mark Fearn for all that you do. You are the fastest reader ever and always pen the most splendidly written reviews.

Finally, I would like to thank my family and friends who have been behind me since my first book was published in 2017. I am so lucky to have you. I'll try to not cancel so many engagements from now on and give a bit more time to living. After all, coffee and cake doesn't consume itself.

I am available on social media and love to chat to readers.

www.facebook.com/thewriterjude

www.instagram.com/jabakerauthor

J.A. Baker (@thewriterjude.bsky.social) – Bluesky

Best Wishes

J.A. Baker

ABOUT THE AUTHOR

J. A. Baker is a successful writer of numerous psychological thrillers. Born and brought up in Middlesbrough, she still lives in the North East, which inspires the settings for her books.

Sign up to J. A. Baker's mailing list here for news, competitions and updates on future books.

Follow J. A. Baker on social media:

facebook.com/thewriterjude

x.com/thewriterjude

instagram.com/jabakerauthor

tiktok.com/@jabaker41

bookbub.com/authors/JABaker

ALSO BY J. A. BAKER

THE *Murder* LIST

**THE MURDER LIST IS A NEWSLETTER
DEDICATED TO SPINE-CHILLING
FICTION AND GRIPPING
PAGE-TURNERS!**

**SIGN UP TO MAKE SURE YOU'RE ON
OUR HIT LIST FOR EXCLUSIVE DEALS,
AUTHOR CONTENT, AND
COMPETITIONS.**

**SIGN UP TO OUR
NEWSLETTER**

BIT.LY/THEMURDERLISTNEWS

Boldw**oo**d

Boldwood Books is an award-winning fiction publishing company seeking out the best stories from around the world.

Find out more at www.boldwoodbooks.com

Join our reader community for brilliant books, competitions and offers!

Follow us
@BoldwoodBooks
@TheBoldBookClub

Sign up to our weekly
deals newsletter

https://bit.ly/BoldwoodBNewsletter

www.ingramcontent.com/pod-product-compliance
Ingram Content Group UK Ltd.
Pitfield, Milton Keynes, MK11 3LW, UK
UKHW040611071125
8795UKWH00009B/99